Hot Damn

Hot as Puck

Book Three

Rhian Cahill

Hot Damn
Hot as Puck Book Three
By Rhian Cahill

For more information visit:
www.rhiancahill.com

For Schellie

CAMI

"Hot damn!"

I barely avoid a fist to the face when the guy next to me punches the air. He can't be more than five four and at five eleven in bare feet I tower over him.

The last thing I need—or want—is a black eye. Leaning back as far as the wall behind me allows in case he comes up swinging again, I warn, "Hey, watch it next time."

He whirls around like he's under attack, one arm out, palm up to hold off the threat while the other hand presses his phone to his chest, his eyes darting this way and that before landing on me.

His assessing gaze takes me in for a few seconds and I see the moment he dismisses me, a sneering twist of his lips overtaking his face. The smirk doesn't do anything to improve his looks. In fact it does the opposite; the predatory smile makes me think of serial killers.

Before I can ask what has him so excited, he shuffles backward putting a good four feet between us, his creepy gaze never leaving me as though he thinks I'll follow him to snatch the phone he's cradling like it's a bag of crack and I'm an addict looking for a fix.

Idiot.

I know most in the industry and he's no different. There is

not a chance in hell I'm going near Herman Draper by choice. In the world of journalism he's a bottom feeder, a freelancer after any story he can sell to the highest bidder. He'll peer through windows and hunt through garbage cans in search of some tidbit to reveal about any celebrity of interest to the public, especially those his information would tear down.

I'm pretty sure he was nabbed on a break and enter a few years ago.

The man gives respectable journalists a bad name.

I didn't realize who he was when he slipped into the room and settled beside me a few minutes ago. Now I have to wonder why he's here. Sports reporting isn't his thing.

Then again, it's not mine either.

I'm here because the usual guy called in a favor I'd been dumb enough to owe him. I should have known Bas would send me to a stinky locker room.

Okay, fine, it's not the locker room, but close enough.

I'm not a fan of professional athletes for a number of reasons, the least of which being they smell. Although this room the press is jammed into lacks the usual athletic aroma, instead it's filled with a mix of expensive and cheap perfumes and colognes as well as a slight trace of BO.

That last could be attributed to Draper though. The man looks like he's slept in his clothes for more than a few days straight.

Noise at the front of the room draws everyone's attention, and looking up I see Coach Walker Alcott step into the room. He's followed by assistant coach Blake Watts, and players Beckett Higgison, Chase Hawkins, and Branton Lattimer Watts. While flashes pop all around the room, I watch the group get settled in seats behind a long table lined with microphones and wonder what questions they'll be asked.

As I said, sport isn't my thing and I'm a little out of my depth here, but a favor is a favor and Bas is a cool guy, and if I'm honest,

I'd probably have said yes to anyway. And that's what I am—honest—in my job and life.

I had my fill of liars before I hit double digits and I've no plans to live that way again.

Besides, it's not like I'm here to interview anyone. I just need to pick up some highlights, a few soundbites we can use on the network and paper's websites. Bas watched the game at home where he's recovering from a sprained ankle and will already be pulling together the article to go in the sports section of Sunday's paper as well as the one the network will use in their sports roundup.

I don't plan on asking questions. I'll leave that to the experts in the room. Of which there are many.

Except one.

Herman Draper.

He's more of an expert in gossip, the dirtier the better.

I glance over and see Draper worming his way closer to the front. He's got a look on his face that has me standing straighter, my gaze focused solely on him now.

"What are you up to?" I murmur, moving closer.

I'm not sure why I'm following him. The action is at the front of the room with the players and coaches answering questions about tonight's game. I've got my ears on them, listening for anything I can use, but my gaze is locked on Draper. Whatever he's up to, I don't like it.

Can't say why.

Maybe it's the way his flinty eyes glint or the smarmy smile on his face. Whatever he has planned, I know it's not going to be good. Shit usually gets flung when Draper is around.

From what I know, it's been his stock-in-trade his entire career. We might not run in the same circles—professional or social— but I'm still well aware of his reputation.

I'm a few reporters to his left, back a bit so he doesn't catch me in his peripheral vision. I don't want him to notice me. The last thing I need is for him to work out who I am and aim that devious smirk my way. Best to keep out of his line of sight.

Not that I should be worried. He didn't recognize me before when he was sizing me up as a threat and now he's got his eyes glued to the front of the room.

On Higgison I think.

As I move closer, questions are tossed out about the game, the team, the coaching staff being inexperienced, and being two games into pre-season with two wins under their belt. My brain is cataloguing some possible bites when Draper shouts above everyone else.

"Beckett, you've played for Calgary, Montreal, and the last five years Toronto. Now you're here with the league's newest, and some would say most controversial, franchise team, the Baton Rouge Rogues."

"Right?" Higgison nods with a frown, obviously not hearing the question and I don't blame him, I don't hear one either. It sounds like Draper is reading the man's bio.

Draper grins and I'm stepping closer, my body coiling tight, bracing for what, I don't have a clue, when the next words out of his mouth stop me in my tracks and send my gaze whipping to the man at the front of the room.

"How is it no one knows you have a kid?"

There's a collective gasp, heads turn, and the team officials spread around the room snap to attention, but nothing comes from Higgison. His stony gaze is on the man to my right, and if looks could kill that's the one.

It's razor sharp and ice cold.

I can't help the shiver that raises goosebumps all over my body. I'd hate to be on the receiving end of that look.

Higgison shakes his head slightly and says, "I'm not sure where you get your info—"

"It's right here." Draper waves his phone above his head. "An Instagram post from WhitHigg, a high school senior. It's a pic of the Rogues on the ice after tonight's final horn and the caption reads 'So proud of my dad, leading his new team the Baton Rouge Rogues to victory. Winning their way to the cup!' with a bunch of hashtags and two account tags. You and the Rogues."

I rack my brain trying to recall who on the team has kids, teenagers specifically, and what their names are. I can't think of anyone with a teenager and the look on Higgison's face tells me I won't.

Higgison shakes his head. "No idea—"

"Funny how the post was taken down moments later. And WhitHigg now seems to have switched their account to private."

I can see the anger and fear in Higgison's eyes, the greed and triumph stamped on Draper's face, and as much as I'm clueless when it comes to reporting sports of any kind, never mind at a professional level, I've had a bit of an education in hockey the last few years thanks to my BFF and I'm a reporter. Questions are what I do, so I'm able to at least think up something to ask that will hopefully slow this speeding train down.

My phone is vibrating like crazy in my back pocket and, ignoring it because let's be real, it can only be one of two people— or both of them—trying to reach me right now, I step forward.

Someone needs to stop this press conference from becoming a train wreck.

"Coach Alcott," I call out, waving my hand to get everyone's attention. "You must be pleased with how the team is shaping up. You've had your share of detractors since you took the job as head coach for the Rogues—do you feel vindicated now that your second outing proved the first wasn't a fluke?"

Walker gives me a smile of relief before he answers. "The team played well tonight. The score reflects that, but there's always room for improvement so we'll be studying video footage, talking with coaches and players, before getting back on the ice to work on those areas. As for the detractors, everyone has an opinion— they're entitled."

I don't miss the flick of his gaze to my right.

From the corner of my eye, I see a couple of security guards flank Draper who's still shouting questions and demanding answers from Higgison about WhitHigg.

And because everyone else in the room seems to be watching the action surrounding the reporter, I throw out another question in the hope of blocking out the drama unfolding because I'm pretty sure Draper just threw a punch which isn't good, or is. That will definitely get him ejected from the room quicker.

"How are you finding the team off the ice, and by that, I mean the players, management, and the owner?"

There's a flare of something hot in Walker's gaze but he quickly masks it and smiles. "We're a team from the ice to the front door. Everything is working like a well-oiled machine. Everyone here brings years of experience and the Rogues are benefiting from that. Our performance tonight demonstrated that with favorable results."

I keep the questions rolling as the scuffle on my right increases. "Being a new franchise has to have put more pressure on you and your team. How are you dealing with that? On and off the ice?"

"We're concentrating on what we do best. Hockey. Sure, there is an expectation that we'll fail, but when you take it down to the bones, we're all professionals and it's our job to play hockey, coach it, maintain equipment, or run the administrative end of a professional hockey team, and that's what we're all dedicated to doing. It's what we'll continue to do, win or lose on the ice."

"Coach!" A reporter closer to the front sticks his hand up, a mini recorder held out. "There are rumors of tension in the ranks, in particular surrounding the new owner, Oakley James, who somehow managed to get a franchise without any media attention or prior hockey experience. What do you say to those?"

"I'm in the business of coaching a group of elite athletes, not standing around the water cooler gossiping. Do you have a question about the game?"

A smile tugs at my mouth. I like Walker. I've spent enough time with him outside of the Rogues facility to know he's a stand-up guy. The fact Oakley married him within weeks of meeting him says enough for me anyway.

I trust her with my life. I trust her with the team.

The plan was for me to meet more of the players and staff after tonight's game but I'm pretty sure after Draper's questions, she'll be in damage control mode. Which is probably why my phone hasn't stopped vibrating.

My brain is already running through possibilities to keep this media storm locked down but when I hear the guy next to me say into his phone 'get me everything you can on Beckett Higgison right down to his time of birth', I know it's too late to keep things contained. It's a matter of battening the hatches and hoping for the least amount of damage.

If anyone knows how to do that it's me.

I can't say what the best course is yet, but one thing is clear.

I need to get out of here and find Oakley and Nat.

BECKETT

Ducking out of the conference room I scan the corridor, my thoughts consumed by one thing.

Whitney.

I can't see her in the crowd. Where is she? She's supposed to be here, waiting for me outside the locker room.

"Beckett." Natalie Redding, the Rogues General Manager, comes rushing toward me. Grabbing my arm as she passes, she drags me into her race along the corridor—how she moves so fast on her stiletto heels is mind-boggling. "We've got her up in the owner's box. Oakley is with her, and right now we need you out of sight for a few minutes while we clear the arena of reporters and fans."

"What the fuck?"

"Let's get out of this echo-y cement tunnel, shall we?" She shoves open the locker room door with one hand and pushes me ahead of her with the other. She's stronger than she looks and I have no choice but to step into the room or land flat on my face.

Not that I'm protesting. Every instinct I have might be screaming at me to get to Whitney, but I'm not stupid. If she's in the owner's box with Oakley James, she's in good hands.

For now.

It takes me a second to realize a lot of the guys and staff are still here. No wait, they're all still here sitting around as though waiting for something to happen. "What's going on?"

"What's our official statement?" the GM asks.

"Statement?"

"We need to make one and every member of the Rogues from staff to players needs to know what it is before they go out there. I can guarantee you that little shit show is already all over the internet and while security *accidentally* dropped and stepped on that reporter's phone, I'm pretty sure whatever he had is now splashed across the net."

Fuck!

I put both hands on my head.

It's my worst nightmare come to life. I've spent almost two decades keeping Whitney and our life out of the spotlight. It hasn't been easy, and I never planned for it to be a secret but it is.

Whatever the hell happened tonight to reveal her existence happened because in the last couple of years we've both relaxed.

I let her open accounts on a few of the popular social media sites because I didn't want her life to be any more isolated than it had been before she'd started high school.

She promised to be careful and I trust her. Besides, she's almost an adult. Soon I'll have no control over what she does and I'm okay with that. I think I've done a good job of preparing her for the world outside our little bubble.

In all the years I've limited her social interactions she's not once complained. But homeschooling meant she missed out on those important friendships a teenage girl needs and we'd talked about it repeatedly before I'd moved her to a private high school back in Toronto three years ago.

We discussed the possible move to Baton Rouge and before I even looked at the new contract with the Rogues, we found a local school we were both happy for her to attend.

"Beckett!"

The GM's sharp voice pulls me out of my head.

"What's our official line?"

"No comment."

She draws in a breath and I know the argument is coming but I can't think right now. I need to see Whitney. See that she's okay. Then I can get my head straight and work out what to do.

Before the GM can get a word out, I'm speaking. "I need a few minutes. It's not going to change anything to rush this." I swallow. "I need to see Whit."

She eyes me for long seconds, her gaze softening before she nods. "Okay. Give me a minute and I'll get you there or her here." She barely steps away when the door behind her swings open and Whitney races in.

"Daddy."

I spread my arms wide and lock them closed around my daughter's body the second she crashes into me. I do what I've done her whole life. I hold her tight and rock.

"It's okay, baby," I murmur into her coconut-scented curls. "I've got you."

"I'm so sorry. I didn't even think about it because I've never posted anything like that about you before," she speaks in a rush against my chest where she's burrowed her face like she's done a million times before.

"Shh..." I stroke my hands up and down her back. "It'll be fine. I'll fix it."

Whit pulls back but I keep her in my arms, can't bear to let her go. "But that's just it, Daddy, it won't be. I'm already getting messages from my friends. It's all over the internet. I've ruined everything." The last word hitches and tears fill her eyes.

My heart clutches. If there is one thing guaranteed to bring me to my knees, it's my daughter's tears. I release my hold on her and bring my hands up to cradle her cheeks, lowering my face close to hers I say, "Whitbee, you gotta trust me on this. It will be fine."

When she gives me a small nod I drop a kiss on her forehead, my eyes closing briefly, as once again I suck in the sweet scent of her hair.

"Beckett, we need to get on this."

I look up to find Oakley James and... "What the fuck?" I let go of Whit's face and shove her behind me. "What the hell is she doing in here?"

I glare at the woman beside the team owner. I have no idea why Oakley thinks it's okay to have that woman in here, but she's gone. Now.

"Get out. I've got nothing to say to you or your kind." Every inch of me is vibrating with anger. This woman—this reporter—is the reason I'm in this mess. The reason everything I've worked toward my whole life is being threatened.

She doesn't budge. Just pops one slender eyebrow and eyes me with amusement. Like she knows a secret that I'm not privy to.

"Didn't you hear me?" I growl.

"Oh, I heard you. But it's not your call whether I'm here or not."

I glance at Oakley. "Why would you think bringing her in here is a good idea? She's the reason this shit is happening."

"Actually, I'm not personally the reason your secret is out but I can see why you might think that." She steps forward, ignoring the scowl on my face, and extends her hand. "Cami Nelson."

Her even tone and calm make me want to yell at her—shake her. But Mama Dot raised a gentlemen and those well-honed manners have me extending my own hand without thought. "Beckett Higgison."

One side of her mouth kicks up. "I know," she said with a firm shake.

I don't acknowledge the heat of her hand in mine, the smoothness of her skin as it slides over mine.

And I'm definitely not going to take notice of the zip of electricity either.

Good looking women are a dime a dozen in the world of

professional hockey, and I've never succumbed to a fleeting flash of attraction. I won't be giving in to this one.

But I'm not dumb either. I'll accept it later—when I'm alone —then let it go. It's the only way to keep Whitney safe.

"Cami, how should we deal with this?"

My gaze darts to Oakley. Why is she deferring to this woman? She's the owner, it's her call, probably more than mine, and that thought grates already raw nerves.

Oakley knows where I stand on the subject of my daughter but now that the secret is out, I'm going to have to give the press something other than my usual 'no comment' or refusal to speak about my personal life at all. Not that I've faced this particular question before.

"You need to control the narrative."

"What the fuck does that mean?" I demand. I hate that this reporter's words confuse me. This is my life, not some article.

"It means you've got no choice but to publicly acknowledge you have a daughter. You can't keep Whitney a secret any longer and if you want to get back to the peaceful life you had before tonight you need to tell the world about her—"

"No! No fucking way. Not happening. I'm not giving those vultures anything."

Cami shoots me a dismissive smile before facing Oakley again. "It's the only way to control this."

"Okay, so he does what? Gives an exclusive interview?"

"That would work."

"I'm not giving squat. Whitney is off limits. Period."

Both women sigh but it's Oakley who speaks. "You don't really have a choice, Beckett. It's the only way to keep things under control." She nods at Cami. "Tell him."

"Beckett, I understand your need to protect Whitney but if you don't give them what they want to know, and believe me, after years of knowing nothing about you having a child, they'll want to know everything about her, about you. They'll dig. And dig. They'll dig so deep and so far they'll find the nurse who was there when she was born, the girl she was friends with at day-care, the next door neighbor of the woman who cleans your house, the guy who delivers your pizza, the checkout clerk who serves you at the grocery store to find out what Whitney eats."

Cold sweat breaks out along my spine. "That's ridiculous."

"Unfortunately, I can tell you from experience, it's not. But if you give them something to talk about, what *you* want them to talk about, you take the mystery out of it because Whitney's no longer a secret. And without a juicy secret to uncover, you stop the digging. Why dig when they're being handed what they want?"

"And what do they want?" I know. Of course I know. They'll want to know how I ended up a single father at sixteen, where Whitney's mother is and why I've kept my daughter hidden her entire life.

"Besides the basics, name and age, they'll want to know why you chose to hide her away."

I close my eyes and drag in a breath. "How?" I don't expand. Everyone knows what I'm asking.

"An interview, preferably on camera, not paper."

I glance at Whitney. "On camera. With Whit?"

"That would be wise. If you let them see her, they won't go hunting for her," Cami explains.

Fuck.

The thought of cameramen lying in wait for Whitney drenches my entire body in cold sweat. "When?"

"I'd think as soon as possible," Oakley answers. "But I'm wondering... Cami, what if we did a series of interviews with every player on the team? Coaches, management, the families of those who moved to join the team..."

Cami's eyes light up, I can almost see the idea developing in those dark blue orbs.

Shit.

This isn't going to be over quickly. If I'm reading these two correctly, and I make my living reading people, then we're about to be splashed across screens countrywide for more than a few minutes.

"Okay, okay, give me a second." Cami paces. Two steps, spin, two steps. It's the tightest pacing track I've ever seen but it's her facial expressions that have me mesmerized. "We can start tonight. Do the exclusive reveal of Whitney Higgison and the lead-in to the series of ten, fifteen minute interviews that we will air every night throughout the pre-season."

"That's only a couple of weeks' worth of airtime. If we agree to this, and Nat, weigh in on this please, then I think we would want far more than that in publicity. We're giving full, exclusive access to the entire team. Something we haven't allowed to date."

Oakley's brain is turning as fast as the reporter's and I'm not ashamed to admit that watching these women plot and negotiate is fascinating.

"Full season." The GM joins the discussion. "Pre and regular season as well as playoffs."

Cami holds up her hands. "It's not me you should be negotiating with. I'm not the head of the network's sports department. Or the paper's."

The GM holds out her phone. "Get me whoever I have to talk to then."

"You'll need to call Fenton Barnes."

"You don't want to call him?" Oakley asks as the GM says, "We're going right to the top?" and my head is swiveling back and forth like I'm at some weird three-way tennis match.

Shaking her head, Cami says, "He'll want to negotiate this."

"What about Derrick Whitehall?" the GM asks.

"He'll be who you get after you negotiate the terms with Barnes."

With each new name my skin pulls tighter and the lead in my gut grows heavier. If I'm doing this, and god help me I'll admit I'm out of options, then I'm doing it on my terms. "I want you to do it," I say, my gaze on Cami.

"What?" she asks, her eyes wide when she turns to look at me.

"You." The more I think about this, the more I'm getting comfortable with the idea. "If I'm going on camera with Whitney, I want you across from us."

"But—"

"No buts. Either you're asking the questions or I'll release a statement giving basic facts and a single photo of the two of us." I turn to the GM as I pull Whit close. "Take a pic now, with your phone."

"Jesus. You're going to be a pain in my ass, aren't you, Beckett?" Oakley shakes her head. "Fine. Cami does the interviews."

"Oakley! I can't."

"Why the hell not?"

"You know why."

Oakley shrugs. "We'll worry about that later."

I have no idea what passes between the team owner and reporter but the stare-down lasts almost a minute before Cami gives in with a shoulder deflating sigh. "Fine. But when it blows up in our faces, I'm saying I told you so and I want your mesh lace-up booties."

"My Gianvito Rossi boots?" Oakley asks with a frown. "Brown or black?"

"Both."

"Shit. Fine. Deal." Oakley sticks out a hand. "But I want borrow rights."

CAMI

I'm in the owner's box. Waiting. I know the call is coming and to make sure I'm alone when it does, I told Oakley I wanted some time up here to decide if the suite would work for filming the first of the team's exclusive interviews.

My phone vibrates in my hand. I still haven't switched the sound back on and I'm not inclined to do it now because the damn thing has been blowing up since the press conference earlier. I've ignored all the calls so far. Except I can't ignore this one. I have to decide how to answer it though.

Am I Cami Nelson, features reporter for the *Baton Rouge Times*, or am I Camilla Nelson Barnes, daughter of Fenton Nelson Barnes, owner of the *Times* and the FNB network?

I decide to let my father make the decision. Accepting the call, I bring the phone to my ear but I can hear him talking before it's even next to my face.

"Cam, I'm putting you in charge of this. I want TV and print copy. If I'm giving in to that shark of a woman, I'm getting as much out of it as I can."

"Ah...okay." What the hell did Oakley do? Or maybe it was Nat, she's gone up against Fenton before and won. Something not a lot of people can say.

"Do your interviews on camera but I want a series of feature articles for the *Times* Sunday edition separate from the TV footage. After they've run each weekend, we'll put them up on the network website. I've spoken to Derrick and Bas. They've agreed you are the best reporter to do both, and you should be the point person between the team and FNB."

"You don't think it's a conflict of interest?" My father is well aware I'm a silent partner in the company that owns the Rogues' hockey franchise. And while my connection isn't a secret, my name is rarely mentioned when the team is in the press.

I've had very little to do with the Rogues in any capacity except fronting twenty-five percent of the money Oakley needed to make the franchise happen as well as a quarter of the money needed to build the state-of-the-art arena the team trains and plays in. I gave my three partners complete control; I'm silent in every way.

Which I'm sure is going to bite us in the ass at some point.

"You don't have anything to do with running the franchise, Cam."

"But surely the interviews and articles won't have the same weight if someone remembers I'm a joint owner of the company that owns the team I'm interviewing?"

"Let me and Oakley worry about that. And let me tell you why you're the perfect choice. You're good. At your job. And that's not a biased father talking. Sure, there are a few other journalists I could send in but none of them are female, and I think when we look at the team, the owner, the GM, the assistant coach, we need a woman on this. I want you to punch up the female angle on this, show that having women in charge doesn't take away from the men on the team or the sport."

I close my eyes. I'd thought the same thing earlier when we were in the locker room discussing how to calm the storm Draper had stirred up but I couldn't come up with a name, another journalist I trust to do this.

"You're right. I know you're right about it needing a woman, about taking that angle, but isn't there someone from the network who can do it?"

"Who? The ex-cheerleader Derrick has on the sidelines during football season? No. Definitely not. She knows football, is great at reporting it, but she doesn't have the journalistic skills needed for this." I can all but see him shake his head and frown. "I want a serious journalist on this. One used to getting into the hard questions, finding the best in the subject. And I want you."

"Dad."

"Oh, now I'm Dad, huh." There's a smirk in his voice. "Baby girl, if what I'm hearing is true, you're in a unique position to help these two navigate the media storm that's coming."

I should have known he'd pick up on that. "I wasn't as old as Whitney."

"No. You weren't. And I never chose to hide you, Andrea did, and this is a completely different situation to the one we found ourselves in but it doesn't take away from the fact that you can relate to the media frenzy that's already winding up."

"Fine." I draw in a breath. As much as I don't want to do this, I do. I *can* relate to Whitney and Beckett. I might have been young but I remember every second of the nightmare Andrea caused when she went public with my real father's name. "But I want to do this my way. I don't need a crew tonight. I want to do a series of informal interviews filmed on my phone."

"What are you thinking?"

"What makes you think I've got anything in mind?"

He laughs and I can't help the smile turning up my lips. "You are your father's daughter."

"According to Andrea anyway."

"Don't. She's right though, you are like me. And it pisses her off that she had nothing to do with the way you are. You might look like her, hell you could pass for her clone, but you are *nothing* like her in nature and she knows it. Resents it."

I hate talking about my biological mother. We have a fractured relationship at best, and considering how often she hits me up for money it's definitely better that way. In fact I wish it would break apart completely. I've accepted I was—*am*—nothing more than a means to an end, or in our case, the pot of gold at the end of the rainbow.

"Cam." Dad's voice brings me back from the edge of the dark pit that holds my thoughts about Andrea. "Don't go there, baby girl."

"It's hard." I feel the sting of tears but they're not because the woman who gave birth to me never loved me. They're because this man did. No questions. No matter what I threw at him in those early years, no matter how hard or far I tested him, he held steady. "Thank you."

"Cam. You have nothing to thank me for. You were born for me to love."

Sniffing, I scrub my fingers over my eyes. "And I was born to love you."

Those words? They're our thing. Even before Dad managed to get me away from the toxic Andrea and the man I'd thought was my father, he'd insisted on those words passing between us.

They've given me comfort from the first time we spoke them. As they do now. They also gave me confidence. An intrinsic trust in myself that no amount of self-awareness could deliver.

"I'll come into the office tomorrow and lay it all out for you and Derrick. Nine work for you?"

"I'll make it work. When do you want to air the first interview?"

"Can I do it tonight? Before the ten o'clock news?"

"I'll meet you at the station. After it airs, we can have a late dinner together."

"You haven't eaten yet?"

"No. And now I'll get to eat with my favorite daughter."

"I'm your only daughter."

"You'd still be my favorite girl."

Laughing, I say, "I bet. I promise not to tell Mom." And by

Mom, I mean my step-mother, Dana. The woman who raised me as her own from the minute my father brought me home.

"Mom knows you're my favorite," he murmurs with a smile in his voice. "You're her favorite girl too."

I'm her only as well but I don't say it because I know how much they tried to have children before and after I came along at eight. It used to upset me that I wasn't hers but not because I felt less loved. No, I'd gone to sleep every night wishing with every-thing I was hers, that Dana was my real mother.

It wasn't until my sixteenth birthday that I realized she *was* my real mother, the only one who mattered. From that day forward she was Mom, and I never went to bed without saying thank you for that.

I may have had a seriously warped biological mother but the one who raised me, the one who loves me unconditionally with everything she has, shaped me into the woman I am.

"Will Mom have dinner with us?" Maybe it was Beckett and Whitney Higgison's situation but suddenly I need to spend some time with both of them.

"I'll give her a call as soon as we hang up."

"Okay, then don't bother coming into the station, I'll meet you at home." The home I no longer live in but still think of that way. Despite living in my own place for three years, my two-bedroom condo isn't home. "I'll stay the night," I add.

"Excellent. We'll have breakfast together too."

"Blueberry pancakes?"

"You bet."

My eyes sting and, blinking rapidly, I pull in a slow breath and fight off the tears. "Dad..."

"I'm proud of you, Cam."

"Thanks, Dad."

"I'll see you later at the house."

"Okay." The door opens behind me, and I turn to see Oakley, Nat, Walker, and the Higgisons enter the suite. "I gotta go. See you later."

"You were born for me to love, baby girl."

A smile curls my lips. "And I was born to love you."

As I hang up my gaze collides with Beckett's and the flash of angry heat in his eyes takes me by surprise, gives me a jolt.

He's pissed. I get it. He doesn't want to do this, and I can't fault him for that, which is why I'm going to make this as pain-free as possible.

Waving at the chairs I've pulled into a semi-circle I say, "Why don't we all have a seat and talk before I film anything."

"I'd rather get this over with," Beckett grumbles but he ushers Whitney into a chair then takes the one beside her.

"I understand that. But I thought if I ran through what I want to ask and what your answers are, if you'll answer, we'll be a little more comfortable on camera." I smile at Whitney. "Do you want a cola before we start?"

"I'm good, thanks."

"Are you sure?" I indicate the bar behind me. "You can have whatever you want."

"She said she was good," Beckett barks.

"O-kay." I give him a tight-lipped smile. "Let's get started then."

"What do you want us to do?" Oakley asks from behind me.

"Nothing. I'm going to chat with Beckett and Whitney then we'll decide what questions and answers we'll put on video." I glance around. "I think I'll set my phone up on that side table when I'm ready to record."

"You don't want one of us to hold it?" Nat asks with a frown. "Wouldn't it work better that way?"

"No. I want these ten-minute recordings to be completely informal. I want it to appear as though the only people in the room are the ones in front of the camera." I turn to Walker. "If you don't mind, I'd like to do your interview after Beckett and Whitney."

He glances at Oakley before agreeing. "Sure."

"What time is practice tomorrow?"

"The guys get in anywhere from six to use the training room, but we're suited up and on the ice at eleven."

"I'd like to get some candid shots and video. I won't interview anyone before practice but if you could ask a couple of the players, I'd like to bring them up here one at a time and record their informal interviews after training is done."

"I want to see everything before you air it," Nat demands in her tough GM voice. "Nothing goes live or into print without my approval."

"Of course." Nat knows me. She knows I wouldn't put the team or any of the people involved in a bad light but I get that she needs to be the hard-ass GM right now. Although I am surprised the team's marketing and media manager isn't here. I'm not going to ask because I don't want anyone else in here right now.

Beckett is agitated enough without adding another possibly hostile person to the room, and Dwight Mitchum would definitely be hostile. I'm still shocked that Oakley hired my ex.

Then again, the man knows what he's doing when it comes to marketing. It's the media part of his job I'm not happy about.

But then I'm the silent partner so I have little say in who works for the team my company owns. And I trust Oakley. If she thinks Dwight is the best for the job then he is. I've got other things to worry about than a man I dated for four years back in college.

"Okay. Beckett, let's start with you. Are you happy you made the move to the Rogues?"

He cocks an eyebrow at me. "I was..."

A laugh. "I can imagine you're not too happy about it right at the moment but then it's not really the team's fault your secret daughter has been outed."

"No. It's mine." Every eye swings to Whitney. "Dad has always kept our life and his job separate and I joined them together tonight in a very public way."

I like this girl. She's not backing away from her involvement in the scandal of the hockey season. We might only be into the first few weeks of pre-season but there hasn't been anything news-worthy before tonight. Except the Rogues franchise itself of course.

"Did you do that on purpose, Whitney?"

"Hey!" Beckett launches to his feet. "That's enough."

I tip my head back and lock my gaze with his. "I'm not accusing her, Beckett, I'm asking."

"It's okay, Dad." Whitney puts a hand on her father's arm. "I get why she's asking and we're not recording yet."

He glances down, the frown on his face smoothing out slightly when his eyes land on his daughter. "I don't like where she's going with that question. You'd never do something like that without talking to me about it."

In one simple exchange, father and daughter have demon-strated their love in a way that tells everyone watching they're a tight unit.

It's Beckett and Whitney against the world and as the adult, Beckett has protected her from the harsh realities of that world.

Until now.

BECKETT

It takes every ounce of control I have not to fidget in my seat. Whitney sits beside me as though she isn't about to expose herself to the world, and I'm struggling to keep from picking her up and carrying her out of here.

I don't want her to do this. Except at seventeen she's making adult decisions that I might not agree with but have to accept. I'm proud of her. She's a remarkable young woman and I want to shout that to the world, I really do, I'm just not sure this is how I want to do the shouting.

Cami is on the other side of me, her chair turned a little so she faces us both and we're in a sort of semi-circle. She's relaxed and moves easily through our conversation. And that's what this has felt like, like a conversation between friends.

All the questions have been okay so far. Nothing outside of what we went over before she set her phone up to record and yet I'm still waiting for the other shoe to drop. I can't relax. Unlike Whit who is chatting with the woman like they've known each other for years.

I want to be angry about that except I can't seem to dredge up that emotion. I want to believe this reporter who seems to have a connection with the team owner I can't figure out, isn't trying to catch us in a lie or make a spectacle of me or my daughter. But I can't quite get there either.

I'm so used to being the only one taking care of Whitney that it's hard to believe this stranger would have her best interests at heart.

"So, Beckett. How do you feel about the world knowing about Whitney?" Cami asks.

I frown, I can't help it although I know I should because the camera will catch every emotion crossing my face. Taking a breath, I try to relax my face and gather my thoughts. "To be honest I'm not sure yet. Maybe ask me again in a day or two."

Cami laughs softly. "I'll be sure to do that next time we talk. But maybe I can help you decide how you feel now. Are you angry that your secret has been discovered, effectively forcing the two of you to sit down with me and talk about your lives?"

"Yes and no. Whit's never been a secret per se. I've kept her out of the spotlight for so long it's hard to remember when it became a hidden fact."

"You've always been one of the league's elusive players when it comes to media attention off the ice and some are likely to suggest it was to hide the fact you're an unmarried single father."

"It was to protect someone who couldn't protect herself." I swallow. Lick my lips. I have no idea where those words came from, I certainly hadn't thought it before saying it even if it is the truth. "Look. I'm not saying all reporters are bad but everyone has seen or heard the lengths some of them can go to for a photo or something they consider scandalous. I wanted to protect my daughter, and myself, from that."

"But you weren't in the league when Whitney was born."

"No."

"Then you wouldn't have needed to protect her from the press."

"No." I'm sweating now. I can feel it beading across my forehead. I'm sure the camera is picking it up but I can't wipe my face. There's so much I don't want to reveal to the world about my daughter. I need to apply the same principles I apply to my game. Never let them see you sweat. Never show your fear.

"So why not tell everyone about her?"

"How was I supposed to do that? Take out an advertisement in the paper? I'm not one to want the spotlight. Even if I didn't have Whit to protect I wouldn't seek out media attention. When I leave the ice and the arena, my job is over and I leave that behind. I go home, or to the hotel if we're playing away, and I'm just a man, a dad, who wants to spend time with his daughter."

"You're saying you're no different than the average Joe who goes to work then goes home? Is that possible when what you do for a living is in the public eye?"

"I think I proved exactly that." I don't mean it as a slap but the flash in Cami's eyes seems to indicate she's taken it that way and the urge to soften my words is impossible to ignore. "I never set out to deceive anyone. All I wanted was to give my daughter as normal a life as possible. It's hard being a single parent without having the media put you under a spotlight, without the public judging you for every decision you make."

"Let's talk about that, being a single parent and having a job that takes you away from home so often. How hard was it leaving Whitney so much?"

I smile. "In spite of no one knowing about her before now she accompanied me on most of my away games over the years. There were plenty of days, before and after an away game, where I was in a hotel room helping her with school work."

"You home schooled her?"

"Yes. She was enrolled in a system that allowed her to travel with me until high school when we both decided attending a physical campus would be the best way to finish her schooling before college."

"I'm impressed. It takes considerable effort and discipline to homeschool. For the parent and the child."

"The program made it easy for both of us and Whit's smart.

Smarter than her dad, that's for sure." I laugh. "She's definitely taught me a thing or two over the years."

"It's clear you love your daughter, Beckett. What's one thing you want the world to know about her?"

"Just that. I love her more than anything. If what I do for a living put her in jeopardy, I'd quit in a heartbeat." I reach over and grab Whit's hand, giving it a squeeze. "She's my reason for being."

The room goes quiet while I stare at the woman across from me. She's got a smile curling one side of her mouth and her eyes are sparkling with the liquid pooling in them.

"We'll end it there," she murmurs a long moment later. Getting up, she retrieves her phone and stops the recording.

Letting go of Whit's hand I push to my feet and ask, "Can we see it?"

"Sure. Or you can take a break, get something to eat or drink while I record Coach Alcott's interview, then we can watch them both."

"Do you need a laptop?" the GM asks, reminding me we aren't alone in the room.

"That would probably be good for viewing. I can edit the footage on my phone though."

"Let's get this over with," Coach growls. "I'd like to get out of here before midnight."

I reach down for Whit's hand. "C'mon, Whitbee, we'll grab a drink and sit over there."

We get settled in a couple of chairs by the closed glass doors that overlook the ice. I turn my back to the view and watch Coach take a seat, his back stiff, his face in that serious scowl he gets when he's not happy with what we're doing on the ice.

I'm glad I'm not the only one who isn't happy about this turn of events. Then again, do I have the right to be pissed off about this?

It was my daughter who caused a media storm. A storm I don't see blowing over even with these 'control the narrative' interviews Cami insists will take the mystery out of my daughter's revelation.

"Coach Alcott, your team is looking great on the ice. There doesn't appear to be any friction or missteps for such a new team, and I have to assume the coaching staff has a lot to do with that. Has it been hard? Pulling it all together?"

"Not really. Ms. James and her scouts knew what they were doing when they picked each player on the team. That includes the coaching staff."

"Let's get the hard question over with. Were you upset when they named your assistant coach?"

Coach laughs. "Are you kidding me? Blake Watts was born to play hockey. She's third generation in a family who is arguably hockey royalty, has three Olympic medals and coached the Canadian women's gold medal team in the last Olympics. Who in their right mind wouldn't want her at their side?"

"So you could say you're a fan?" Cami asks with a smile.

"I'm a fan of winning. And I firmly believe Blake is one of the critical components of the Rogues' determination to make the playoffs."

"Is that a prediction, Coach?"

"Damn straight, it is."

"I'm not sure others are such believers."

"I'm sure they're not. But here's the thing, Oakley James might not have a history with hockey but she's an extremely smart woman. She's pulled together people with passion and one goal in mind. Winning. I have no doubt we'll make the playoffs and if I were a betting man I'd say we'll be taking that trophy home sooner than anyone predicts."

A kick to my shin pulls my gaze from the interview to Whit. She's holding her phone out and I can see she's got something on the screen she wants me to see. I'm not sure I want to look. If it's something to do with the post she put up that started this whole thing, I don't know how I'll react.

I know she didn't mean to cause a drama or to out herself, or me, but she has to know we wouldn't be here if she hadn't been careless. She tips her head to indicate the device, and I reluctantly take it.

I steel myself for what I'll read except it isn't what I expect. It's a message, although she hasn't hit send, and I can see it's to me.

> W: I'm really sorry about what happened tonight. I honestly didn't mean to tag you. It was an automatic response because that's what you do on Instagram. You post a pic, add a comment and a billion different hashtags so people searching can find your post. It wasn't until I got a message asking me how long I'd known you were my dad that I realized I'd really screwed things up. I didn't delete the post like that reporter said but I did switch my account to private. I know what I'm going to ask next is going to probably piss you off more but I'd like to switch back to public. I'd like to have that post on there because I'm proud of you dad. I'm proud to be your daughter and I know you've kept me hidden to protect me but after next year I'll be on my own and I don't want to be a secret anymore. Not that that's how you think of me but it's how it seems. And yes, I know you always say it's not what anyone else thinks, it's what you or I think about us, except I want to tell the world I'm yours, that I'm proud of you. I want to show my pride in this team, in our life. I think I'm old enough to make that decision, but I won't do it without your blessing.

Fuck. My eyes are blurry and my nose tingles with the emotion clogging my throat.

"Whitbee," I murmur and reach for her hand.

This girl makes me so proud, so humble. She's far more adult than she should be. I said in our interview that she was smart, but my daughter's brain blows me away. I can't take all the credit for this incredible woman in front of me. Mama Dot had a lot to do with the way Whit turned out.

Hell, she's the reason I'm the way I am too. Without that guidance in the early days of my daughter's life, I'm sure I would have failed.

No. I know I would have failed.

Hitting send on the message, I hand Whit her phone and pull mine from my pocket. I keep it on silent from the minute I change into my gear before a game and don't turn it back on until I leave the arena whether we're at home or away. The earlier fiasco, and the fact I'm still at the arena means I receive Whit's message without a sound.

Tapping in my passcode, I pull up her message and reply.

> I'll agree and respect any decision you make. I don't know what I did to deserve you but I'm thankful every day that you are mine and if you want the world to know that I'm your dad I'm happy for you to do that any way you want to. I love you more than anything, Whitbee. I'm proud of you.

Mindful of the interview taking place across the room Whit reads my message and replies. This isn't the first time we've communicated via text but it's definitely the first time we've been in the same room doing it.

> W: We should wait until Cami tells us what time the interview airs then post a few selfies on both our accounts.

Shit. I forgot about my account. I rarely use it. In fact, until I took the contract with the Rogues I didn't have to bother because my old team had a social media expert running it. After signing with the Rogues, I changed the password and made an announcement about the change of teams for this year and haven't touched it since.

> We should ask Oakley what to post.

> W: Cami too. She might want us to do some posts about the interviews. And we should do some regular posts about the team and us too.

I want to argue about that except I'm not even sure how much I used to post during the season. I didn't lie when I said I leave the ice and my job is done. I'm clueless with all of this. I guess this means I'm going to have to make an effort.

The world knowing I have a daughter isn't the only thing changing tonight.

CAMI

"Cam!"

I've barely cracked the door of my car when Mom comes racing across the driveway to meet me. The second I'm on my feet, her arms are around me and her cheek is pressed to mine.

"I missed you."

I laugh. "You saw me three days ago."

"Two days too many to go without a Cam hug." She smacks a kiss on my forehead then lets go. "Come on. I've got dinner ready. Your father is in his office on a call. He's been fielding them since the interview aired. Great job, by the way."

"I didn't stick around the studio to watch it once we got it cued to go." I wanted to but I also didn't. I saw it. Lived it. I knew it was good. And I was still nervous as hell about it anyway. "Is Dad happy or..."

"Oh, happy doesn't come close to describing it. He's got rival networks throwing money at him to get their hands on it."

I stumble to a stop. "Really?"

She palms my face with both hands, her own face split wide with a huge grin. "The interview isn't all they're trying to buy. You, my dear, are as much a smash hit as the secret you were privileged to reveal."

"I didn't reveal it."

"No, but you got the real scoop, didn't you? Draper is making noise about you stealing his story, but no one is listening."

"Shit. I don't need him coming after me."

Mom shrugs. "He'll do what he does, and we'll do what we do." She gives me a wink. "I know a really good lawyer."

"She won't need one." Dad stands just inside the front door, a smug smile on his face. "C'mon, we're having your favorite for dinner."

"Hot dogs?" I ask smiling.

"No." He shakes his head with a laugh. "Your other favorite."

"I thought we were having pancakes for breakfast?"

"Get in here." He wraps his arm around my neck and yanks me close. "You did good, baby girl, so good."

"Mom was just telling me the feedback on the interview is good."

"Good? Lord, baby, that thing is blowing up the airwaves. I've got national networks trying to get their hands on it and you."

"And those are good things?"

"They are if you want a national platform." He leans back and our eyes lock. "But *you* don't want that."

I shake my head. "No. I'm happy at the paper. I'm happy for the interviews to go national though."

"Okay." Dad lets me go and grabs my hand. "We've got a lot to talk about then. Good thing you've got your legal rep here." He sends a wink over his shoulder at Mom.

"I need a lawyer?"

"Not like you're thinking."

When we reach the kitchen, I see Mom has set the table in the breakfast nook and there is a pile of paperwork to one side. "What's all that?"

"Your new contract with FNB."

"New contract?"

"Sit down, Cam. Let's not spoil dinner with work talk. We'll deal with it after we eat." Mom moves toward the fridge. "What do you want to drink."

I glance at the table. At the new contract. "Water." I want wine but I'm going to need all my wits to get through those pages. With a sigh, I slip into a chair and reach for the paperwork. "May as well get this over with. Letting it sit here while we eat is going to spoil it anyway."

Dad smiles at me from across the table. "That's my girl."

"We'll see if you still say that after I've read this." I hold up the bundle. Dropping it back to the table I start to read. "I'm freelance?"

"It's the best for you. FNB and KAW and its associated investments too," Mom says, putting a glass of water in front of me. "If someone digs and publicizes your involvement with KAW they'll connect you to the Rogues. I spoke to Oakley earlier and she's getting your lawyers to draw up a contract between you and the Rogues to cover the interviews."

"So even though I technically own the team, we're drawing the line between ownership and journalist?"

"Exactly. And, we were talking about possibly donating your earnings from the interviews to one of the Rogues' designated charities or one of your choosing."

"Hmm..." I glance back at the contract. It doesn't take me long to work my way through it in spite of it being twenty pages long. There's nothing I see that worries me and the monetary value is more than acceptable. In fact... "Don't you think the dollar amount is a little high?" I ask Dad.

"It was less until this one got involved." He points at Mom. "Good thing she's on our side. She had valid arguments as to why I should up the figure to that amount."

"You'll notice the clause about income received from the pieces too. Anything FNB brings in from the interviews or articles will be split between you, FNB, and a charity of your choice."

"If I donate my earnings I'll effectively be working for free."

"You don't need to work, Cam."

I look at Dad. "I know. You made sure of that, but I still have bills to pay, and you know I haven't touched my trust fund for anything other than the start-up money for Rogue sportswear and the Rogues franchise."

"I do and yet, you've barely dented it."

"Half a billion is more than a dent Dad."

"It is, but not when you put it up against what you have."

I can't argue with him. My trust fund has been invested well over the years and while I've taken money out of it, there's still well over a billion in there. And then there's my personal accounts. The ones holding my share of the Rogue sportswear profits.

Looking at Mom, I ask, "You think I should make everyone aware I'm donating my earning from these interviews or keep it on the quiet until someone starts pointing fingers?"

"Up to you."

"I have an idea."

I turn to Dad. "What?"

"You probably won't like it but I think you should leave the owners of the Rogues until last."

"But Blake and Nat work for the team, I can't leave the assistant coach and GM out of these interviews."

"No, you can't. And that's not what I'm saying. I think you should interview them as GM and assistant coach. Don't mention them being part of KAW."

It takes barely a moment for his words to form a picture of what he's suggesting. "The owners, Oak, Nat, Blake, and me."

"Yes."

"And who would do that interview?"

"You."

"How the hell would I do that?"

"The same way you do the players and staff, except the girls can turn any question back on you or ask something else."

"The interviewer becomes the interviewee?"

"Yes."

I mull that over. I can see how it would work. But then something else comes to mind. "What if I let Walker and Branton, no, wait, what if we got Andrew Watts to interview us? He's arguably the most knowledgeable and respected name in the hockey world."

"Do you think he'd do it? Because I really like that idea."

"I think so, but I'll ask him tomorrow. And it might be a good idea to have Walker and Branton there with us or for them to join us at some point..."

"Okay, enough shop talk." Mom moves the contract to the side. "Let's eat dinner and come back to this discussion. Although you can leave the final interview decisions for now. Who knows, by the time you're ready to film it, there may be a couple more partners to add."

"Nat's divorcing Johnathon."

"Oh, I know. She's been working on it for a while now." Mom smiles at me.

"You knew?"

"Yes. Although I thought she would have done it before now."

"She hasn't said much but I think he's being a dick."

"He was always a dick. So was her grandfather."

My eyes dart to Dad. "Huh?"

"Redding was a fucking prick who treated the women in his family like property."

"I. Um." My gaze bounces to Mom and back. "You knew Nat's grandfather?"

"Yes. I know him. Wish I didn't. Waste of air, that man. I hoped when he died his antiquated ideas would die with him. But then Natalie married Johnathon."

I sit back and stare at Dad. "I had no idea you knew Nat before I met her in college."

"I didn't know her. I knew her grandparents and I'd met her parents a couple of times. Her father was a spineless waste of air too. I wasn't sad to hear he'd died."

"Wow. This is...I don't know what this is."

"Tell Nat if she needs any help getting Johnathon out of her life to give me a call."

"What could you do? She already has enough evidence from the PI to cut him loose with minimal damage. But I think she's going to sweeten the pot for him to walk away. She's already giving him the house in New Orleans, but Oakley said something about five hundred million to convince him to walk without looking back."

"Not the family home?"

"No. They never lived in that. And something in her grandfather's will means she can't without being married so she's leaving that as is."

"She can't sell it?" Mom asks.

"Again, something in the will stops that from happening."

"Fucking prick. Did he at least leave money for the upkeep on the monstrosity?"

"Yeah. And Nat thinks she may have come up with a way to use it without living there. I can't remember exactly what and with the start of the season on us she's been distracted."

"They've lived separate lives as long as I've known her. I honestly didn't think he'd make things difficult for her."

I look at Mom. "She's his unlimited credit card. He's got no money of his own and never had a job that I know of."

"He worked for his father before they were married," Dad explains. "Now that I think about it, I'm pretty sure Whitman senior cut him off around that time."

"It would explain why he married Natalie."

"You don't think they were in love once?" Mom asks.

I can't help the bark of laughter that breaks free. "Hell no. She told us she married him to unlock her trust funds. Although I will admit that's new information. In all the years we've known her, she's barely talked about him or their marriage. As you say, they've lived separate lives. I remember the documents we had to sign to guarantee he couldn't touch Rogue sportswear and now the Rogues franchise."

"With the money the Redding family has, I'm surprised she worried about that."

I glance at Dad. "I think she worried about us, not herself."

"Ah, yes, I can see that."

"Speaking of deadbeat family."

"Was that what we were doing?"

"In a roundabout way, yes." I lock gazes with Dad. "You know she's going to come out of whatever hole she's in, right?"

"She can crawl out, but it won't affect you."

"I'll be the first one she heads for."

"Don't talk to her. If you accidentally pick up a call because she's got a new number, hang up and send me the number before blocking it."

Dad's words are firm, no room for argument, and to be honest, I'd probably do what he asked minus sending him the number anyway.

I have no inclination to talk to my biological mother. As far as I'm concerned, she doesn't exist.

"Cam?"

"I won't entertain her in any way. Call, in person, no matter how she tries to contact me, I won't give her the satisfaction of getting to me."

"If she does contact you, we'll have another restraining order put in place."

"We know that won't stop her."

"No, but it will make it easier to get her to go away."

"I can get the paperwork drawn up, ready to go." Mom laughs as we both look at her. "What? We all know she's going to remember who she gave birth to once she sees you splashed all over the TV and internet."

"Draper might dig."

"He probably will, but I can blacklist him from a few outlets.

I can't really stop the gutter press from taking whatever he has to offer and that might be information on you."

"Thanks, Dad, but I think we'll see what happens before you call in any favors."

"Say the word and it'll be done. Of course he's already black-listed from the entire FNB network."

"Since when?"

"Since Natalie called me with her demands."

"She told you what happened?"

"Of course she did. It made her demands more acceptable."

"Why?"

"Because he chose to attack my girls."

"He didn't attack us."

"He went after Higgison. You own Higgison. Therefore, he went after you."

"Dad."

"Baby girl, I will do anything and everything to make sure you're taken care of."

"But—"

Dad holds up a hand. "I couldn't protect you for eight years."

"That wasn't your fault."

"No, it wasn't, but it's a father's privilege to take care of his daughter."

"I want to argue I'm a grown up, but I know it must be hard for you, even after all this time, to accept you weren't there for me."

"It guts me every day to think she left you without food, in dirty clothes." He shakes his head. "And don't get me started on Muskin. I can't make that go away, can't erase the trauma you went through, but I can damn well try to make up for it no matter how old you are."

"I was born to love you."

Dad's frown instantly turns to a grin. "And you were born for me to love."

BECKETT

A whistle blows and every one of my teammates stops whatever drill they're on and turns toward the bench.

"All right, that's enough for today." Coach Alcott waves us in. When we're all close, he says, "I need a couple of volunteers to head up to the owner's suite in the arena after you get cleaned up."

"Don't panic, no one is in trouble," Assistant Coach Watts adds. "The team is doing a series of interviews with each player. If you haven't seen the one with your captain that went live last night, I suggest you search for it and watch it."

"We all have to do it?" Mikel Vinter asks, his accent heavy.

"Yes. Eventually." Alcott turns to me. "If you've got a minute, Cami wants to see you too."

"What? Why? I did my interview."

"I have no idea, but she specifically asked if you could spare her a few minutes after morning skate. Seeing how you know the way to the suite, you can show the others where they need to go." He leans in closer, lowers his voice. "Maybe give them a few tips, some reassurance that this isn't a witch hunt, more of a sit-down chat with Cami on camera."

"Sure. I can do that."

"We've got Mikel and Noah for volunteers today," Coach Watts says. "The rest of you get out of here."

I wait for everyone to leave the ice before I move. There's no point rushing if I have to head over to the arena.

"You good?" Alcott asks as he steps beside me. "Whitney okay?"

"She's fine, handled last night's drama better than I did."

"Are we openly saying you have a daughter now?"

"May as well. The world knows about her and I never tried to keep her a secret to begin with." I shrug. "Just turned out that way."

"I don't know how. Your previous teammates knew you had a kid, the Rogues org knew." Alcott shakes his head. "I don't understand why Draper thought it was such a big deal."

"Draper?"

"The guy from the press conference. Herman Draper. From what Oakley tells me, he's the scum of scum kind of journalist who will dig in your trash looking for any dirt he can expose. Usually sells to the gossip columns."

"Does anyone believe those?"

"Probably." Alcott claps me on the shoulder. "Listen. I know you like to keep to yourself off ice but I'd—we'd— appreciate it if you were a bit more social with the rest of the team. You'll find the owners are friendly and want to be involved in the players' lives."

"Why? They're paying us to do a job, not be their friend."

"True. But they have a philosophy that has paid off big-time in their other business."

"What business? To be honest, other than Oakley, I don't know who the owners of the Rogues are."

"You didn't read or see any of the stuff when the franchise was announced?"

"Maybe. But at that point it had nothing to do with me, and when my agent came to me with the offer to play here, all I was concerned with was whether it would be suitable for Whit. I can play anywhere."

"Huh." He's quiet a moment before saying, "I don't know if anyone else warned you or not and maybe that's what Cami wants to see you about today, but you didn't mention Whitney's mom in your interview."

"Why would I? She's not in our lives. Hasn't been since Whit was born."

"Okay." Alcott stops me, turns to face me. "If I'm calculating right, and I'll be the first to admit math isn't my favorite subject or in my skill set but even I can minus seventeen from thirty-three."

I swallow. I know what's coming. The judgement, the curiosity. I was forced to face both when Whit was first born but as she got older—as I got older—the looks stopped, so did the questions, and I found it easier to lay it out. Reveal enough information to stop whoever was asking from digging deeper.

"I was sixteen when Whit was born. Her mother didn't want her but I did. Luckily I had Mama Dot, my foster mother, to help me."

"Jeez, Blake has a fifteen-year-old nephew. I can't imagine him becoming a parent next year."

"It wasn't easy. I never thought about being a parent until I found out she was on the way, but once I knew about her, I did everything I could to protect her." The fierceness of my voice has Alcott raising a brow and I have to think of something to say that will stop any more questions. "I have first-hand knowledge of a parent who doesn't protect you. I didn't want that for my kid."

Alcott nods. "I understand that. Micky isn't mine, he's my cousin's son, but I'll do anything to keep him safe, make sure he has everything he needs."

I know a little about the boy Alcott and Oakley James are raising. I might not have taken much notice of the new team in the league when it was announced but once I knew I'd sign the contract with Rogues, I did some research on the coaches. I admire them both for taking on the little boy. Although at five I guess he's not that little.

Glancing at his watch, Alcott says, "And speaking of Micky. I need to head out. He's got a school thing on."

I smile. "I've only dealt with those in recent years. When Whit was homeschooled, our school things were more excursions for one. Well, two. Someone had to go with her. Usually me."

"This is an art showing. Apparently I *need* to be there because he wants all his family with him when he unveils his painting."

"Sounds like a fun afternoon."

"Oakley promised ice cream after. Can't pass up ice cream."

"Better get going so you're not late or she might renege on that."

"That's exactly what she'd do." Alcott laughs. "Although Pa will slip me some on the sly if she does."

I have no idea who Pa is and I know I should ask if I'm going to be more friendly with the people involved in my new team but my natural inclination is to not ask. If I don't ask, they don't ask. It's how I've kept myself and Whit out of the spotlight.

"All right, get in there,"—he indicates the locker room with a chin lift—"get cleaned up, and help Mikel and Noah with their interviews."

"Not sure what help I'll be but I'll try." Again, my inclination is to not get involved but I need to. Especially now the world knows about Whit. "I'll see you tomorrow."

"Tomorrow." Alcott waves as he heads down the corridor toward his office and I wait until he's behind his door before pushing into the locker room.

I've spent eighteen years protecting Whit, protecting myself, and now, with her on the cusp of adulthood, I'm going to have to learn to be more open. More friendly. More involved in life outside of hockey and home.

"Hey, Bex. Ready to head over to the arena?"

I glance up to find Noah Hubert dressed, hair wet from his

recent shower. Looking down at my skates, I bring my gaze back up and raise an eyebrow.

"Right. No. Not ready. I'll wait in the lounge." He smiles sheepishly as he passes me. He's young. Good on the ice but green off it. He'll get there. Being twenty and finding yourself playing for a national team is daunting, and overwhelming at times.

"I'll be quick," I say to his back.

He waves in acknowledgment as he pushes out the door. Turning back to the locker room, I see the team is all still here. Most are showered and getting in their street clothes. The only one beside myself who isn't either showered or in one is Mikel.

The scowl on his face should scare people away. His perpetual grumpiness does what the frown doesn't. I've been training with the guy, playing alongside him, for a few weeks now and I still can't work out if he's pissed to be here, pissed in general, or missing home.

The last would be understandable. He's playing in the US for the first time in his short life.

At twenty-four he's not that young but he's not old either. He's seasoned, played for the professional league in Europe, so it's not that being here is much different to what he's used to.

Well, except for the whole speaking English thing.

"Mikel. You good?"

I get a nod before he shoves to his feet and starts to strip. "I don't want to talk to person."

"It's not that bad. She's just going to ask you some questions but more in a conversation way than an interview."

"You be there?" The pleading in his gaze has me answering before thinking.

"Yes." I'd planned to talk to Cami and get out of there but with Alcott's words about connecting with my team better echoing in my head, I realize staying while Noah and Mikel do their thing with Cami is the best thing to do. "I'll stick around the whole time."

He grunts, snatches up a towel, and heads for the showers.

Shaking my head, I walk to my locker and sit. I've got one skate unlaced, the second half undone when Branton sits next to me. He's quiet as I get my second skate undone and pull both off. Looking up I ask, "Need something?"

"No. Just wanted to say I know what it's like to want to protect a child with your life. I don't think you did a bad thing hiding your daughter from the world."

"I didn't hide her. That was never my intention." Except it was. Because if anyone found out about her mother, if someone dug deep enough, they'd find the trail and the trail leads to a time in my life I buried along with the woman who birthed my daughter.

"I get that. I didn't mean to imply you were being sneaky or anything." He scrubs a hand over his head. "Shit. This isn't coming out right."

"Why don't you keep going and maybe we can work it out between us."

"I just want you to know I have your back. You need to keep to yourself, keep Whitney from the public eye, I'll do—we'll do" —he indicates the men around us—"whatever you and she need to feel comfortable."

"At this point I can't keep her out of the public eye. Both Oakley and that reporter, Cami, thought it would be best if we got in front of any possible bad press by doing last night's interview. I'm sure there will be more in the future. I'm not dumb enough to think that ten minutes of conversation will satisfy everyone."

"Blake explained about the videos they want us all to do. What did they call it... A conversation with a Rogue?"

"Yeah, that's what they called mine and Coach's. It fits with promoting the team."

"It does. And Cami knows her shit, so you're in good hands there. We all are."

"Hope so."

"You are. Cami would never do anything to make the team or anyone associated with it look bad."

"That's not my experience with journalists."

"But Cami...wait. You don't know?"

"Don't know what?"

"Um, well, she's um, one of—"

"Bran!" Coach Watts sticks her head in the door. "Five minutes before we need to go."

"Shit!" He launches to his feet. "Sorry. I'm ready. Coming. Two seconds."

I have to hide my smile when Coach sends him a scowl before disappearing.

"Sorry, the wife calls. I'll catch you tomorrow."

It's amazing to see Branton and Coach Watts working together. If you didn't know anything about them, you'd never guess they were married. They keep their personal life personal and their professional life professional.

Come to think of it, so do Coach Alcott and Oakley James.

I really need to do more research on the team I play for. Find out all the connections within the team because if I'm going to be more involved in the Rogues, I should know who's who and what's what outside of the men I take the ice with.

I'll start by getting to know Noah and Mikel.

CAMI

The second Beckett Higgison enters the suite my whole body goes tense. In spite of the success of last night's interview, he still emanates hostility whenever he looks my way.

I don't know what I did that would cause his dislike—and let's be real, it's more disdain than dislike—and for some reason my natural instinct to duck and run isn't there.

I've thought about it for the last hour. The presence of Noah Hubert and Mikel Vinter hasn't helped temper Beckett's distrust.

And that's it in a nutshell. He doesn't trust me.

I can't blame him. He barely knows me and our first introduction was at the press conference where Draper attempted to tear him down. Even with my treatment of our casual interview yesterday, Beckett shouldn't blindly trust me.

I respect that.

Even if I want to do everything in my power to change his mind about me.

The aversion I have toward athletes isn't throwing up the usual red flags or walls. And where I'd normally keep my distance, especially from the ones who are contracted to represent Rogue sportswear and now the Rogues, I find myself wanting to get closer to Beckett.

I don't understand the draw. He's good looking, I can admit that, and he seems like a nice guy, hell, the man has protected his daughter from the spotlight for seventeen years. Maybe that's it.

Maybe, the fact he's done his best to shield Whitney, to keep her from being the center of scandal, is what has me wanting to get closer.

Whitney is the other reason I want to get to know this man. His daughter is intelligent, brave, not above standing up for her mistakes even if the one she made isn't really one.

I like her. And if I like her, then it would stand to reason that I would like her father.

If only her father would give me more than heated glares.

He's been nothing but polite to me, but the two men he walked in here with have received smiles, conversation, laughter. Neither Noah or Mikel seem to notice the barely veiled indifference Beckett sends my way and I'm glad for that, because while I'm upset by his behavior toward me, I'm thrilled with the way he's brought both men out of their shells.

Especially Mikel. The big blond man struggles to speak English, and obviously feels out of his depth with the way he fidgets in his chair, and without Beckett I doubt I would have gotten more than a few words out of him.

Noah was easy enough. He's like a new puppy. Excited to talk about this amazing experience he's been given. Even before he revealed he'd grown up in a small town with only his grandparents to support him, I'd have said he was sheltered. I hope playing in the NHL doesn't tarnish his boy-next-door persona.

After I film both ten-minute conversations we play them back and I make small adjustments but like Beckett's last night, neither needs more than a little sound tweak and the addition of the intro and end credits. I'm more than pleased with what I've got and both men are happy as they head out the door.

With the click of the lock, the suite seems to be sucked bare of all the fun of the last sixty minutes. Beckett is an indomitable life-force, his presence filling the space with heavy tension. It doesn't quite feel menacing and even though I want to leave, I stand in place and wait for him to acknowledge me.

He gave me a chin lift on arrival but I had to introduced myself to Noah and Mikel. The hi I sent Beckett's way was ignored in favor of conversing with his teammates.

I can't decide if I should break the tension between us or let him suffer.

"Coach said you wanted to talk to me."

His words pull my gaze off my laptop screen. "I. Yes." I lick my lips, swallow in spite of my tight throat. "I wanted to check in with you and Whitney. See if you were both okay after last night."

"Why?"

"Why what?"

"Why did you want to check on us."

His question confuses me. "Because you were both sent into a situation you weren't prepared for?"

"And? What's it to you how we are?"

Jesus. This guy isn't giving me any slack. I push to my feet. "Well. First, I was genuinely concerned for you both and wondered if I could offer help with anything. Second, I hate that one man can blacken my chosen career with his behavior and I want to assure you we're not all the same. And third, I was involved in the situation and it's the right thing to do to follow up with you, check you're both doing okay."

"We're fine. Is that all? I've got stuff to do before Whit gets home from school."

"No. It's not all." I take a step closer. "I want to warn you that it's likely other reporters are going to want to know about Whitney's mom."

"Other reporters or *you*?" he sneers.

"I'm not interested in her mom, but I can guarantee others won't feel the same way, Draper in particular. Especially when neither of you mentioned her last night. I'd like to add more interviews to—"

"No!"

"Whoa." I put up a hand. "Let me explain a little before you bite my head off."

Beckett crosses his arms making his biceps bulge bigger. "Fine. Explain. Not that my answer will be any different."

I'm not a violent person but the urge to shove him into a chair and make him listen steals through me like the cold of the arena sinking in. To the bone.

Matching his cross-armed stance I say, "Look. I get you don't like me. I even get you have reasons in spite of them not really being my fault. *But*, I think you need to prepare yourself for more questions and I'd hoped I could help you divert them, possibly avoid them altogether."

"The only thing you've helped do is put my daughter's face all over the internet and TV." His words are a growl through clenched teeth.

"Yes, I'll grant you that, but I did it without hiding outside your house or in front of her school, without harassing her at a local restaurant or in her own driveway." I suck in a breath and try to curb my anger. The whole time I speak, my voice rises in volume, and like my stance on violence, I'm generally not a yeller.

"Okay. I see that *maybe* you were trying to help us."

"Trying! I did help you, you idiot!" Tossing up my hands I spin around. "You know what, screw it. I rescind my offer to help more."

"What's in it for you?"

His question has me turning back around, a frown pulling at my brow and mouth. "In it for me? Nothing. What could I possibly gain from helping you other than being nice?"

"Ah, I see, you're a do-gooder. I don't need one of those. Got my gut full of them when I was a teenager."

His words remind me of something else I wanted to warn him about. "You were sixteen when Whitney was born."

Beckett takes a half step back, his fists now clenching at his sides. "And?"

"I think that will be a big topic the press will want to dig into as well as her mother."

"Fuck!" He slams his hands on his head and looks at the ceiling.

"I get that you don't like me or trust me, but you have to believe me when I say I would never do anything to hurt you or your daughter," I try to soothe his frustration and anger. "And if you can't take my word for it, think about Oakley, Natalie, Blake, and Walker. None of them would let anyone close to this team or its employees if they thought they were up to no good."

His head lowers, his eyes meeting mine as he drops his arms. "I'll agree with you on that."

I want to say thank you but it feels weird to voice it. "I promise. I would never do anything to hurt Whitney. Or you. Or m— this team."

I don't know why I cut myself off, why I don't want him to know I'm part owner of the team. I assumed he knew, that everyone on the team knows, but the more I interact with them, I realize that piece of information has slipped through the cracks.

And I want Beckett to like me for me, not because I'm his boss.

Shit!

Since when do I want this man to like me?

I don't need to be his friend, I don't even need to like him. I'm a silent partner in the team, I have nothing to do with the day-to-day running of the Rogues and honestly, every member of the team from ice to front of house could hate me and it wouldn't matter.

Except it does.

I want Beckett Higgison to like me.

I have no clue why. He's a professional athlete, something I've always avoided because of my past. The man my mother passed off as my father for the first six years of my life played in the NFL and was a grade A asshole. Violent and mean, he did everything he could to make my life miserable.

The only consolation I have is he didn't treat Andrea differently. She was subjected to his callous cruelty as much as I was.

But Beckett? I can't even imagine him hurting an adult, never mind a child—*his* child.

And I have to remember that his hostility comes from his love of Whitney, of his need to be sure she's protected, taken care of. In some ways, he reminds me of Dad.

Even now, at thirty-three, I still find myself the recipient of my father's protection. The conversation about my biological mother last night is just the most recent example of my dad taking care of me.

I can't blame Beckett for being the way he is. Having Whitney so young had to have been hard and not just the fact he was a kid raising a kid part. People must have been horrible to him when they found out he was a single dad.

I can only imagine the fear he must have endured every day, fear of someone taking his daughter away…

"I'm sorry." The apology is out before I can stop it.

"For what?"

"For everything you've dealt with while raising a remarkable young woman. She's a testament to you, to your parenting, and you should be proud of what you've done."

His head cocks to the side and he studies me for a long moment before he straightens and says, "Thank you. And thank you for checking on us and warning me we might face more intrusive questions from others."

"My offer stands. If you want me to help you navigate those possible questions, I'm here."

"At this point, I'll say thanks but no thanks."

"I'm a phone call away if you change your mind. Ask either of your coaches or Oakley or Natalie for my number but I'll be around a lot doing these interviews." I want him to know he has full access to me. Short of handing over my number now—which I doubt he'd take—this is the best I can do.

"Sure. Thanks. I gotta—" He tips his head at the door.

"Of course. Thank you for your help with Noah and Mikel."

His mouth lifts on one side in a slanted smile. "It was pointed out to me, it was the thing to do as captain of the team."

"It is." I nod. "But I doubt you needed to have it pointed out to you."

"Oh, I did. I've never even been assistant captain of a team. I have no idea what I'm supposed to do." He shrugs. "Well, other than yelling at the guys to move it, shoot it, or block it, when we play…"

This small glimpse into Beckett's insecurities surprises me. Maybe we can move past his hostility toward my profession and forge some kind of friendship. "I'm sure you'll be great once you get the hang of it."

"We'll see." He stares at me a moment longer before he seems to remember he doesn't like me and frowns. "Bye."

The word is quickly followed by his exit. The speed with which he leaves is enough to cause a breeze when he closes the door behind him.

Beckett Higgison is an enigma.

Or maybe it's the emotions I feel around him that are.

Or the fact I could have—should have—told him I own the team.

BECKETT

"She owns the team!"

I look up from the steak I'm searing on the grill to see Whit racing through the back door. "What?"

"The team! She owns the team!"

She's grinning and dancing around like she's got ants in her pants, and I can't help the smile that tilts my lips. "What team and who? Oakley?"

"No!" She stops moving, stares at me like I'm the dumbest man on the planet. "Well, yes, Oakley James owns the team too. But there are four of them!"

"Four of them...?" I return my focus to our dinner—there's nothing worse than overcooked steak.

"Yeah, the Rogues are owned by KAW. And KAW also owns Rogue sportswear—you know the workout clothes I buy?"

I nod. "Yes, I'm aware the people behind Rogue sportswear also own the Rogues NHL team."

"But did you know that KAW is made up of four women who met in college and started making sportswear in their living room?"

"No, I'm not aware of the history of your sportswear." I have no idea why we're having a history lesson except since two nights

54

ago when the shit hit the fan and Whit outed herself to the world, she's had an insatiable need to know everything about my new team. "Hey, grab that plate for me and pass it here. These steaks are done."

"Ewe... They're not done, they're still red. I'm not eating that."

"They're medium, and you will eat it because it's good for you." From the moment Whit was born I've been a little—or a lot—obsessed with making sure she gets all the vitamins and minerals she needs to grow up healthy and strong. I never wanted her to go without nutritious food the way I did.

Whit cocks an eyebrow at me. Without words she conveys her thoughts on my continued insistence she eat red meat with the amount of iron she'll be ingesting in mind. She's never liked red meat. Complains it tastes like blood no matter how it's cooked. And considering her last yearly physical showed she's in perfect health, I need to give in on this one.

"Fine, I'll leave yours on a little longer but I'm taking mine off now. It won't hurt for it to sit while I char yours to black ash."

Rolling her eyes, she holds out the plate and waits for me to put my steak on it. "Do I need to do anything else for dinner?"

"No, I made a salad and there are baked potatoes and grilled veggies keeping warm in the oven."

"Set the table?"

"I thought we'd eat out here. It's not too hot and the bugs aren't biting."

"They will now you've put that out there." She puts the plate back on the outdoor table and heads toward the house. "I'll get the bug spray and those candle thingys you bought to keep the mosquitos away."

"Citronella candles," I call after her. "Grab our plates too."

When Whit comes back out, she's carrying a tray loaded with our plates, the bowl of salad, the pan of potatoes and veggies, and I can see the bug spray tucked under one arm.

"Here, give me that." Rushing over, I take the tray from her and put it on the table.

"I was fine, I didn't need your help, and you saved me all of five steps, Dad." She might not have rolled her eyes but it's in her tone.

Looking up I stare at my daughter—the one I swear just yesterday was asking me to carry her but is now telling me she can carry things on her own—and I wonder where the years went.

When did the little girl who relied on me for everything turn into this beautiful young woman?

Cami's right. She's a remarkable young woman and I should be proud of myself for having a hand in that as much as I'm proud of her and all she's accomplished.

"I'm proud of you."

"What?"

"I'm proud of you. I love you. I don't say either enough."

"You tell me you love me every day, Dad."

"I do?"

"Yes. Not always in words, but every day you take care of me, you show me you love me, and actions are far more believable than words most of the time." She moves beside me and wraps her arms around my waist. "I love you too but if you try to serve me bleeding meat again, I'll smother you in your sleep."

"That's a little extreme."

"Meh." She shrugs. "I couldn't find those candles."

"I think I left them in the garage when I unpacked the groceries."

"Should I go get them?"

"No, the spray should be enough. I'll dig the candles out tomorrow, put them in the utility room so they're closer to the patio."

Whit glances around. "We really should do something with the garden. Make it more usable."

"What's wrong with how it is?"

"It's too... Pretentious."

"Goes with the house."

"Yeah." She looks over her shoulder, her expression one of concern. "We need to fix that too."

"Okay, I think your steak is black enough now. Let's sit down and talk about what we want to tackle first."

"Our bedrooms, or mine, since you don't care about that."

"I can tell you right now that I do care about the fact my walls are covered in pink floral wallpaper."

"It's not as bad as the psychedelic crap on my walls."

"I told you to pick a different room," I remind as I transfer the steaks to our plates.

"But I want that one. It's got the window seat that overlooks the garden."

"The pretentious one?" With an arched brow, I pull out my seat and sit. At her unimpressed glare, I say, "Okay, first thing is getting someone to remove the wallpaper and paint the walls."

"Can I choose the color for my room?"

"Of course. Didn't I let you choose at our last house?"

"Yes, but you complained about it the whole time we lived there!"

"Well, you have to admit mustard yellow isn't exactly the best choice."

"It worked perfectly with the rest of my stuff."

"Okay, you're right, it did. The question is, have you outgrown mustard yellow or are we recreating your room in Toronto?"

"I'm thinking pale pink, like barely a tinge of pink, on three walls and a dark pink, bright but not fluoro, on the fourth one. The one behind my bed."

"If that's what you want." I cut a piece of steak and swipe it through the butter melting over my baked potato.

"You're not going to complain about it?"

"I don't think so. At this point I should be preparing myself for all your choices being your own and just accepting them."

"What do you mean?"

"You're eighteen soon. That makes you technically an adult."

"And?"

"I should stop making decisions for you."

"Dad. You don't make decisions for me. We've been discussing everything for years now, and you never discount my opinion even when you know I'm wrong."

"I can't remember a time when you were wrong. Well, there was the mustard yellow incident." I grin.

"Ha, ha. Speaking of decisions. I'm sorry I made the one that had that reporter yelling questions at you about me. I know you like to keep your work life and family life separate."

She doesn't know why I keep our family life out of the public eye, and I don't want to imagine how she'd react to that information. "It's not that I keep it separate as much as I didn't—don't—want you, or me caught up in a media frenzy."

"And I dropped us both into one with that post."

"It's okay. The Rogues helped us navigate it and I'm sure as soon as someone does something scandalous, we'll be forgotten."

"Ah, um." She ducks her head to avoid my gaze. "There were photographers outside school today."

"What?" My fork clatters on my plate.

"Yeah, but it's okay, I didn't talk to them and the principal made them leave the grounds."

"Why wasn't I told about this? Why didn't you call me. I would have come to get you."

"And give up my sweet ride?" She grins.

"Oh, funny. You know why I got you that hunk of junk."

"It's not junk; you made sure it's mechanically sound before you let me drive it."

"I did."

"Hey, speaking of the Rogues, we didn't finish talking about who owns the team."

"KAW owns it."

"Yes, but guess who owns KAW?"

"Oakley James."

"Yep. And…"

"What do you mean and?"

"I told you KAW is made up of four women who met in college and started Rogue sportswear in their living room."

"You did, yes. Okay, so who are the other three women?"

"As you said, Oakley James. Your assistant coach, Blake Lattimer Watts." She holds up a finger with each name. "The Rogues GM Natalie Redding and…"

"The GM and Assistant Coach? Isn't that a—"

"Wait, wait. I saved the best for last."

Rolling my eyes, I motion zipping my lips.

"Camilla Nelson Barnes."

She looks at me like I should know who that is, but I don't know anyone in the Rogues org named Camilla.

With an exasperated sigh and roll of her eyes, she says, "Also known as Cami Nelson."

"Cami? Reporter Cami? The woman who did our interview?"

"Yep."

"What the fuck!"

"Hey!"

"Shit. Sorry. Sorry." I wave my hand. "But what the? Cami is co-owner of the Rogues?"

"Yes. From what I can find, she's a silent partner. Has no job within the organization. Either the hockey team or the sportswear business. She's just a reporter. She works for her father's network on the local paper here."

"Her father's network?"

"FNB. Her father is Fenton Nelson Barnes." Whit leans closer. "He's worth billions. But get this. Cami is worth more. One, she's his only heir, and two, Rogues sportswear is a billion-dollar global business and KAW paid cash for the franchise and the development of the arena and surrounding area. The info I found said they've poured over three billion dollars into developing Baton Rouge, both the area around the arena and downtown."

"She's an owner." I shake my head. "How did that not come up in conversation?"

"Why would it? We were talking about me. You."

"Yes, but..." Why wouldn't she tell me she was an owner? When she was trying to get me to believe she wouldn't hurt Whit or me she could have easily slipped that nugget of information into our conversation and that would have put an end to my hostility toward her. "Jesus. I own her an apology."

"Why? You weren't rude. Much." Whit grins at me. "Honest, Dad. You have nothing to apologize for."

"Not for the other night no. But yesterday. After training." I put my hands on my head and roll through my memories from yesterday. "Shit. I'm a dick."

"What happened yesterday? You didn't mention it last night."

"I saw her when she did a couple of interviews with two of the players."

"Why were you there?"

"Because I'm the captain of the team and Coach thought it would be good for me to be there and because Cami asked to see me."

"What did she want to see you about?"

"To ask if you were okay. If I was okay." And now, with this new information, her inquiry doesn't seem nefarious. Not like it did at the time. "To warn me we might get some reporters asking questions about you. And me."

"What questions? Didn't we tell them what they want to know?"

"Some, yes, but neither of us mentioned your mother or that I was only sixteen when you were born."

"Oh. I guess they might want to know that. But that's not something to worry about. There are plenty of teenage pregnancies."

"Yes, but not many fathers take responsibility for raising those children."

"But my mom died. She couldn't raise me."

My insides clench when she talks about her mother. All I've ever told Whit is her mother died before she was two. Which is true. The way she died has never come up and I've waited years for Whit to voice the question. Except she never has.

"Don't worry so much. There's nothing there to drag up. I researched that reporter too."

"And when did you do your schoolwork?"

With another eye roll, she says, "I did that as well. But I wanted to know who he was. He's not a very good journalist. More of a gossip collector."

"Yeah, well, at the moment anything out of the normal concerning the Rogues is good fodder."

"It'll be fine now we've done that interview."

I hope so. With everything in me, I hope no one questions where Whit's mother is. How I came to be a single father at sixteen. Why the woman who birthed the best thing in my life never held her, never saw her. Never wanted her.

Or why the mother's name listed on Whit's birth certificate is a fake one.

CAMI

Pulling my ringing phone from my bag I look at the number on the screen and frown. There's no name so it's not in my contacts and with Dad's warning about my biological mother possibly seeing me and trying to make contact, I'm unsure if I should answer.

Except this isn't the first time I've received a call from an unknown number this week. Since the interviews started going live each night I've fielded numerous calls about rights to air them and job offers. And honestly, I'm tired.

It's late in the afternoon and I've been on the go since before the sun came up but in spite of my urge to ignore it, I swipe to answer and put the phone to my ear.

"Hello."

"Is this Cami Nelson?"

"Yes, who's this?"

"Hi, Ms. Nelson. My name is William Dalton and I'm principal of Hannon Grove high school. I've got Whitney Higgison in my office. Her father isn't answering his phone, and she assures me you're able to come collect her."

"Of course, but why. What's wrong?"

"Nothing too bad. Her car has a couple of flat tires and only one spare."

"Oh. Okay." I glance at my watch. "You're on Barker, right?"

"That's correct."

"I'm downtown, at the FNB building. It will take me about fifteen minutes to get there, is that okay?"

"Yes. I'll be here until after six. And she's happy to wait in my office."

"I'll be as fast as I can."

"See you when you get here."

Hanging up, I drop the phone back in my bag as I snap my laptop shut. I have no idea why Whitney chose to call me or how she got my number, but I do know most of the Rogues are out of town at an away game. And that thought brings up another one.

Who is Whitney staying with while her father is away?

From everything I know about Beckett, he wouldn't leave her at home alone even if she's almost an adult. Especially after the few instances of photographers hanging around outside the arena and her school.

Not that I have first-hand knowledge of the photographers. Oakley called two days ago and asked if I knew who was still hunting for information and how they might stop it from happening moving forward.

I gave her the same suggestion I gave Beckett last week, give them what they want before they know they want it.

I pointed out posting pictures on their social media accounts and adding the fact he's a single dad to his bio on the team website would be another way to keep them at bay.

Honestly, I don't know why they would be lying in wait to get pictures of Whitney or Beckett with her. I haven't been paying attention to any gossip doing the rounds with other reporters, but then sports isn't my area of expertise.

Making a mental note to message Bas to find out if he's heard anything, I shove my laptop in my bag and grab my keys from the top drawer of my desk. A desk that won't be mine after this week. Neither will the office be mine.

Now that I'm working for the paper as a freelance journalist I can work from anywhere, and while I'll miss chatting with Deb from reception, I've never formed friendships with my colleagues. It doesn't help when your dad owns the network we all work for.

It took years for everyone to feel comfortable with the owner's daughter working beside them. Not that I blame them. In the beginning I did get a job here because of who I was. But I started at the bottom. And I haven't moved further up the ladder than feature writer because I don't want to. I like diving into a story and bringing it to life.

Dana says I should write biographies or even fiction, but I like the short form of feature articles and I don't always write about people. Just last month I did an article about the history of Baton Rouge's river industry. So few of the men and women who worked in the heyday of the shipping industry are left to talk to and it's a part of my hometown's history that I didn't want to see slip away.

"Hey. You heading out early?"

I look up to see Deb in my doorway. "Yes. Did you need something?"

"No. Was just passing by on my way to get a coffee when I saw you packing up." She steps into the room and shuts the door. "I wanted to have a quick word before you leave."

"Can it wait 'til tomorrow? I'm in a bit of a rush."

"Oh, you're not packing up, packing up?" She glances around my office.

"No. Not for a few more days."

"Okay, yes, it can wait until tomorrow. Why don't we head down the street to that Mexican place for lunch around one?"

Smiling, I shoulder my bag. "Sounds great."

"Good." With a smile she opens the door and holds it. "I'll let you get out of here."

"Thanks." I pass her and don't stop, just look back over my shoulder and ask, "Can you lock that for me?"

"Sure. Talk tomorrow."

"See you then." Without a second thought to what Deb could want to talk about, I head for the elevators.

At this time of day, pedestrian traffic is light in the elevators and the parking garage, so it only takes me five minutes to be on my way. And seven minutes after that I'm pulling into the school parking lot and right up beside what I'm assuming is Whitney's car. Frowning, I see the front passenger tire is flat as a tack.

Switching off the car and climbing out, I walk around to the other side of Whitney's car to see the rear tire is as flat as the front one on the other side. It seems odd that the opposite tires are flat. If she'd run over something, wouldn't tires on the same side be flat?

I don't bother looking closer, I'll get the tow company's opinion on it when they come to collect the car. Turning, I head for the front of the admin building. Once I'm inside out of the heat, it's a simple task to find the principal's office.

It's directly on the right after you come through the doors. And through the large window behind a desk I assume belongs to the principal's secretary I can see Whitney, head down, fingers tapping away at a laptop, and I have to smile.

The one and only time I found myself in the principal's office in high school, I was not looking as relaxed as Whitney.

No, I was shaking in my shoes waiting for Dad to arrive because Oakley had gotten us into trouble for letting out all the mice in the science labs.

The memory has me smiling in spite of the grounding I got after Dad took me home.

Tapping on the doorframe I wait for the principal to stand before stepping inside.

"Cami Nelson?"

"Yes." I walk to his desk and hold out a hand. "Thank you for contacting me."

"Sure. Whitney would have done it herself but her phone is dead." He smiles at Whitney as she packs away her things. "And it's been a pleasure talking with her. We've been discussing the history of the area and what things I think she and her father might enjoy exploring."

"Mr. Dalton has lived here his whole life." Whitney zips up her backpack and puts it over one shoulder. "He was telling me the house we live in was once owned by a man who had plantations further south and a shipping line that used to carry his cotton up and down the Mississippi River to the rest of the country and the world."

"You should talk to Oakley about that if you're interested. Her family owns one of the biggest shipping companies in the country."

"Really? Cool." Turning to the principal she says, "Thanks for letting me use your phone and for letting me sit in here out of the heat."

"I'd say any time, but I don't want you to have flat tires again."

"Me either." Grinning, she turns to me. "Can you take me home now? I'm going to leave the car here and wait for Dad to get back tomorrow."

"No need to wait. I'll have a tow company come get it tonight so my mechanic can get it fixed tomorrow. If we're lucky, it'll be done before your dad gets home and then he won't have to worry about it."

"Okay, that would be great. I've got a credit card to use for payment."

"We'll worry about that when we pick the car up tomorrow. I've been going to the same guy since I was a teenager. He's trustworthy and trusts me to pay after he does the work." Facing the principal again I hold out my hand. "Thanks again for taking care of her."

"You're welcome. When I saw her out there beside her car, I offered to help with changing the tire but then we realized it wasn't only the front one that was flat. And it was too hot to be out there for however long it took for someone to come."

"Well, thanks. We'll get out of your way now." Putting a hand on Whitney's back, I urge her out of the office. It isn't until we get outside the building that I ask, "Why did you call me and how did you get my number?"

"Should I not have called you?"

"No. Yes, of course you should, I'm just wondering how I'm the one you thought of."

"Ms. James gave me a list of Rogue people to call if Dad's playing away or even here and I can't get hold of him. The top four are the owners of the Rogues."

"Huh. Makes sense, I guess. And everyone but me is out of town at the game."

"Yep."

"Okay, let me call my mechanic and get your car sorted. Then I'll take you home—wait, are you staying on your own?"

"No, I'm staying with the lady next door. She's ninety-two and about half my size but apparently Dad thinks I'm safer with her than on my own."

The eye roll she does has me holding in a laugh. "Do you need to call her and tell her you're running late?"

"No. I was supposed to go home and get ready for school tomorrow before heading next door. She's not expecting me until dinner time."

"All right. How about this? We get your car sorted, then we hit the grocery store, and I'll cook for all three of us at your house, and if we can get hold of your dad, we'll see if he's okay with me staying with you overnight. That way you don't have to drag all your stuff next door and you're not putting your neighbor out."

"I like that plan."

I have no idea where the idea of staying with Whitney came from. I know Beckett isn't my biggest fan and I'm not even sure he'll agree to it, but I'll cook for Whitney and their neighbor no matter what Beckett decides.

We have to wait thirty minutes for the tow truck to arrive and we spend that time sitting in my car with the engine and air running. There's no shade in the school parking lot and the sun has spent all day baking the ground and parked cars to the point you can see heatwaves rising off the blacktop.

When the tow driver—Gary—looks at the car and scratches his head, I'm reminded of my own puzzlement on seeing the two flat tires. I want to question him about it but I don't want to say anything in front of Whitney in case it's just a coincidence and not something nefarious like I'm thinking.

After Oakley told me about the photographers hanging around, I pushed it and any concern I had for Whitney and Beckett aside. But now I have to wonder if I should have taken more notice.

I spent some time when we first came out here looking around to be sure no one was hanging around with a camera in hand. Seeing no one I relaxed and enjoyed getting to know Whitney better.

I already liked her after our first meeting and I told Beckett he should be proud of the woman he's raised. What I didn't tell him is I'm proud of him for raising her on his own. I don't know their full story—no one does—but what I do know, and what I can speculate on, is that he's a shining example of what a father should be. Single or otherwise, he's one of the most dedicated, loving fathers I've ever met.

And I know I shouldn't take things at face value, that anything could be happening behind closed doors, but I don't think I'll find anything scandalous about Beckett and Whitney Higgison.

BECKETT

It's late when we get to the hotel. We're all wired, pumped from another pre-season win, and I can tell a few of my teammates are going to hit the bar. As captain I should probably join them, but all I want to do is get to my room and call Whit.

I can't believe I left my phone behind when we left for the arena. Granted I was a little distracted when I couldn't find my lucky underwear but I'm never without my phone just in case Whit needs me. Especially when she's not traveling with me, which she's done less and less now that she's in high school.

Before we left Toronto, I had full confidence in her staying with a teammate's family overnight. Jenny Ruston was the perfect person to take care of Whit for me after Mama Dot passed. It helped that Whit attended the same school as the Rustons' sons. The boys treated Whit like a little sister and even when I wasn't away, we spent a good deal of time with them.

Cory Ruston is the closest thing to a best friend I've ever had and leaving him and his family behind when we moved to Baton Rouge is proving harder than I thought it would be.

"Hey, Bex, you getting a celebratory drink with us?"

I should. But I need to touch base with Whit. Glancing at my watch I see it's later than her usual bedtime and if I called now I'd probably wake her...

"Yeah, I'll have one but we've got an early flight out in the morning so we shouldn't make it a late one."

The need to talk to Whit and the promise I made Coach to connect with the members of the Rogues org compete but I have to remember my girl is almost an adult and if she needed me and I didn't answer she'd have found another way to get hold of me.

Stepping into the hotel bar I see it's packed with Rogues and I smile. Even if there were some fans that wanted to hang out with players, there's no room for them to get in here.

I lift my chin at Coach Alcott and Oakley. They're sitting at a two-seat high table near the entrance. The vantage spot gives them a view of everyone inside and anyone entering and I wonder if it's so they can keep an eye on the players.

At the beginning of the season, when everyone rolled into Baton Rouge, our GM, Oakley, Coach Watts, and Coach Alcott, along with the rest of the coaching staff made their expectations clear. They don't want any scandal outside of what the franchise already caused.

Their plan is to concentrate on winning and they want nothing to detract from that. The older, more experienced guys on the team, particularly the married ones, aren't going to be a problem, but there are a few younger players. A couple of them mere boys, who might prove to be a problem.

Coach asked me to keep an eye on things, give some of the younger guys a guiding hand in navigating the sometimes treacherous waters of professional sportsmanship.

I'm sure he thinks because I've kept myself out of the spotlight other than on the ice, I know how to handle the attention, the sometimes over the top adoration hockey players receive, and by adoration I'm pretty sure he means puck bunnies.

I've never dealt with any of it. Even in my younger days I steered clear of the late-night partying because my sole focus was on playing well to keep my position on the team and raising Whit.

I'm not sure how much help I'll be but I'll put in the effort because the more I look at where I am in life, where Whit is, the more I realize this is my last team. I signed a three-year, no trade contract, and at that point I'll be thirty-six. I don't even know if I'll be able to play that long.

"Bex!" Tasman Culler calls me over. He's our top defense player and he's sitting with Cutter Jepson and Mike Ferro, two other defensemen.

"Great game, guys. We couldn't have won it without you," I say as I pull out a chair at their table. "Let me buy you a round."

"No need. Our illustrious owner and her husband have opened a tab. We each get two drinks then they're shutting down the bar," Tas explains.

"Oh, I didn't realize they were doing that."

"She got the hotel to open the bar just for us. It's normally closed this late on a weeknight," Jep adds.

"Explains them perched on that table by the door."

"Right?" Mike pours a beer from the pitcher in the middle of the table and hands me the glass. "And the win isn't only because of us. You were smokin' out there tonight, Bex."

"I did have a good game. But it's not just on me either. I think we're meshing as a team and as much as on paper we don't look like we'd play as good as we have been, I think it's because we all want to play well. We're making more effort to learn each other's tells and to be honest, I think the way the org treats us, and I'm including the coaches, has a lot to do with our success so far. Not that we should get complacent at all."

"Definitely not!" Tas slams his glass on the table. "Complacency loses games."

Jep and Mike lift their glasses up over the middle of our table and I quickly do the same.

"To the Rogues," Jep offers as a toast.

Tas joins in and as we each take a sip the sound of clapping fills the room. All our heads turn in the direction of the noise and see Oakley James standing on a chair, her hand on Coach's shoulder for support.

"Now that I have your attention I'd like to say a few things." Her eyes scan the room, making sure everyone is looking her direction before she continues. "We're kicking pre-season butt but we can't sit on *our* butts because we've won a few games."

The fact her words echo our sentiments doesn't surprise me. After my conversation with Whit the other night, I did some research into the four women who make up KAW.

They're remarkable. Each of them comes from money, none of them have to work a day in their life, and yet they went balls to the wall on their Rogue sportswear brand and are still doing it with innovative production facilities and materials.

And now they've turned that drive to succeed to their NHL team.

"I want to thank everyone for their efforts. I know you've all given everything you have to this team so far and I hope you continue to do that going forward. If you have any concerns or need help with anything, professionally or personally, my door is always open to you. Same goes for any member of staff, from your coaches to management to arena staff to front office staff. We're all in this together!"

A round of cheers goes up and most of us raise a glass when Oakley raises hers.

"I know this is not a new phrase, I know it's been the motto of a business that has been around for a few years but as you've seen, that business is tightly woven with this one, so..." She holds her glass higher. "Go Rogue!"

The chant of Go Rogue is loud enough to raise the roof and the smiles on the faces around me bring one to my own. I feel a connection to this team I haven't with any other. Maybe it's the underdog vibe or the dirty stepchild in the corner attitude some have had toward the new franchise.

Whatever it is, I want to get to know these people.

I know a few from playing with them or against them over the years, but some of the younger guys are new faces and I understand why Coach would ask me to be a guiding influence.

And standing here, surrounded by them, I want to do that. I'm no longer resigned to doing it. I *want* to do it.

I want to build close relationships with these men

I want to build us into a team—a force to be reckoned with.

I want to build this team into a Cup winner.

I know we can do it. Whether we do it this season or next doesn't matter. We will hold that Cup.

Oakley, Blake, Natalie, and Cami will hold that Cup.

And they'll do it with their heads high.

"All right, all right. Quiet down." Oakley smiles out at us and even from this distance I can see her eyes are wet. "Win or lose, you're all the best players I could ask for and I'm honored you agreed to join us on this journey. I know it hasn't been easy, and there have been some not-nice things said about us as a team, and individually, *but*, we are a team, we'll stick together, you always have someone at your back, and we'll keep winning games. Now drink up and get to bed. Our plane leaves at seven, I want everyone out of their room and on the bus by six."

A round of cheers and groans echoes off the ceiling and I have to grin. I've never played for a team that felt this close. It's strange, a little uncomfortable, and yet it feels right.

I walk toward the door as I finish my beer. I make sure to acknowledge each player as they leave, some with a chin lift, some a few words, but when I'm the last one besides the coaches and management, I step forward and offer my hand to Oakley.

"I want to thank you for everything you're doing."

"I'm not doing more than any other owner," she says as she shakes my hand.

"You're wrong. I've played for three teams over my career, so I know what owners do and don't do. You're a cut above what I'm used to, what I've observed in others. Thank you. Some of these guys know different, some haven't a clue that this org isn't the normal. As the captain of these men, I want you to know we appreciate what you're doing and you have our support, our loyalty, our gratitude."

"All I ask is you give me your best on the ice and embrace the Rogues as an extension of your family."

"You can count on it. Now, if you'll excuse me, I've got an early wake up and I'd hate to be late and disappoint my boss."

"Say hi to Whit for me and tell her to join us in the owner's box next home game."

"I'll tell her but now that she's not keeping a low profile, she's talking about sitting by the glass."

"Well, if she wants to sit there, I'll join her. She's a remarkable young woman. You should be proud of her."

"You're not the only person to point that out recently. I am proud of her. She's the best thing in my life, no offense."

"None taken. Now go. I've got to close out the tab in this place."

"Already done," our GM says as she moves beside her. "I'm heading up. See you all tomorrow."

"You still heading to Atlanta?" Oakley asks before the GM can leave.

"Yes. I'll be back in Baton Rouge by tomorrow night, morning after at the latest."

"Okay. Call if you need anything."

"I will." She shoots a smile my way. "Good game, Beckett."

I'm surprised enough to stumble over my words. "T-th-thanks."

A hand claps my shoulder and I turn to see Coach Alcott. "I'll echo her words. Good game. And thanks for doing as I asked."

"I'm not sure how good I'll be at guiding some of these guys, but I'll do my best with that the same as I'll do my best on the ice."

"Good man. Now go talk to your daughter. I know you would have preferred to do that than come in here."

I smile. "Yeah, but I need to remember Whit isn't a kid anymore. She's almost at the point of making decisions without discussing them with me, never mind letting me weigh in on them."

"I'm told they grow up fast and if I hadn't had the last eighteen months with Micky I wouldn't believe it, but man, that kid is growing like a weed."

"And eating like a horse!" Oakley adds.

"Enjoy this time. Before you know it, you'll be going over college choices with him."

Coach frowns and Oakley shivers before saying, "I'm not ready for that."

I laugh. "Ready or not, they take life at their own pace."

"I'm sure they do. And maybe we can convince Micky to stick close to home when the time comes."

"I'm trying to do that with Whit but then I want her to have everything I never did and that includes going to the college of her choice."

"I don't envy you your situation but you can bet I'll be taking notes." Coach glances at Oakley. "Hopefully Micky isn't our only child to navigate that time with."

"On that note, I'm out of here. See you in the morning."

Following words with action, I head out of the bar and across the lobby. The place is quiet compared to earlier and I'm the only one on the elevator when it's rising to my floor.

The corridor is quiet and when I slip into my room and switch on the light, I'm glad I have the room to myself. I offered to room with one of the younger players but Coach told me I'd be on my own this first away trip. Come regular season and he'll be switching me between players—all of us will—to help build the connections between us.

It's not something I've done before, but then like I told Oakley, this team isn't run like any other I've played for. Or heard about. She's building camaraderie more like a family unit and I have to admit it's working so far. This team is closer than any I've played with or against and I have to conclude it has a lot to do with our undefeated standing.

Not that I expect that winning streak to continue all season but I think we're looking good to be at the top of our conference this year. And I cross my fingers that means we make the playoffs.

Spotting my phone on the floor by my bag I walk over and scoop it up. As soon as the screen lights up, the band I wasn't aware of around my chest loosens.

There's a text from Whit.

> W: Congrats on another win! You had a great game! Love you!

Smiling, I reply knowing she's probably asleep.

> Love you too, Whitbee. See you soon!

Besides Whit's message I've got a missed call and a voicemail. I don't recognize the number and in spite of being tired and ready to call it a night, I dial in to my voicemail and retrieve the message.

"Hi, Beckett, it's Cami. I tried to call but you're obviously playing. Anyway, I just wanted you to know I'm at your house with Whitney"—my heart jerks into my throat—"She's okay, fine. Nothing wrong with her. I promise. But there was an incident I'd like to talk to you about it. Can you call me on this number when you get the chance? Doesn't matter how late. Okay, thanks. Bye."

With palms sweating and my heart in my throat, I hit the unknown number from the missed call.

CAMI

I jolt awake when the phone in my hand rings. Sitting up I hit accept before the noise wakes the girl sleeping upstairs.

"Hello?" My voice is croaky, raspy from sleep.

"Cami?"

"Yeah." I clear my throat as quietly as I can.

"What happened? Where's Whit?"

"She's asleep." My gaze flashes to the stairs. "She's fine, like I said in my message."

"Then why are you at my house and why isn't she staying with Mrs. Gerber?"

"Hang on. Let me go into the garage."

"Why are you going into the garage?"

"So you don't wake Whitney up with your yelling," I snap. The man's voice can be heard without me holding the phone to my ear.

"Oh, sorry. I'm worried."

"I understand that. But I promise you, there's no need for immediate concern."

"That sounds like I should be concerned though."

"I think so. Maybe. I'm not sure. It's why I want to talk to you about it. Explain why I'm sleeping on the couch in your house."

"Why are you sleeping on the couch? There's a perfectly good bed upstairs."

"The only bed beside Whitney's is yours and I wasn't about to impose by sleeping there."

"Well, you should. I don't want you uncomfortable while you watch over Whit. I give you permission to sleep in my bed. *After* you tell me what the fuck is going on."

I can't blame him for yelling. And I need to tell him what happened to relieve his mind as quickly as I can. Pulling open the door into the garage, I step through and close it quietly behind me. "Okay, I'm in the garage, we shouldn't wake Whitney up now."

"You said she's okay?"

"She is. More than okay. But then she doesn't know everything, and I haven't told her because I wanted to speak to you first."

"Jesus, get on with it, you're not building confidence with this roundabout way of telling me what happened."

"Sorry, sorry, I'm half asleep. Okay, I'll start at the beginning —try not to interrupt until I'm done."

"Go."

I don't point out his directive is an interruption. "This afternoon I got a call from the principal of Whitney's school, I can't remember his name—"

"Dalton. It's William Dalton."

I frown at his lack of silence but choose to keep going. "Anyway, he was calling on behalf of Whitney because her phone was dead and she needed someone to come get her becau—"

"What's wrong with her car?"

A grumble of disapproval rattles in my throat. "I'm getting to that," I say tersely.

"Sorry. Go on."

"She has two flat tires—"

"Two? How the hell did that happened?"

"Beckett, I understand that you're concerned for your

daughter and if I didn't think it would wake her up, I'd go upstairs and take a picture of her sleeping soundly in her own bed, not a scratch on her."

"Okay, okay. I'll wait until you're finished."

"Right. When she came out of school this afternoon, she discovered she had a flat tire. Not a minute later the principal walked up and offered to help her change it. The problem they found when they went to retrieve the jack and spare from her trunk was that the opposite tire on her car was also flat."

"What the fuck?"

"Yes. That was my thought when I arrived but let me tell you the rest first. So the principal suggested she get the car towed and call someone to come get her except when she pulled her phone out, her battery was dead. The principal offered to make the call for her. Luckily, Oakley saw fit to give her a list of numbers to call if she ever couldn't get hold of you. Hers, Nat's, Blake's, and mine are top of that list. Unfortunately, the other three are away with you so they called me."

"Thank you."

I pause, the genuineness in his voice making me forget the interruption. "You're welcome. Anyway, when I got to the school and saw her car, I was puzzled by the two flat tires. Didn't bother asking her about it because I wanted to get the car sorted and her home. I offered to cook her and Mrs. Gerber dinner then stay here because those two opposite flat tires didn't sit right."

"I appreciate your help even if it sounds like I don't. I'm not used to anyone else taking care of things with Whit."

"Again, you're welcome. But let me get to the part about why I wanted you to call me. I had her car towed to my mechanic. I've been using him for years and he's trustworthy. The tow truck driver was confused by the tires and asked Whitney if she'd run over anything; she assured us she hadn't. On the side to me, he said he'd speak to Cal and get him to call me. Cal called me after dinner."

"And?"

"Someone let those tires down. There's nothing wrong with them. No nails in them, no tears from hitting a gutter, nothing. They're in perfect condition. Cal said they aren't even wearing unevenly or anything."

"They were let down on purpose?"

"That's Cal's guess. Mine too."

"Who would want to do that?"

"I wanted to ask Whitney if she'd had a fight or disagreement with anyone at school but she's not my daughter; it's not my place to ask."

"Right. Okay, and she's all right?"

"She's fine. No hint that something might be wrong. Although we did talk about the two times reporters were waiting for her outside school and here at the house."

"At the house? She didn't tell me about that. I knew about the school incident and spoke to the principal about it and he promised to be more vigilant."

"Explains why he was out there when she left this afternoon."

My mind spins with possibilities and explanations and the only thing I can come up with other than another kid doing it as a prank or revenge is someone did it to strand Whitney outside her school.

"It might have been someone hoping to catch her there. Possibly a reporter looking to strand her there to get to ask questions or take pictures?"

"Is that a question?"

"Kind of. I'm not sure I buy that explanation but it's a possibility as much as another kid doing it."

"What reporter would do that? You told me you're not all like the guy from the other night."

"I did and it's the truth but he's still around somewhere. He seemed too invested in digging up dirt on you for my liking. Besides, he's still trying to get the Rogues to pay to replace his phone." A smile curls my lips. Nat is giving him the runaround on that. Although she intends to have it replaced, just on her timeline, not his.

"I don't know what to think. Or what to do."

"If I were you, I'd ask Whitney about anyone she might have argued with at school. It seems like a prank to me. Something a boy might do if he wanted her attention…" The more I think about it, the more possibilities I come up with. "Maybe a boy likes her and wanted to come to the rescue?"

"Again with a question." I can hear the smile in Beckett's voice. "It's late and I've got to be up early to fly home. Can you stay at the house with Whit until she goes to school?"

"I can. I'll even drop her off. Cal said he'll have the car ready to pick up in the morning but if you want, I can swing past your house and grab you after lunch and we can get it before Whitney finishes school."

"Okay, yeah, that will work. We've got tomorrow off because of the thing tomorrow night."

"Ah, yes, the fan barbecue. You don't sound too keen on going."

"I'm not. It'll be our first public appearance as father and daughter and I'm not sure how that's going to go. Are you going to be there?"

"I am. Although I'll be working. I'm going to do some interviews with the fans, weave them into the ones I'm doing with the players and management and staff of the Rogues."

"Other reporters will be there."

"They will, but only a couple. Nat doesn't want it turning into a press conference; it's about the fans."

"Any advice for answering questions about me and Whit?"

"Tell the truth. You don't have to tell them everything but don't lie either. If you don't want to answer a question, give them something else."

"Like what?"

"Well, if they ask about being a teenage single dad, talk about changing dirty diapers and how you never thought you'd be wiping someone else's butt, something like that."

"Okay, I can do that."

"And tell Whitney she can come find me if she feels uncomfortable being near you. Most people don't know who she is and won't recognize her so she should be free to move around the event without getting hassled."

"No one better hassle her."

The vehemence in his voice makes me smile. He really is a great dad, a great protector. "She'll be fine. There's going to be a lot of security and staff wandering around; they'll be keeping an eye on everything and everyone."

"I hope so. I'd hate to get into trouble for punching someone."

"You don't strike me as the violent type."

"I'm not. Except when it comes to Whit."

I can see that. His love for his daughter is fierce, a palpable energy that surrounds them when they're together. I saw it the night I interviewed them. Feel it whenever he talks about Whitney and from her when she talks about him. "I'll be sure to give everyone a heads up. Do I have your permission to tell them about her car?"

"You think you should?"

"I don't know, but I'd rather be safe than sorry."

"Okay, but I can pull Oakley and Natalie aside to tell them in the morning."

"All right, I'll leave that with you but tell them to call me if they have any questions. And they both use the same mechanic so they can call him if they want more details."

"Thanks. I better let you go. We both need to get up early."

"Yeah, Whitney said she leaves for school at seven so she can work in the library before class."

"She loves school. It made homeschooling her easy as hell. Never any fights over doing her lessons."

"I can see that about her. She had a heap of questions about my job while we ate dinner."

"She's naturally curious, which makes me wonder how I ever kept her off social media."

"I was surprised when she told me she's only been on there a couple of years; these days everyone is on one platform or another. Especially teenagers. Then again, Whitney isn't the average teenager. She's wise beyond her years."

"Which makes me think she didn't miss the weirdness of her flat tires."

"Huh. Now that you say that, I bet she's just as curious about it as I am."

"That makes three of us. But we can't do anything about it now. I'll let you get some sleep. And please, don't sleep on the couch, use my bed. And I'm sure you've only got the clothes you were wearing today, there should be a shirt or something in my wardrobe for you to sleep in."

"Thanks. But Whitney already set me up with a pair of her pajamas."

"Good. And thanks again for looking after Whit. I'll see you tomorrow after lunch."

"About two? That should give us time to pick up her car before you have to pick her up from school."

"Can we touch base on the time tomorrow? I might need a nap after tonight. I'm sure I won't get much sleep with what you've told me rolling around my head."

"Sure. Message me. I've got a lunch date but other than that I'm free all day."

"You're not working on your next big scoop?"

I can hear the grin and imagine the way it tilts his mouth. The vision is clear as day in my head and I have to shake it to dislodge the image.

"No. That's not how I work."

"Really? You'll have to explain to me what it is you do when I see you tomorrow."

"If you're interested, sure." I press a hand to my mouth when a yawn cracks my jaw. "Sorry. The day is catching up with me."

"My fault. Go, get some sleep and I'll talk to you in the morning."

"Bye." Hanging up I stand in the garage and ponder our conversation.

In spite of Beckett's initial raised voice, our talk didn't go the way I expected it to. We haven't really been on friendly terms. In fact I'd say our interactions have been quite hostile. But the last few minutes were relaxed. Like two friends catching up on each other's lives...

I don't understand the shift. We haven't had any interaction since the day after I interviewed him and Whitney, and his level of dislike was still blatantly obvious.

What changed?

Oakley hasn't mentioned talking to him; neither has Nat or Blake. If he'd gone to them like I suggested I could understand the shift.

Then again, it could just be that I came to Whitney's aid today. In my experience actions are always more believable than words. It's possible, with time to think, to replay our previous encounters, Beckett Higgison no longer sees me as the enemy he first perceived.

Shaking my head as another jaw cracking yawn sneaks up on me, I head back into the house. I lock the door between the garage and the utility room for good measure although I'm not worried about someone breaking in.

That doesn't stop me from checking all the doors and windows on the ground floor. As I said to Beckett, better to be safe than sorry. And the safety of the girl in my care is a priority I have no intention of slacking on.

Once I'm happy the house is secure, I head upstairs to the master bedroom. The walls are covered in the girliest wallpaper I've even seen and I can't hold back my laughter.

The thought of big brawny Beckett Higgison sleeping in here, surrounded by all this femininity, is hilarious. I'm still chuckling as I snuggle under the soft bedding on Beckett's bed, his masculine scent surrounding me, and drift off to sleep.

BECKETT

I'm dragging ass. Two hours sleep is not enough on the tail end of a tough game. Especially after the adrenaline drop of winning that tough game.

Scrubbing a hand down my face, I debate talking to Oakley or Natalie before we board the plane. If I'm lucky I can grab a quick catnap on the flight home. But if I talk to them before that I'm sure they'll want to dive deep into what happened.

With that in mind, I push last night's discussion with Cami aside and join the guys lining up to get on board. I'm the last in line and as I pass the coaches, I tip my chin up in silent greeting. They move in behind me and I can't help overhearing their conversation.

"Nat not flying home with us?" Coach Watts asks.

"No. Oakley said she's got to go to Atlanta before returning to Baton Rouge," Coach Alcott replies.

"That fucker." Watts's growled curse brings a smile to my face. "He's making her work for it in the hope she'll give in and give him more money."

"Not happening," Alcott answers, his words tinged with a growl of his own. "She's got him over a barrel. Oakley said the last report from the PI is the final nail in his coffin."

"Shame it's a metaphorical coffin and not a real one."

"He keeps it up, I might find a way to make it a real one."

"You do, Bran and I want in on it. Although if Nat would just let Cami off the leash." Coach Watts laughs what can only be described as a cackle. "She's been his biggest non-fan the whole time we've known Nat."

I have no idea who they're talking about, but their conversation shows how close the women are, how much they'd go to bat for each other. And how strong and independent they are. Our GM isn't letting anyone do her dirty work for her. Whatever that dirty work is.

"With any luck, Nat will be in Baton Rouge tonight with signed divorce papers in hand." Coach Alcott's words clue me in.

Natalie Redding is in the middle of a divorce, and from the little I know about the situation, and it's just hallway chatter, her husband is trying to bleed her dry of money. Although the consensus is he's been doing that for years already.

The flight crew greets me with a smile as I leave the jetway and enter the plane. We don't have assigned seats, the plane a private charter, but there is a crew to serve us meals and drinks if we want either.

As I walk further down the aisle, I see most of my teammates have the same idea as me. The three-hour flight is a good chance to rest our battle-weary bodies and catch up on sleep.

I head to the last row, toss my bag up in the overhead locker, and flop down in the seat next to the window. Buckling my belt, I lean my head back and shut my eyes. With any luck I'll be out before we take off and only wake up when we land.

My seat shakes as someone takes the one next to me and I inwardly cringe and hope they don't want to talk. The feminine clearing of a throat tells me I'm out of luck.

"I'll only talk for a few minutes."

I turn my head and crack one eye. Oakley James is doing up her seatbelt as she settles in beside me. "You don't want to sit next to your husband?"

"I will after we chat." Her gaze snags mine. "Cami called me this morning."

"Ah." Opening both eyes, I sit up straighter and twist a little toward her. "What did she call you about?"

"Whitney. Or more specifically her car."

"Right, well, you probably know as much as I do."

"After we hung up, I called the PI we have on retainer and asked him to do some investigating. I also asked him to see if he can get any security footage from the school."

"I should have thought of that."

"At midnight? I think you're forgiven for not. And this isn't the first time I've dealt with this kind of thing. Amos, our PI, is good. Really good. I expect to have an answer as to how Whitney's tires got flat in the next day or so."

"Okay. Thank you."

"You're welcome. Now, about Whitney. What are your plans for her when you're playing out of town?"

"She's supposed to spend the night with our neighbor. Mrs. Gerber."

"I'm told Mrs. Gerber could blow over in a stiff breeze."

I chuckle, the description of our elderly neighbor spot on. Although Mrs. Gerber is tiny, she's tough as nails. The first time I met her she tried to beam me over the head with a broom. If I didn't have quick reflexes she would have got me, and with the power behind her swing she'd have cracked my skull open too.

"She's small but don't underestimate her. And Whit doesn't really need a babysitter, it's more about her not being alone."

"I have a proposition for you."

I grin. "Does your husband know you're propositioning players?"

"Oh, funny. And yes, he knows what I'm going to offer. At the moment Chase Hawkins' sisters stay with Nat when he's out of town. If she's with the team, like this trip, they stay at my house with Mikey and Pa. I'm offering Whitney the same. She can either stay with Nat and Pa, or just Pa. You might also see if Cami is up for staying with Whitney or alternately, she can stay with Cami."

"I..." I blink a couple of times, my brain trying to roll through the options she just laid out. "Thank you. But I don't want to put—"

She holds up a hand. "You—*she*—would not be putting anyone out. It gives all the kids someone to hang with when their parents, or in Chase's case, guardian, aren't there. We're a built-in family and I'd like you to take advantage of that because if the situation is reversed and someone needs help, I'd expect you to offer it."

"That goes without saying."

"Then it's settled. She's got lots of choices for the next time we have an away game. I'll make sure she meets everyone tonight at the barbecue. She might already know the twins—they go to the same school as she does. I think they're a grade or two below her though."

"She hasn't mentioned anyone at school being involved with the team." I'd have remembered if it had come up, she hasn't talked about many kids since she started at the beginning of the school year. I make a mental note to ask her about it.

"The rest of the kids are in middle school or below. Summer and Autumn are the only ones besides Whitney in high school. Which brings me to another offer. Is she up for earning a little money? I'd like to offer her a job at home games helping wrangle the younger kids."

"She'd do that for free. Or food. You don't have to pay her."

"We can talk about it tonight." She pats my hand. "You're no longer an island, Beckett. I know you had friends you could rely on before you came to the Rogues, but now you have a whole bunch of us to help when you need."

"We're normally self-sufficient. Especially now that Whit is older. But I'll keep it in mind. And please, if I can help someone in any way let me know."

"You're already helping by guiding the younger team members."

"I'm not really doing much there."

"Nonsense. I've seen you with the team, on and off the ice. I like your style because it's not obvious that you're doing anything. I don't want being in the NHL to have a detrimental effect on the boys we've brought in. And yes, some of them are boys. Hell, one of them is barely out of high school."

I know exactly who she's talking about. "Kallan."

"Yeah. And he's still learning English. Whoever was teaching him before did a shitty job."

"I can work with him on that, get Whit to help me. I'll make sure all the guys know to make sure he's understanding what they're saying and him in return."

"We might have a talk about that tomorrow at training..."

The seatbelt light goes off with a ding and Oakley unbuckles hers. I hadn't even noticed we'd taken off.

"I'll leave you to catch up on sleep. I'll talk to you later about what we've discussed."

"Sure. Okay."

My brain is foggy from lack of sleep and we covered a few things I'm still trying to process but as the cabin lights dim I decide to worry about everything after a nap.

Closing my eyes again, I tip my seat back and lean my head against the side of the plane.

I'm out seconds later.

The first thing I do when I get home is toss a load in the washer. I managed to sleep the whole flight once Oakley left me. Those couple of hours have set me up for the day and as we don't have practice or a skate today, I'll be fine to make it through until tonight.

When I hit the utility room I find a pile of clean, folded

laundry on top of the dryer. Scratching my head, I try to recall when I did the washing. I'm positive the last load I did didn't have Whit's neon green yoga pants in it. Which means my daughter finally took it upon herself to help with the laundry.

I grin. How she can prefer scrubbing the bathroom over washing clothes is beyond me but over the last few years we've gotten into a routine and split those chores. With only the clothes in my bag to wash I contemplate leaving them but then I remember the last time I left a bag of away clothes and the stink that took two washes to get out.

Putting in a small load, I pick up the pile of folded clothes and head upstairs. Whit's stuff is on top of the pile and it's easy to put them in her room and continue to my own.

The second I step through the doorway I'm assaulted with a fragrance that is unfamiliar. It's a subtle sweetness that sticks and pulls up several memories.

Cami.

My bedroom smells like Cami Nelson.

Which is to be expected seeing how I told her to sleep up here instead of on the couch.

My gaze moves to the bed.

The quilt is perfectly smooth and the pillows piled against the headboard. I don't think my bed has ever been that well made. I usually toss the quilt up off the floor where I've inevitably kicked it during the night.

An image of Cami, snuggled under my covers, bursts to life in my head and I jolt with the vividness of it. I don't miss the movement in my groin either. The visceral reaction to my imagination is interesting. I'm not a fantasy kind of guy. If I feel the urge, I wait until I'm able to take care of it in the shower.

The last thing I want is my daughter walking in on that!

Thinking of the shower sparks my imagination further and I'm walking toward my bathroom before I know I'm moving.

Pushing open the door, I take a deep breath and find the scent from the bedroom is stronger in here. Two steps has me in front of the shower door, hand on the rail that passes for a handle. With a tug, the glass panel swings out and an even stronger wave of Cami hits me.

And the movement in my groin becomes a rush.

I put my clean clothes on the counter and strip out of my dirty ones. I'm in the shower, water running, hand on my dick seconds later.

Closing my eyes I breathe deep and conjure Cami's pretty face. I might not have acknowledged her looks before now but my subconscious isn't stupid. In my mind she's as clear as she'd be if she was right in front of me.

My hand tightens and a grumble of pleasure rolls through my chest. Firm strokes, a gentle twist to skim the top, and my dick is pulsing, pre-come oozing.

I lean into the hand I have on the wall, rest my forehead on my arm, and concentrate on the image of Cami in my head.

She's on her knees, her hand replacing mine, her tongue sweeping out to drag across the swollen tip of my dick and it's game over.

I'm shooting my load on the tile with sharp jerks of my hips.

Spent, I stay, dick in hand, for long moments as the water beats down. I should be ashamed of what I just did, using someone I'm not sure I even like as fodder for my own pleasure, but I'm not.

I'm still aroused.

More than I've been in so long I don't remember the last time a hand job was more than a quick release of pressure and nothing more.

Fuck.

I don't remember the last time masturbating made me feel so good.

Or so unsatisfied.

Shoving off the wall, I move under the spray and try to wash away the feeling of dissatisfaction. It doesn't work.

And the more I think about what I just did—think about the

woman I imagined while doing it—the more I realize I'm in deep shit.

I was sure I didn't like Cami Nelson. Her career is what I've avoided since I was a teenager. Getting close to her would be dangerous. Not for me—I've come to grips with the way I became a father and I wouldn't change how Whit became mine for anything.

Whit is the innocent in all of this and while I've always thought I'd have to tell her about how she came to be eventually, I thought I'd wait until she was older.

Except she is older.

And if that scumbag reporter—or any other reporter—keeps digging, it won't be hard to find out the name in the mother section of Whit's birth certificate is fake.

Or that the name in the father section isn't the one I was born with.

CAMI

Offering my hand across the table to Deb I say, "We'll talk later. Let me know how you go at work."

"They'll probably walk me out the door as soon as I hand in my resignation."

"Then you'll be able to work with me sooner." I smile. "I'm really excited about this. I had no idea you had a degree in film."

"I have multiple degrees. I thought I wanted to be in front of the camera but the more time I spent at FNB I changed my mind."

"Listen, I've got a thing with the Rogues tonight. It's a barbecue for the fans and I want to wander around asking random people questions as well as get some footage of the whole event. Feel like barbecue for dinner?"

"If I get walked this afternoon, definitely."

"Even if you don't, you can still come. I'll get Oakley to get you a press pass so you can go anywhere but what I'd like is for you to shadow me and take some video. I'll film any interviews the same way—"

"How will you make that work? From what I've seen, you set your phone up on something then sit down to talk with the players."

"Hmm...I do..." Ideas roll until one takes. "What if you record? Nothing fancy, just use your phone camera, the same as the video I want of the event. I want this series to be natural, candid. Nothing staged or put together if that makes sense."

"It makes perfect sense. You want the audience to feel like they're there with you and whoever you talk to. Make it like they caught you talking as they walked past."

"Yes." I grin. "I think this is going to be a brilliant working relationship."

Deb smiles back. "Me too. I can't wait to get started."

"Well, lunch is done and you've got a resignation to submit so..."

She pushes her chair back while rummaging in her bag.

"Don't worry, I've got this. We'll put it down as our first planning lunch."

"Oh gosh." She looks up, eyes wide. "This is really happening."

"It is."

"I can't thank you enough for giving me this chance."

"All the thanks I need is for you to do a good job."

"I'll do the best."

I smile at my new partner. "I'm going to send you a number, it's for my lawyer, I'll apprise her about what we're doing but I want you to get your own to go over the contract with. I also think you should form a company. Instead of being my employee I'll contract you to work for me."

"Like freelance?"

"Yes."

"I can do that. I already have a company set up. I do the occasional job of videoing. I have a photographer friend who uses me as a videographer when her regular guy can't do it."

"Perfect!" I stand and shoulder my bag. "I'll have my lawyer contact you later today with a contract for tonight."

"I can't wait. What time do you want me at the arena?"

"Can you swing five-thirty?"

"Yes. If you're okay with me wearing this?" Deb indicates the business skirt and blouse she's wearing.

"Do you have anything else? Not that there's anything wrong with what you're wearing but it's a bit formal for tonight."

"I have a pair of jeans in my car...but no shirt."

"That's okay, I'll get you a Rogues jersey or shirt. Meet me at the arena, staff parking entrance, at five-thirty and I'll get you set up."

"Gosh, I really hope they walk me this afternoon but I'll go for weeks without sleep if it means getting to work with you on this."

"I don't normally do this but..." I grin. "I know someone who might expedite your resignation."

"Your dad? You'd call your dad for me?"

I shrug. "Sure. I'd never do it for myself but I don't see why I can't do it to benefit you."

"Thank you. But I should probably just work my two-week notice."

"You could or..." The more I think about it, the more I know Dad will get on board with me pulling Deb across. He was harping at me yesterday about this being too much for one person. "I'll call him. See what I can work out. You go back to the office and hand in your resignation now, make out like you intend to work out your notice, and we'll see what happens."

Deb walks around the table and throws her arms around me. "Thank you!"

"I should thank you. I love the suggestions you had and I'm sure between the two of us we'll come up with some great stuff." I pat her back as I pull away. "Now go. I'll see you later."

With a huge grin on her face, she says a squeaky "Bye" and leaves me standing here smiling.

My phone buzzes with a reminder that I have somewhere else I need to be. It takes me a few minutes to settle our check but then I'm out of the restaurant and heading for my car.

The first thing I do when I get behind the wheel is turn the car on and get the air going. Then I check that my phone is connected to the car's Bluetooth system and call Dad.

"Cam! We were just talking about you."

"Who was?"

"Mom and I."

"Oh?"

"We were saying what a fantastic job you're doing with these intimate interviews of the Rogues."

"Speaking of them, I have something of a request but don't feel as though you have to say yes."

"What do you need?"

"I've got a videographer lined up to work with me on the rest of the conversations and some other things but she needs to give two weeks' notice at her job before she can really dive into it with me."

"Okay. How do I play in this?"

"It's Deb. The FNB building receptionist."

"I didn't realize she was a videographer."

"Neither did I. And not to malign anyone, but every time she's tried to apply for a position more suited to her skillset, she's been told she didn't have the right experience."

"And does she?"

"Yes. She showed me some of what she's capable of."

"And you wouldn't hire her to work for you if she couldn't do the job."

"Right?" A thought occurs to me. "Wait, you said you were talking with Mom. Is she with you?"

"Yes, we're at home having lunch."

"Put me on speaker please."

"You're already on speaker, Cam," Mom says.

"Oh, good. Okay, so Dad, the favor I have is for you to somehow get Deb's two-week notice waived. She's handing in her resignation as we speak with the intention of working the notice but..."

"If I could get that dealt with, she could start full-time with you."

"Yes. And, Mom, I need a contract for a freelance videographer. I'll get the details of her company to you by this afternoon. She's going to work with me tonight at the Rogues' Fan Day barbecue."

"And you want the contract drawn up before then?"

"Do I need to? Could we back-date it?"

"We could but I can also get it done before tonight. I've got the afternoon off. I was planning to spend it in the garden but it's hot out today. Too hot for what I'd planned."

"Are you sure? I know I'm rushing but she's good and I want her in on this with me. Sooner than later if I can. Although I hate using my connections to make that happen." The guilt weighing down my stomach proves my words aren't a lie. And I've never done this before. Not once in my life have I asked Mom or Dad to smooth the way.

"Done."

"I'll call head of HR. Get Deb free this afternoon."

"Thanks!"

"Why don't we meet you at the barbecue?" Mom asks. "We don't have plans for dinner, and you know we've become hockey fans since you got the franchise."

"You were fans before KAW got the franchise."

"We were but it's our home team."

"Nothing beats supporting your home team."

I can hear the pleasure in their voices. It makes me proud in so many ways and all I did was hand over money to make the team happen. I've had nothing to do with building the team or the arena.

My phone beeps with another reminder. Shit! If I don't get moving, I'll be late.

"I gotta go. But I'll call later. About four."

"Talk then. Love you," Mom says.

"Love you too."

"Need me to do anything else?" Dad asks.

"No. That's all I need."

"Don't hesitate to ask if something comes up."

"Will do. See you later."

"You will. I'm so proud of what you're doing, what you've already done."

"Thanks, Dad."

"And, Cam?"

"Yeah?"

"You were born for me to love."

I grin. "And I was born to love you."

The call disconnects and I check my mirrors before pulling out in traffic. I've got just enough time to get across town to Beckett's house to pick him up before we head to Whitney's school.

His message this morning was straightforward, almost clinical. I don't know if he's not comfortable texting or if we're still in the not liking each other phase of our relationship. Not that we're in a relationship.

Shit.

Why the hell did I think that word? We're acquaintances, nothing more.

Okay, fine, technically I'm his boss but that doesn't affect the way we deal with each other. Although I suppose I changed that dynamic yesterday when I rescued his daughter and stayed with her.

After our call last night, I thought maybe we'd cut through his initial hostility. And Whitney let me know they're both aware I'm an owner of the team even if I don't advertise I am.

But this morning's message was weird. Or maybe I'm being weird because after sleeping in Beckett's bed, showering in his shower, I'm feeling a little off-kilter. The excited zip of anticipation I got when I saw his name flash on my phone screen didn't help.

I admire him for what he's done with Whitney and his career, but I'm not sure I like him. I like him as a father. I can't deny that.

And he reminds me of Dad so that could account for the buzz of pleasure I got when his text came in.

Except he kind of ruined it with his words. So abrupt and sterile.

Pick me up at 2:30. We'll get Whit before her car.

I'm not sure what I expected. If I should have expected anything more than I got. It's hard to put a finger on how I feel about Beckett because in the short time I've known him, in the scant minutes I've spent in his presence, I've run a gauntlet of emotions.

Defense. Anger. Amusement. Dislike. Like. Concern.

It's better with Whitney.

I really like her. She's such a pleasure to be around. And she's an extension of Beckett so how can I like her and not him?

I swear, I'm getting emotional whiplash from this man and I don't like it.

Everything about it reminds me of my biological mother and the see-saw of contradicting behavior she's displayed my whole life.

I don't need that upheaval. I cut all ties—well, I tried to cut them all—with Andrea years ago because I didn't want that kind of turmoil in my life. Especially after Mom gave me unconditional love and stability the way my birth mother should have.

Except I can't deny I'm drawn to the Higgisons. It's like an invisible tether, with a retraction mechanism slowly winding me closer and closer.

On one hand I want to get closer.

On the other I want to run far, far away.

I've never been wishy-washy like this. Never found it hard to make a decision about something. But I can't decide what to do about the father and daughter duo.

I know one thing though.

I'm stuck with them for now. I need to see this thing through, need to be sure someone isn't out to hurt either of them.

Because for some reason I think they've been hurt before.

Beckett more than Whitney. But there's something about him that trips a switch inside me, has me wanting to protect them both.

It could be because of the way Draper went at him that first night or it could be something else. Whatever it is, as an owner of the Rogues it's kind of my job to make sure they're okay. Safe.

I'm invested more than that though.

Every instinct I have is telling me they need me to stick close.

It's puzzling and exciting and confusing.

I've never lost my head over a guy. Not even Dwight and we dated for four years before calling it quits.

Beckett Higgison and his daughter are going to turn my life upside down.

Hell, they already are.

Beckett

I wipe down the kitchen counter.

Again.

And curse myself an idiot.

Cami has already been in my house. She's seen it in less than a sparkling clean state so why the hell am I cleaning the place from top to bottom before she arrives?

And she's probably not even going to come inside!

We're cutting the timing close to pick up Whit when school gets out. I did that on purpose because after my jack-off session in the shower this morning I need to put some distance between me and the woman who has me thinking things I haven't in over seventeen years.

She's just a lift. Like a share-ride without the cost, she'll pick me up, take me to get my daughter, then we'll go get Whit's car.

That's it.

She'll drive away, leaving us at the mechanic to pay for the repairs or air or whatever the guy decides to charge me for.

My house doesn't need to be clean.

I'm not out to impress her.

I don't like her.

Hell.

That's a lie.

I don't like her job and by extension I don't like her, but I don't know her.

She seems genuine. She helped Whit when I couldn't. She even came to me with her concerns about what happened and she didn't have to. She could have just dropped Whit at home after helping get her car towed and that would have been acceptable.

Except she didn't.

She cooked dinner.

For Whit and Mrs. Gerber, who came by earlier to thank me for the meal and the leftovers Cami sent her home with last night.

The woman confounds me. She's nothing like I assumed she would be.

Then again, the worst time of my life involved reporters digging for dirt, trying to invade my life and take away my chance to love my daughter.

To *keep* my daughter.

I scrub a hand down my face and sigh.

I'm laying someone else's misdeeds on Cami's shoulders.

I shouldn't. I know I shouldn't. I'm the first to understand how someone else's actions can affect those around them. How finger pointing and laying blame aren't always in the right places.

Cami has done nothing to reinforce my first instinct to protect myself and Whit from her. In fact, she's done a number of things that prove I *can* trust her.

And I trust Oakley, Coaches Alcott and Watts, even the Rogues' GM is in the trust column. I can't see any of them being friends, never mind business partners, with a woman who would set out to hurt others.

I need to dig up some of her work. See what type of articles she writes. Get a feel for the way she treats people and their secrets.

Not that I will ever reveal mine.

Not until Whit knows the whole truth about her mother.

That's another reason I'm struggling with my feelings toward

Cami. She makes me realize I need to tell Whit the truth. I've put it off for long enough thinking it best to wait until she was an adult, out of college.

But my girl is smart, well adjusted, and mature enough to know now. She'll be eighteen in two months. It's time I told her everything. Told her how she came into my life.

The doorbell echoes through the house and I glance at the microwave.

"She's early."

Only a few minutes, but it's a good sign. She either doesn't like to be late or she knows we don't have time to waste. Scooping up my keys from the bowl on the counter along with the garage remote Whit took out of her car before letting it be towed, I head for the front door.

I'm a few steps into the foyer when the doorbell rings again and I smile at the woman's impatience. It's barely a minute since she pressed it the first time.

I pull the door open with a grin on my face that quickly dies. "Can I help you?"

The guy on my front step jumps and turns back to face me. "Oh. I didn't think anyone was home."

It's not an answer to my question and I'm standing here which proves his assumption is incorrect so there's no need to say a word. Something that makes the guy squirm.

He's in his twenties, mid to late if I were to guess, but I'm more interested in what he's doing here. When he stares at me for another few seconds, his feet shuffling and his eyes shifting, I want to slam the door in his face.

Except at that moment Cami pulls into my driveway. At least I think it's her. I have no idea what type of car she drives but the high end SUV seems to fit. And when the driver's door opens and Cami steps out with a frown on her face my suspicion of this guy ramps up a notch.

Cami wastes no time getting to us and the frown on her face

turns into a downright scowl with laser-eyes that should have this guy dropping to his knees.

"Kenneth. What are you doing here?"

"Oh, hey, I..." His gaze darts back and forth between us. "Hi, Cami."

She walks around him and stops in front of my door, kind of blocking me and the house from Kenneth, whoever he is. Her arms are crossed, her feet are shoulder width apart. The stance is a defensive one that makes me smile.

How she thinks she can protect me from this guy is anyone's guess but I have to say the pleasure her protection delivers is one I'm not accustomed to but find appealing.

I cock my head and arch an eyebrow, sizing up the possible threat at my door. "So, Kenneth, you haven't answered mine or Cami's question."

"Oh, right. Well, um—"

"For god's sake, Kenneth, get to it." Cami's voice is laced with exasperation without a trace of concern and I have to think she's no longer worried this guy is here with nefarious intentions.

"I..." He licks his lips and swallows. "IwonderedifImightge-taninterviewwithHiggison."

His words roll out in one long rush and it takes me a few seconds to separate them. "An inter—"

"No!" Cami takes a step toward Kenneth, making him back up. "And you know better than turning up on someone's doorstep to ask. If you want to interview anyone on the Rogues' roster you contact head office. They'll either grant or deny your request. If they grant it, they'll tell you where and when the interview will take place."

"But—"

"Nope. No buts. That's the way it works with professional athletes, and you know it."

"It's not against the law—"

"No, it's not, but being on private property without invitation is trespassing. And that *is* against the law."

"Aw, c'mon, Cami. The Rogues aren't letting anyone interview their players."

Turning her head slightly, Cami says, "Beckett, can you call the police and then the Rogues' GM please?"

"Okay, okay." Kenneth holds up his hands as he walks backward. "No need to go that far. I'm leaving."

"Good." Cami's attention is back on the guy retreating with his shoulders hunched and a frown on his face. "And, Kenneth?"

She waits for him to look right at her.

"Don't come back."

He shoots her a dirty look that has my fists clenching. I'd like to punch this guy in the nose, hopefully break it, for looking at Cami like that.

The violent urge surprises me. Physical altercations have only even been inspired on the ice, or in defense of Whit.

This woman, one I claim to dislike, is pulling on instincts previously reserved for my daughter. And let's be honest, I don't think Cami needs me to protect her. She's fully capable of doing it herself, and if she can't she's smart enough to find someone or something that can.

"Wait until he leaves." Her voice is low even though Kenneth is too far away to hear anything we say.

Quietly we watch him get into a car parked across the street. It's a beater, a little worse for wear than the car I bought Whit, and it sparks an idea.

"Do you think he let the air out of Whit's tires?"

"Before today I'd have said no. Now I'm not so sure. I'll send his picture to our PI and see if he can get a connection between what happened to Whitney's car and Kenneth."

"He's driving—"

"I took a picture. I'll send that to Amos too."

Tipping forward, I peer over her shoulder. Sure enough, she's got her phone out and she's zooming in on Kenneth's car and snapping photos rapidly.

Once he's out of sight, she spins around and faces me. "Here."

I look down to see she's holding out her keys. "What are those for?"

"Go get Whitney, bring her back here. I'll have Cal bring the car to you."

"What? Why?"

"Because I don't like that he was here. It's strange to see a reporter on your doorstep when I know the Rogues put out the word to all media outlets that players are off limits unless they go through official channels."

"So what you told him is true, the org decides who we speak to?"

"You didn't get the email?"

"I..." I shake my head. "No. I haven't checked my inbox since before getting on the plane this morning."

"Okay. Well, basically you've all been banned from talking to the media, and that includes influencers and bloggers, until further notice. Nat's on a tear. She's pissed but not at the team, or the media really, but it is what it is, and she calls the shots on these things."

"You don't get a say?" It's the first time I've brought up her involvement with the team.

Her mouth opens and closes. With a shrug, she says, "It's not my place—"

"Bullshit. You own the team."

She sucks in a breath, her eyes going wide as her eyebrows shoot up her forehead. "Right. Okay, yes, I'm *part* owner."

"You don't advertise it."

"No."

"Why not? Why keep it a secret?"

"It's not a secret. I'm not involved in the running of the team, frontend or back. I'm a quarter of KAW and that's it."

"So you don't care about the team?" I know she does, but I want to poke at her. Find out why she stays away from something the others seem so proud of.

"I do." Her gaze skitters to the side. "I'm just not a sports fan."

"But one of your best friends played hockey her whole life. Went to the Olympics."

"Yes. I'm aware." Her eyes are back on me and I can see she's moved back into defense mode after that brief display of vulnerability.

"So. You don't get a say? In the media ban?"

Cami blows out a breath and her shoulders slump. "I suggested it."

"You. Why?"

"Because they want the Conversations with a Rogue to be in the spotlight and if you all go around talking to any reporter, there will be multiple articles and interviews floating around. Plus we need to steer the narrative, particularly with you right now, and the way to do that is to control all information being put out."

Shit, she's so fucking smart. If the only thing coming out of the Rogue camp is Rogue approved, there's less chance of things being uncovered that should remain private.

"Okay, I get it. No talking to anyone about anything."

"It's going to prove difficult because we want the fans to have access to the players, want you all to be able to sign autographs if a fan stops you, but you'll need to be careful about what you say."

"Is there any direction concerning that in the email you talked about?"

"No. But I'm meeting with Nat, Oakley, and Blake after this before the barbecue tonight. I'll run the idea of holding a media dos and don'ts with everyone tomorrow. Before or after training."

"And the reason you're giving me your keys and telling me to go get Whit?"

"I don't think you should leave your house empty at the moment. And my car isn't yours so it won't draw as much attention as yours would."

"Mine isn't exactly flashy." It's a BMW SUV. Plenty of those on the road around here. Especially in the parking lot of Whit's private school.

"No. But we have the ability to disguise you, so why not. Just to be safe."

"Better safe than sorry."

"Exactly!" She grabs my hand and turns it over so my palm is up. Dropping her keys into it she says, "Now go get Whit before you're late and I'll call Cal to get her car brought over."

"I haven't paid him."

She waves her hand. "Don't worry about that. Whitney gave him her card details yesterday. He'll charge that."

"Oh." I keep forgetting I gave Whit a card for when I'm not around. "If that guy comes back, do what you asked me to do, and call the police."

"Don't worry, I will. I'm also going to call the Rogues' head of security and see about beefing up yours."

"I've got an alarm."

"Yes, except it could use an update and I noticed the door to the garage isn't alarmed and neither is the garage."

"Huh." I lean forward and look at my roller door. "I never thought about that."

"It's okay. I've got experience in needing to cover every angle of security."

Her words have my gaze back on her, curious about her tone and what she's implying. The thought of Cami needing security or finding breaches in it through any means other than a security specialist telling her has my entire body tensing.

"Lock the door behind me," I say as I move past her and urge her through the doorway. "I'll be as quick as I can but don't open the door to anyone while I'm gone. Unless it's the police."

"Beckett, I'm fine. I'll be fine."

"Of course. Just don't take any chances." I reach into the house and grab the front door handle. As I pull it closed, she takes a step back. "See you when I get back."

"But I—"

I snap the door shut and call out, "Lock it!"

Ignoring her protests about something in her car, I step back and repeat, "Lock it, Cami."

I hear her huff through the door but I also hear the tell-tale click of the deadbolt sliding into place. With a smile, I head for Cami's car, pleased she's safe inside my house.

The alarm might not be the best but I doubt anyone, especially reed-thin Kenneth, will break in at this hour of the day. Then again, most burglaries occur during the day while the occupants are out at work or whatever.

That thought has me picking up my pace and when I jump behind the wheel and crank the engine, I slam the gear into reverse and accelerate so fast the tires give a little squeal against the driveway's concrete surface.

And I'm not ashamed to admit I went a few miles above the speed limit all the way to Whit's school.

CAMI

Pacing Beckett's house I notice a few things are different since I left this morning. For one, the clean laundry I left in the utility room is gone, and the dishwasher had been run and everything put away.

The small amount of last night's leftovers I put in the fridge are gone too.

It pleases me to think Beckett ate them for lunch. Or breakfast. And I can't help wondering if he liked what I made. It wasn't fancy, just a chicken, bacon, and leek bake I've made for years because it's great for freezing leftovers. And when you're cooking for one all the time, meals that have more than one use are better and more efficient than cooking a single meal every night.

Not that I cook as much as I should. Years of living at home meant Mom took care of that most nights and now I'm out of their home, I find myself back at Mom and Dad's a lot of the time.

Except recently.

I might not have had much say—or any—in the way the Rogues came together but I've been there. Which shocks me that most people don't seem to know I'm part owner. Like I told Beckett, it's not a secret and I've been at every press conference about the team from the announcement of the franchise nearly two years ago.

Although I tend to stand toward the back. And I never speak. I leave that to Nat, Oakley, and Blake. They're all front and center whenever something happens. It's the same way with Rogue sportswear. I'm not comfortable in the spotlight, not after spending my childhood being thrust into it.

The thought of my life before Dad took me away from it makes me shudder. Crossing my arms, I rub my hands up and down my biceps in an attempt to ward off the chill.

I hate thinking about that time in my life. Hate that no matter what I do the memories are as clear as the day they happened and still have the ability to affect me.

Resentment and hate are all I feel for the two people I spent my first eight years with. The last two the worst of them because Andrea finally admitted I wasn't Gun Muskin's kid.

I'm pulled from my thoughts by the door to the garage bursting open. For a moment my instinct is to reach for a knife in the block sitting prominently on the kitchen counter. The urge is squashed a second later when Whitney's voice echoes off every surface.

"Cami!"

The girl races toward me and throws her arms around my neck. Shocked by the show of affection I stare at her father with wide eyes. His indulgent smile has me snapping out of my daze and reciprocating the hug.

"Hey. How was school?"

"It was school." She pulls back, her arms still around me. "But guess what?"

"What?"

"Dad said if it's okay with you I can stay at your house or you can stay here whenever he has an away game from now on."

"Oh." My gaze darts to Beckett for confirmation. The look he sends me is sheepish, and I have to believe there's a reason he offered me up as babysitter. "That sounds like a plan. But I have to work things out with your dad first. There might be conflicts in my schedule and his—"

"That's okay. Oakley said I could also stay with Pa or Natalie with the twins." She lets me go and walks to the fridge. "I'm starving, are those leftovers still here?"

"I ate them for lunch."

Whitney eyes her father over the fridge door. "Of course you did. But I'm not going to last until the barbecue tonight. I need something to tide me over."

One thing I noticed about Whitney last night was that for someone so slender, she has an appetite. One to rival a teenage boy. "I can whip something up."

The offer is out and I'm moving toward her before I think about what I'm doing.

"Oh. Sorry." I glance at Beckett. "Cal said he's going to be another thirty minutes so I've got time to make you both something before then."

"You don't need to get going?"

Glancing at the time on the microwave, I calculate what I have to do before the start of the Rogues' Fan Barbecue and shrug. "I've got time."

"Sure. Did you talk to the head of security?" Beckett asks as he comes closer. "And tell us what we can do to help you pull something together."

"Yes. He's going to talk to you tonight and arrange to come over tomorrow."

"I can give him a key and he can come while I'm at training and Whit's at school."

"Why do we need a security guy here?" Whitney eyes us suspiciously.

"Because our system is out of date and I want the garage wired up," Beckett says as though it's no big deal.

I smile at Whitney and ask, "How does a nibble platter sound?"

"Do we have stuff for that?" she asks, peering into the fridge beside me.

"Sure. Give me some room and I'll pass you what will work."

"Okay." Stepping back, she waits, her gaze bouncing between me and her dad.

I noticed a tub of hummus and a bottle of ranch dressing when I put the leftovers away last night and I know I saw a bunch of veggies and fruit in here too. "Do you have some corn chips or crackers?"

"Yeah. I'll get them," Beckett answers.

Passing things behind me I hear Whitney muttering with each one. Once I think there's enough to fill both their bellies, I close the fridge and turn. Both Beckett and Whitney eye the food on the counter.

It's Beckett who voices the concern I see on their faces. "Is this enough for all of us?"

"All of us?"

"You're staying, right? We can't expect you to put something together and then not eat with us."

"Oh. I..." I honestly hadn't thought about it but now that he's put it out there, it seems stupid to put a platter together for them to eat while we wait for Cal to get here with Whitney's car and not join them. "Hold on."

Spinning back, I yank the fridge open again and grab a jar of olives and a block of cheese. I'll cut up one of the apples Beckett has in the bowl on the counter too. Now we'll have cold cuts, veggies, fruit, crackers, and cheese, with two dips to choose from.

"We just lay all this out and pick what we want to dip?" Beckett asks, already getting to work on opening packages.

"Some of it we should cut into sticks. Like the apple, cheese, cucumber, carrots—"

"I get it." He moves away and comes back with a chopping board and knife. "I'll cut, you set it up."

Whitney hands me a large platter. "I don't think this is going to be big enough and it's the biggest we've got."

"Got some foil? Or baking paper?"

"Yeah, that drawer over there." Beckett points his knife toward the fridge.

"What are you going to do with it?" Whitney asks.

"Spread it out on the counter. We'll pile everything on it then we can roll it up and toss it out when we're done."

"Wow, that's a cool idea. I never would have thought of it. Dad and I would probably have used lots of plates."

"We could do that too. Bowls or plates would work but this way there isn't much clean up and it's kind of fun to eat off the counter. A bit of rebellion against manners." I grin.

They're both looking at me. Whitney with awe and Beckett with a curious, confused expression, like he's trying to work me out and can't.

I don't mind that. If I'm honest, I like it. A lot. Having his interest isn't something I've really thought about. Our first few interactions weren't good, he wasn't nice, but with each subsequent one, there's a subtle shift in our demeanor. His mainly.

His hostility is no longer front and center. In fact, I'd go as far as saying it's barely hovering in the background now.

"Are you going to be at the barbecue tonight?" Whitney asks, breaking me out of my thoughts.

"Yes. I'll be doing some filming and asking some of the fans questions."

"Not the players?" Beckett asks.

"Probably. Especially if they're with a fan. I want to continue with the real aspect of the Conversations with a Rogue series."

"I've watched every one so far. They're really good." Whitney smiles at me. "I have to do a project about technology and I was going to focus on the way social media has changed our lives but I want to change it to how devices have made our lives different with a focus on the accessibility to the internet and social media particularly."

"That sounds like a huge undertaking."

"Not really. I did something similar last year but about cars. The evolution of them and their impact on society."

I glance at Beckett. "Wow. Are you sure you're in high school? That sounds like something you'd do in college."

"It's for an AP class."

"I'm impressed."

"Can I use your series as an example of what a phone can do? You used your phone to edit the videos, right?"

"I did. Although, I didn't really edit them much. Mainly tweaked the sound."

"I need to get your permission in writing, and I'll credit you at the end of the assignment."

"Sure. I'll get my mom to draw up a legal doc covering it."

"Your mom?"

"She's a lawyer. You can meet her tonight if you want."

"Your parents are coming?" Beckett asks, a look on his face I can't decipher.

"Yeah. They try and support everything I do but they're both hockey fans so it's a no brainer they'll be at all the Rogue things they can get to."

"And yet, you're not a fan."

"You don't like hockey?" Whitney asks, her mouth agape. "Who doesn't like hockey?"

I laugh. "It's not that I don't like it. More that I'm not a fan."

"What's the difference?"

"Well, a fan goes out of their way to watch it, play it, talk about it."

"And you don't do that?"

"I don't go out of my way, no. But I do watch. And I do talk about it. Kind of hard not to when I own a team in the NHL."

"I don't understand why you own a team if you're not a fan." Whitney shakes her head as we put the last few things out on our makeshift platter.

"It's a business to me. Same as Rogue sportswear. I own them both but I'm not involved in the everyday running of either."

"If I owned them I'd be in everything." Whitney nods. "Yeah, you'd never get me to stop working."

"That's no way to live. It's why we have managers and staff in both businesses. Experts in their field who take care of things we don't have time or skill to do."

"I want to work for KAW when I finish school."

"That's a few years away, yet. You'll probably change your mind." Beckett nudges her with his shoulder. "And there is nothing wrong with changing your mind."

"Oh, I won't. And I'm not talking about after college, Dad. I'm going to start looking for something I can do while I go to college."

"You're sticking close for college?" I ask, curious as to what this blossoming woman has in mind. She seems so set and determined and I've already noticed how mature she is for her age.

"I am. I'm also looking at doing online. I know everyone thinks going away to college is an experience I should want but I don't. I like being close to Dad, and why should I go if I can get where I want to go without it?"

"You have a point." Beckett eyes his daughter. "You really don't want to go away to college?"

"No. I like it here."

"We've been here less than six months."

"I know but as soon as we got here, it felt like home."

"Huh."

"You didn't feel that way?" she asks, her gaze glued to Beckett.

"I did." Something passes through his gaze, something that has an edge of fear to it. And I can't help but think he's not being quite truthful.

"Does it remind you of where you grew up?" Whitney asks before she picks up a cherry tomato, drags it through the hummus, and pops it in her mouth.

Beckett's entire body goes rigid. There's no visible jolt or anything, but the tenseness of every muscle telegraphs his reaction to her words.

"You grew up near here?" I flinch as soon as the words are out because the look he shoots me is one so hostile you'd think we were opposing each other on a battle field. I wrack my brain for any memory of his file. I know the PI gave us an extensive one before we offered him a contract but I don't recall anything about him living in the US.

As far as I remember he's played his whole career for Canadian teams and never set foot across the border for anything other than to play.

He takes a moment to get himself a glass of water, pours myself and Whitney one too before he comes back and looks me right in the eye.

"I was born in Florida, but my mother moved us north, to Michigan, when I was two. So no. Baton Rouge doesn't remind me of home."

He doesn't say anything else and I don't either. The look in his eyes tells me the subject is closed and he won't answer any other question I might ask.

Once again I think he's hiding something.

I can't put my finger on it. Have no idea what it could be or why he feels the need to keep it to himself.

The doorbell interrupts the tension hanging in the air and I breathe a sigh of relief.

"That will be Cal." I go to move but Beckett stops me with a hand on my arm.

"I'll get it in case it's not. Stay here with Whit." His words aren't harsh but they're an order all the same.

I glance at Whitney who shrugs as she stuffs a handful of grapes into her mouth.

She's as clueless as I am and her lack of concern for the weirdness of the last few minutes has me trying to shake it off.

Except the more I think about it, the more I want to dive deeper into Beckett's past. And I can't decide if it's the reporter in me or the woman who's become a little too intrigued by this man and his daughter.

BECKETT

My eyes move over the crowd searching for the familiar curls of my daughter.

She spent about five minutes at my side before Oakley introduced her to Chase Hawkins' twin sisters. The twins go to Whit's school and the three of them instantly hit it off.

Within minutes Whit was begging to take off with them to check out all the carnival type stalls spread out over the practice rink.

I have no idea how much effort it took to cover the ice and put all this together but I have to admit it's been a fantastic night.

The fans have been nice, enthusiastic, but respectful. And not one of them called me out on hiding a daughter for seventeen years.

There are a couple of reporters and photographers, although I think the latter are with the team not the reporters. I've spoken to three so far, all of them sticking to my game and how I feel about living somewhere so hot when I spend my working hours on ice.

I had a good chuckle over that question because it honestly hasn't affected me. I'm sure when we're in the thick of summer, and Whit and I only caught the tail-end of it when we arrived in

Baton Rouge, I might have something to say but for now, it's work as usual.

I spot Ray Denim walking my way and wait for him to reach me. The head of security is in his forties and looks like a man you don't want to mess with. I heard he's an ex-SEAL who started his own security company and now works for the Rogues.

His hand is already out when he gets a couple of feet away and I stretch mine out to meet it.

"Hey."

"Mr. Higgison."

"Shit, none of that. It's Beckett or Bex."

"Okay, Beckett. Call me Ray." His eyes are on a constant sweep, scanning the area and coming back only to do it again and again. "I hear you need some security at your house. What did you have in mind?"

"Everything."

His gaze snaps back to me. "Any particular reason why?"

"I have a system but Cami pointed out the garage isn't connected to it and the door between it and my kitchen isn't either."

"Huh. Well, that's dumb. May as well leave the front door open."

"Yeah, anyway, there was a reporter on my doorstep earlier today that Cami didn't like and I'll be honest, the thought of my daughter being home alone now doesn't sit well. I want to know she's safe inside our house. Then there's the incident with her car."

"I heard about that. Oakley has me looking into some things with Amos on that."

"Oh?" This is news to me.

"He found something and wanted me to take a look."

"What? What did he find and why don't I know about it?"

"Calm down. If it was a threat you would know; it's not. But we think we've found the culprit in the tire incident. Amos is checking on one more thing, then he'll report to Oakley."

"Jesus." I scrub a hand down my face. "How soon can you get something set up at my house?"

"I can get it done tomorrow or the next day. I'll need to see what I'm working with then order the gear. I've probably got most of what you'll need but it'll have to come up from New Orleans."

"Okay. I can give you a key now. The code for the less than brilliant alarm currently fitted. You can go in whenever you have the time."

"All right. I'll grab one of my guys and head over there now." He looks at his watch. "This thing is supposed to go for another few hours. We should be finished before you get home and if I need any info, I'll call."

"You have my number?"

He gives me a look that says that was a stupid question. Then he grins and it transforms his face completely. He's no longer as intimidating. "I could probably get in without the key..."

Leaving the words hanging, he tips his chin and holds out his hand. Except with his words my brain has hit on a thought I can't move past.

"Do that. Get in without a key. Find all the places you can to get inside and then fix them so you can't."

"Is there something you're not telling us?"

"No. But my daughter is the most precious thing in my life and until now I haven't had to worry about her safety because she wasn't known as Beckett Higgison's daughter."

"Ah, I get it. No problem. I'll make a call, you'll get one after I do, from someone on the Baton Rogue PD. Don't want to have to call Oakley James to come bail me out for breaking and entering," he explains with a grin.

Laughing, I nod. "I'll be waiting. And I won't offer my address because..."

"Yeah, don't bother with that either." He offers his hand again. "I'll talk to you when I know what you're up for."

"Don't worry about cost. Whatever it is I'll cover it."

"Figured you would. Enjoy the rest of your night."

In seconds he's gone, disappearing into the crowd which is a feat because the guy has an inch or two on me and I'm six-three.

The crowd isn't large, but it's not small either. I'd say there are twenty people to each player and I'm not counting front office or arena staff. There's about seven hundred people by my estimation and with the way management has set everything up, we're not all crowded inside the boards of the practice rink.

Some of the players are holding court on the seats rising up on all sides of the ice. I'm sure others are out in the foyer where the food is set up. I spot Whit racing toward me and smile.

She's out of breath when she reaches me but the grin on her face tells me she's having a great time and I'm glad. I worried about moving her when she'd barely established connections with her schoolmates back in Toronto.

But my daughter had rolled her eyes and said there was no one she'd miss that much and if she did, they could always stay in contact by phone. I had no choice but to take her word for it and so far I haven't seen any negative changes in her the move may have caused.

"Dad!"

"Whit!" I mimic her tone with a grin.

"Can I go to Mr. Hawkins's place tonight?" Before I can protest it's a school night, she's steamrolling over me. "I know I've got school tomorrow but so do they and we can all go together. I can drive us. Actually, I said I'd pick them up for school and drop them off every day from now on. They *walk!*"

I can't help laughing at her distress over them walking to school. It's all I did as a kid. Even at five I was walking. On my own.

That thought brings up some memories I can do without thinking about so I look past her to see if I can see Chase. "Did Mr. Hawkins offer up a sleepover or have you kids decided on your own?"

"He did. He wants us to get to know each other better and he has to go home now because the baby needs to get to bed. Natalie is coming with us. She lives next door or something. Anyway, she said she'd run me by home so I can pick up my car then let me follow her to where they live even though I already know."

Her words are rushed and her volume rises with her level of excitement. "I'd rather you not drive the car yet."

"What? Why? The mechanic said it was fine."

"Yes, he did, but I'd like to run you to and from school until I have to leave town for the next away game."

"Daaaaad..."

"I know. But humor me. Please. Plus, the security people will be putting in a new alarm system tomorrow or the next day and I want to walk you through it the first few times you use it."

It's not necessary. She's smart enough to remember after being shown once but I can't seem to shake the niggle of fear in my chest.

I don't know if it's Cami's concern playing into my own or that Ray said they may have found the person responsible for letting the air out of Whit's tires.

She quietly stares at me as though she can change my mind and I have to smile. "Please, Whitbee."

"Fine. But can I go home with the twins?"

"Where's Mr. Hawkins? Let me have a quick word with him before I decide."

"He's out where the food is."

"Lead the way."

I follow Whit off the rink and up the stairs until we hit the corridor that winds around the edge of the building to the foyer. A few people stop me to talk, to ask for an autograph, but most let us pass with a smile or in the case of most of the men, a chin lift.

"Hey, Hawkeye. Whit tells me you've lost your mind and want to add another kid to your bunch for the night," I say when we're close enough I don't have to shout.

"Hey! Yeah, the twins are loving hanging out with her and as

I've dragged them away to this 'godforsaken hell' away from all their friends, I figure I should at least help them out when they find a new one."

"Godforsaken hell?" I ask with a grin.

"Cassidy's words. She's the one I'm having the most trouble with." He glances around to make sure his little sister isn't close. "If it wasn't for the fact I know this is the best thing for all of us, I'd pack up and go back to Minnesota."

"You know if you need help with anything you can call me. I might not have had three kids to deal with at your age but I had Whit so I might be able to offer some advice on things."

"Thanks. Gem's been a huge help. She's the reason I'm ducking out of here early. She knows the little one doesn't sleep at all if she's not in bed by nine."

"Need help getting everyone to the car?"

"Nah, we're good. Gem's on her way. She just needed to tell Oakley something." Chase looks at the twins talking excitedly with Whit. "You letting her come with us? I'll make sure she's up and ready for school."

"Yeah. But I'll swing by in the morning and pick them all up. I want to speak to the principal anyway."

"Oh? Whitney's not in trouble, is she? She seems level-headed to me."

"No. There was an incident with her car while we were away and he helped her. I just want to thank him in person."

"Ah, right. Okay, well, I'm good with that plan if you're cool with it."

"I am."

"Here's Gem now." He tips his chin to indicate someone behind me.

When I turn around, I'm shocked by who he's referring to. I thought Gem was a nanny or babysitter or something but it's Natalie Redding. GM of the Rogues...and the name clicks.

I have no idea when Chase started calling her that or if he does it all the time and I'm not sure I want to ask although my curiosity is definitely tripped.

"Beckett. Do I need keys or anything for Whitney to collect her car?"

"Ah, no, I'll come by Chase's in the morning and pick all the kids up for school."

"Are you sure? It's no trouble driving to your house then home," she assures me in her no-nonsense manner.

"I'm sure. I've got some business at the school in the morning and I'd rather let Ray and his man have the house to themselves right now to work out what I need to update the alarm system."

"Did Detective Clark call you yet?"

"No." As if her words conjures him, my phone rings with an unknown number. "This is probably him."

"Take it. We've got Whitney handled. If you come a little earlier in the morning, I'll have some breakfast for you and I'm sure she'll need clothes and her school bag."

"Shit. I didn't think of that."

She waves me away with a hand and says, "Answer that, bring her things tomorrow morning. I'm sure we can find something for her to wear tonight and that's all she needs."

"Are you sure?" I bounce my gaze between them as my phone continues to ring.

"Of course," Natalie says with a smile.

Chase gives me a chin lift before he heads over to his siblings and Whit.

"She'll be fine, and it'll be good for her to spend some time with some of her Rogues family." Natalie cocks her eyebrow in a way that says don't argue, you know I'm right.

Holding up a hand, I chuckle. "Okay, okay, I get it. We need to make the effort to build connections."

"You won't regret doing it. Now go call the detective back before he arrests my head of security."

"Shit. Sorry." I bobble my phone for a second before I pull up the recent calls and hit the last one that came in. Lifting a hand, I wave to Whit who's paying me no attention as I move toward a quiet corner to take this call.

"Mr. Higgison?"

"This is Beckett."

"I understand you have given permission for Ray Denim and his man to break into your house to test for weak spots in your security."

"Yes."

"All right then, now that you've confirmed that, I'll let you get on with your night. I know it's a big one for the Rogues."

"Okay, thanks."

He hangs up without a goodbye and when I turn to look for Whit to give her a kiss goodnight she's already gone. With a huff, I head back inside to do my duty as captain of the team. I want to check on some of the younger guys, make sure the attention isn't too overwhelming or they're not getting themselves into trouble.

I didn't notice any puck bunnies, but you can never tell who's on the lookout for a hook up.

Kallan is the first one I spot and the color of his face tells me the women surrounding him are either embarrassing him or he has no idea what they're saying.

Picking up my pace, I make a beeline straight for him. The relief in his eyes as I draw closer says I probably should have sought him out sooner.

"Hey, Kallan, ladies." I force a friendly smile when I'm not at all in my comfort zone in this type of situation. I'm even more uncomfortable when one of the women steps closer and puts her hand on my chest, purring my name as she looks up at me.

Shit. Looks like Kallan isn't the only one who needs rescuing from this.

And just as I think that, the woman who has proven to be on the spot for me and Whit walks up. Slipping her arm through mine, she leans her head on my biceps and looks at the group around us.

"Well, isn't this cozy? Are you all enjoying your night?"

She doesn't take them to task, just gives of subtle vibes and body language that has the women murmuring their answers before dispersing with words about needing food or the restroom.

I grin down at Cami. "You woman, are a life saver."

"You both looked like deer caught in headlights. How are you doing, Kallan? Do you need a break from all this?"

His nod is enough to get her moving away from me and to him. Hooking her arm in his the same as she did me, she motions me to follow as she soothes him with words too quiet for me to hear.

And like some kind of sap, I trail behind her.

CAMI

Rescuing Beckett and Kallan from the clutches of the lust-dazed women is easy. And once I have them surrounded by a group of elderly men who've been hockey fans all their lives, I look for Oakley.

I spot her across the other side of the rink with Walker and Mikey. Mikey is in Walker's arms, his head resting on his uncle's shoulder and even from here, I can see he's almost asleep.

"Hey."

I turn to face Beckett. "What's up?"

"Nothing. Just wanted to say thanks for back there. Kallan was out of his depth, and honestly, so was I."

"You'd have been fine." And he would have. My need to interrupt their conversation had nothing to do with either man being out of their depth and everything to do with the emotion that rose up in me when I saw that woman put her hand on Beckett. "Kallan's young though, he'd have needed a life preserver."

I try to make light of it because I'm still struggling with what I did. I'd marched over there and basically plastered myself to Beckett's side before my brain had registered what I was doing.

"Either way, thanks."

"Where's Whitney?"

"She went home with Chase Hawkins. Her and the twins hit it off."

"They left already?" I thought Natalie gave everyone strict instructions to stay until the last fan was ushered out the door.

"Yes. Natalie went with them."

"Natalie went with them?" My jaw is slack. Nat has never snuck out of a business event. And to go home with Chase Hawkins...

"Whit said she lives next door to them. She offered to feed me breakfast in the morning." Beckett grins at me like he knows that little nugget of info just blew my mind.

"Natalie Redding, GM of the Rogues, has gone home with a guy, his three young siblings, your teenage daughter in tow, *and* offered to prepare breakfast for you in the morning?"

"That's what I said." His grin widens. "You seem shocked by that."

"Shocked? I'm not shocked. I'm flabbergasted!" What the hell have I missed? Yanking my phone from my pocket I shoot a text to our group chat.

WTF Nat!

Oakley: What? What's Nat done?"

Blake: She went home.

Blake waits a beat before sending a second text.

Blake: With Chase Hawkins.

Oakley: Oh, is something wrong with one of the kids?

Oakley's concern may account for Nat's uncharacteristic behavior but I'm not buying it.

Not that I'm aware. And get this, Whitney
went with them and Nat offered to make
Beckett breakfast tomorrow!

There's silence for a good two minutes before Nat replies.

Nat: The baby is teething. I've been helping
Chase with the older two because she's rarely
let him put her down since she woke with a
fever this morning when he got back from the
game.

I have no idea what to say.

Natalie, the woman who has spent as long as I've known her telling us she doesn't want kids is now playing mother to a pair of teenagers?

Oakley: Let me know if you need anything. We
never went through it with Mikey but I know it
can be brutal for some kids.

Blake: Oh god. Those days suck. Thankfully
Bran doesn't mind walking the floor with
Drew. Also, get him to try a washcloth out of
the freezer. Wet it and stick it in for a few
minutes. Does wonders to soothe their little
gums.

I stare at my phone and try to work out what happened to my three best friends. The women who insisted on talking shop with me even when I didn't want to know what was going on because it wasn't my job to know, are now chatting about teething babies.

"Oh man, I never would have let Whit go home with them if I'd known the baby was teething. Whit was a nightmare with her one- and two-year-old molars. Candace is one, right?"

I shake my head. "I have no idea."

"I think he said she just turned one before they moved."

Oakley: Anything we need to be aware of in
your absence, Nat?

Nat: No. Trevor has things handled and what
he doesn't he's got a minion for.

I laugh. Nat isn't wrong. Oakley's assistant turned Rogues'
assistant has multiple minions scurrying around every day. If Nat
left him in charge of the rest of the night, you can bet things will
go off without a hitch.

"Who's Trevor?'

"You haven't met Trevor?" I glance up at Beckett. "He's the
Rogues' assistant. Used to be Oakley's but since we signed the
contract for the franchise, he's shifted his focus and now runs a
team of assistants who see to everyone's needs."

"I've probably met him." He shrugs. "I've met so many new
people, it's hard to keep them all straight."

"I understand that completely."

"You should get to know more of them now, with the interviews you're doing."

I smile. "It's probably the best way to get to know everyone
because I can use something they tell me to remember them by.
It'll help me keep track of who's who and what they do."

"Who's who and what they do?" He laughs. "Sounding a
little sing-songy there."

I arch an eyebrow. "What the hell kind of word is sing-
songy?"

"Something Whit used to say when she was little."

"Oh?"

"Yeah, she'd ask me to sing nursery rhymes with her but she'd
ask for a sing-songy instead of a nursery rhyme."

I can't decide whether to laugh my ass off or swoon in a
poodle of goo at how sweet this man is. It's one more reminder of
how much he loves his daughter. How much he'd do for her. He

doesn't care that saying a word like that makes him sound silly or could be embarrassing.

Hell, I bet he sang those sing-songies with her whenever she asked no matter where they were.

"That's the sweetest thing I've ever heard."

He eyes me skeptically. "Don't lie on my account. You won't be the first person to laugh at me over it."

"I thought about laughing. But then I thought about how much you must love your daughter to still use the word she made up as a child."

"Don't be fooled. She's still a child and when she's sick, the first thing she asks for is a sing-songy."

"Oh God. Stop." I put a hand on my belly and press against the swirling going on around my ovaries. I've never had a man affect me the way Beckett does. Then again, I've never met a man like Beckett.

His devotion to his daughter, his dedication to seeing her safe and cared for when he was no more than a child when he had her isn't just admirable. It's inspirational. Every father should take notes from this man.

"You're a great father, Beckett."

"Huh?"

"The way you've raised Whitney. It's an inspiration and she's lucky to have you."

"No. I'm lucky to have her and I thank the stars every day that Mama Dot was able to make it happen."

"Mama Dot?"

"My foster mother. Without her I never would have been able to keep Whit's mother from aborting her. Never gotten to take custody of my daughter at the age of sixteen. Never made it through the early years when our whole lives were uprooted. Never—" He stops abruptly, his eyes wide, and I can only imagine he never intended to say all that.

"Don't discount your own input."

He shakes his head, whether in denial or an attempt to clear his mind, I don't know. But I see the second he decides he needs to retreat. I don't need his next words to know this conversation is over.

"I should go check on some of the other guys. Coach wants me to help them navigate being in the NHL."

He doesn't elaborate further, and I don't really need him to. I understand what Walker is expecting him to do as captain of the team. He's the perfect man for the role. His parenting of Whitney gives him an advantage with the younger ones. They're not much older than her and he can draw on his interactions with Whitney to deal with the players.

There's no goodbye. No chin lift. He just spins on his heel and heads away as though his ass is on fire.

I want to go after him. Ask him the million and one questions now filling my head, but I know if I do he'll shut down and I won't get any answers. If I wait, keep doing what I'm doing, he may reveal more about himself, about what he went through raising Whitney.

One thing is for sure. He's hiding something about how he came to be a teenage parent. I'm not sure if I want to know or not. Or if I deserve to know.

Whitney hasn't dropped any hints about their early life. The only thing she's mentioned is that Beckett was born in the US. And the small amount of elaborating he did on that subject isn't enough to curb my curiosity.

I want to know everything there is to know about Beckett Higgison.

I want to blame my reporter instinct.

I want to say it's nothing more than me intrigued by the dynamic between him and Whitney.

Except I'm not a liar. Especially with myself.

I want to know everything there is to know about Beckett Higgison because I can't not know. The more time I spend with him, talk to him, the more I want to do both.

It's like a snowball rolling down a hill. My desire to know him grows with each new piece of information. The longer I spend in his company the more I want to be there.

And that's not including my interest in Whitney.

She's such a remarkable young woman. And when you look at her life, the father who raised her, she's more extraordinary.

They both are.

And I'm not going to lie to myself anymore.

I want to know both of them, but Beckett, he stirs up feelings I haven't felt in a long long time, if ever.

It's like a smoldering fire beneath my skin, in my bones. Glowing and warming from the inside out. A slow burn that if I'm not careful could spark and catch, turning into a wildfire engulfing everything in its way.

I don't want any of us to get hurt in whatever this thing is bubbling through me. I know there's a healthy dose of attraction. I'm not blind or delusional—Beckett is gorgeous, and how some woman hasn't snapped him up and put a ring on it is anyone's guess.

Although, watching him with Whitney, knowing what I know about them, I can see he's kept himself and her secluded in their own little bubble.

A bubble that burst the other week when Whitney posted that picture.

A picture that since she took her account off private has been reposted hundreds of times. Most of the reposts have been good, encouraging. Only a handful have questioned how Beckett Higgison has a seventeen-year-old daughter and where he's been hiding her.

Fortunately there hasn't been too much speculation on why he kept her out of the public eye. I haven't said anything to anyone except Dad, but I've set up some alerts. Any time either Beckett or Whitney is mentioned I know about it. Check it out and make sure it's nothing to worry about.

Dad's also keeping his ear to the ground. Neither of us wants this to turn into the scandal that was my childhood. We're too familiar with how things can go from inquisitive to dangerous in the blink of an eye.

I don't want that for either of them. So I'll keep doing what I'm doing until I don't have to anymore.

When that will be, I'm not sure.

All I know is right now I want to protect them both from anything that could hurt them.

Beckett

Clicking my fob as I walk toward my truck, I wave at a few of the guys left lingering in the players' carpark. Training went well today, like it has most days since we took to the ice together.

We're playing as though we've played together for years and it's lifting our spirits as much as the fact we've remained undefeated through our pre-season games. The day after tomorrow we play our first away game in a week.

The season opener against the Miami Steam.

Everyone will be there. The Rogues org has arranged for any family member or Rogues employee to travel to Miami for our first regular season game in the league.

It's a big day.

For us and the league.

And we're ready.

Excitement, determination, and confidence pump through all of us, and I know being away from home won't change the way we play.

Because we aren't about home turf. Our home turf is the team, the guys, the coaches, the equipment staff, the trainers. As long as we're together, we're home.

Tossing my bag in the back, I hop up into the driver's seat and crank the engine. Hot air blasts through the vents and I quickly hit the buttons for all the windows hoping to rid the interior of the suffocating heat faster.

A glance at the clock has me swearing under my breath. I was supposed to pick up Whit five minutes ago.

Since the incident with her tires and finding out the culprit was none other than Kenneth Dupre, the reporter who knocked on my door the day after, I've been taking her to and from school when I can and someone from the Rogues does it when I can't.

Usually Cami does it. But Chase has done it a few times when he's picked up his sisters, even the Rogues GM picked up Whit and the twins one day and brought them to the practice rink when a video viewing session ran long.

They told me to embrace the Rogues family, and I have, but it's more the other way around. The other players' partners have helped out. Front office staff, even the arena staff have pitched in. And it's not just me they're helping. I saw a cleaning staff member walking Chase's baby sister up and down the corridor the other day. Everyone pulls together when someone needs a hand.

It's the most amazing thing I've ever been part of and I'm happier than I ever remember being.

And Whit is blossoming.

Watching her grow is one of my greatest joys and she's doing it in leaps and bounds here.

Maybe it's her age, but I think a lot of it is the people we're surrounded by. They're the family I could never give her on my own.

A family of cousins, aunts, and uncles. Hell, even Pa, Oakley's grandfather, has taken on the role of grandfather to all. Child or adult, it doesn't matter, and he's in his element doing it.

It's bittersweet.

On one hand I'm thrilled Whit has this now. On the other I'm sad I hadn't found this for her before.

The Bluetooth in my car sparks to life scaring the shit out of me. A look at the screen has my heart lurching into my throat.

Hitting the button on the steering wheel to connect the call, I demand, "What's wrong? What happened?"

"Whitney is fine. Cami Nelson is here with her."

"Why is Cami there?"

"Ms. Nelson was talking to the tenth graders about journalism. We're having a few people from various occupations coming in throughout the year talking to the sophomores in preparation for choosing subjects for future careers," Mr. Dalton explains.

"That doesn't explain your call."

A sigh fills the space around me. "When Ms. Nelson left this afternoon, Whitney was with her, thankfully, because a reporter was waiting outside and tried to speak to your daughter. Unfortunately, he was a little aggressive and when Whitney stepped back, she bumped into Ms. Nelson, who was moving to intervene, causing her to miss the top step and tumble down them."

"Fuck! I'm on my way." Shoving the truck in reverse, I squeal out of my spot then slam the gear stick into drive while pressing down on the accelerator. Screeching tires and a revving engine accompanying me out of the parking lot. "Is Cami okay?"

"Yes. The EMTs are looking her over now but I believe she's come away with only a few bruises."

"And the reporter?"

"Ah, well, he didn't stick around after Ms. Nelson fell."

"Did you call the police?"

"Of course. They're here now. Talking to witnesses."

"I'm ten minutes away but I'd like to talk to the police when I get there—can you make sure they don't leave before I arrive, please?" How I remember that small piece of my manners when my heart is racing faster than my car I haven't a clue.

"Certainly. And I've called the investigator who looked into the incident with your daughter's car. He's on his way too."

"Thanks. I'll be there soon." Disconnecting the call I debate calling Natalie Redding. But then I think about the PI and figure he'll have done that; if not I can do it after I check that Cami is okay. Check on Whit.

It takes a lifetime to get to Whit's school. In reality it's less than the fifteen minutes it usually takes to get from the practice rink to Hannon Grove. I have to remind myself I'm entering a school and slow down even though every instinct I have is screaming for me to go faster.

Pulling up in front of the admin building I barely get the truck in park and the brake set before I'm bounding out the door.

Cami is sitting on the steps, her butt on the third from bottom, feet on the ground and the look she's shooting the EMT would have a lesser person backing away. When I get closer, I can't stop the slight curl of my lips.

"I told you I'm fine. I did not hit my head and the only things bruised are my butt and my pride." Cami sees me coming and her eyes immediately dart to the right.

Following her gaze, I see Whit talking to a couple of men in plain clothes. It doesn't take a uniform to tell me they're the police. Stopping next to Cami, I lower myself to a crouch.

"Hey."

"Hi." The smile she gives me is strained.

"You sure you're okay?" My level of concern for this woman is something I've only ever felt for three people. The first betrayed me in the worst way, the second proved my trust was well placed, and the third is the light of my life.

"Honestly, I'm fine. But I broke my heel. And I think my laptop is toast."

"Your laptop?" I look around and see the computer on the ground about ten feet away. "What happened to your laptop?"

"She had it in her hand when we came outside. Part of the reason she fell all the way down the stairs was because she tried to throw it at the guy who grabbed my arm."

I look up to see Whit standing beside me, a frown on her face. Glancing back at Cami I say, "You threw your computer at him?"

"Well, I didn't have a baseball bat handy, so yes, I threw it at his head." She grins, the curve of her lips somehow wicked and

I'm reminded again how much she's done to protect my daughter.

"I'll buy you a new one."

"Don't bother, I've got a couple and thankfully that's the oldest of my collection. Besides, I'd gladly sacrifice a laptop to protect Whitney." Turning her gaze from me to my daughter she says in a tone meant to convey Whit better not argue, "Sit down and let them check your arm and chin."

"I'm okay. You barely bumped me with your elbow on the way past and his grip didn't really clamp down before I pulled away."

I'm on my feet, finger pointing at the stairs. "Sit. Let them check you out. Now."

Whit rolls her eyes but does as I say.

"I'll be back in a sec. I want to have a word with the police and the principal." Who all happen to be talking over where Whit had been when I first noticed her.

Marching over, adrenaline still pumping through my veins despite seeing Cami and Whit are okay, I'm sure I look like a tiger hunting its prey.

Except these men shouldn't be my target and with great effort I use the skills from years of taking the ice where tempers can flare at the drop of a glove, and tone down the anger vibrating through every cell.

"Gentlemen." I hold out a hand. "Beckett Higgison. Whit's father, Cami's...friend." I stumble over the last because it suddenly occurs to me I don't know what Cami and I are. Technically she's my boss but she doesn't have anything to do with my job and—

"Higgison, we spoke the other night. Detective Clark. And this is my partner, Detective Anders." The tall blond shakes my hand, his grip firm.

Shaking the dark-haired Anders' hand, I say, "I'd say it's a pleasure to meet you both but as you can imagine..."

"Yes. I would much have preferred attending last week's fan event over this."

Not wanting to get sidetracked, I ask about the reason they're here. "So what do you know? Have you found the man who grabbed Whit?"

"No. He's still out there but we know who we're looking for."

"You do?"

"Yes. Ms. Nelson identified the man as Kenneth Dupre."

"Shit." My gaze darts back to the girls. "She's sure?"

"Yes. Is there something we need to know about him?"

I return my gaze to Detective Clark. "He came to my house the other week. Cami arrived not long after. There was a little hostility between them when she asked him what he was doing at my place. He said something about wanting an interview and she reminded him that he needed to go through official channels for that."

"And that's it? He just left?" Detective Anders asks.

"Well, no, it took some convincing, a reminder that he was on private property and if he didn't leave we could call the police because he was trespassing."

"Would you say he felt threatened by that?"

I look Anders right in the eye. "Yes. Because it was a threat."

"Would that explain today's incident?" Clark asks.

"No. Because from what Mr. Dalton told me, he went after Whit, not Cami."

"True. True." Clark rubs his chin, his gaze over my shoulder where I know he can see Whit and Cami. His eyes widen, and he says, "Is that Chase Hawkins running this way?"

I'm already turned around by the time he finishes speaking because his wide-eyed look had fear ricocheting through my chest. With a sigh of relief, I say, "Yeah, that's Chase. His twin sisters go to school here too."

We stand, quietly watching, as Chase races up to Cami and Whit, says a few words, then heads in our direction.

"Hey. When the twins got home, they said something

happened to Whit. Then Gem called and asked me to come over here because she's across town."

I know who he's talking about but I'm sure the detectives are clueless so I explain. "Gem as in GM. Of the Rogues org."

"Ah, right." Detective Clark holds out a hand to Chase. "Detectives Clark and Anders. Nice to meet you. Or it would be if..."

"Yeah, they're both okay, though, right?" Chase glances back at where Cami and Whit sit, heads huddled together.

"They're okay."

"Can I take them, then?" His gaze returns to us. "I can drive Cami's car to my house, take Whitney, if you're all finished with them," he directs at the detectives.

"Whitney has given her statement but we still need to speak to Ms. Nelson."

"Take Whit. Get Cami's keys off her and take her car. I'll wait with her and follow after she's done."

I don't miss the speculative glances the detectives give me but I ignore them. I don't care what they think. I'm not leaving Cami here to deal with this alone, especially when she was hurt protecting my daughter.

"Okay. I'll see you at my place when you're done. And don't worry about dinner, we'll organize something for all of us. Plus I wouldn't be surprised if Blake and Oakley turn up at some point."

"Shit." I look at Cami. "Should I call them?"

"I think Gem's on that."

"What about her parents?"

"Don't know about that but let her do it after she's finished giving her statement."

"Good idea." I put a hand on Chase's shoulder, give it a squeeze. "Thanks for coming. And for taking Whit."

"No problem. Got a cardio workout in." He grins at me and I find myself smiling back.

"You sprint all the way?"

"Of course!"

I laugh. The tension inside me easing with every second.

"I'll leave you to it." He tips his head at the detectives before heading back to the girls.

"You've got a good friend there," Anders says.

"He's more than a friend." I watch as Cami hands over her keys, pauses then hands her bag to Whit. "He's a brother."

It isn't until I hear those words out loud that I realize Whit isn't the only one getting something from our move to Baton Rouge. We're both surrounded by the Rogues family.

Chase dropped everything to run here—*run!*—to support me and Whit in any way he could. He didn't have a clue what he was running in to. Didn't have to come at all. We've formed a bond on the ice, yes, but this...

This is something Whit and I have never had.

A family who supports us unconditionally.

The emotion that sweeps through me is overwhelming, clogs my throat, and makes my knees wobble, and it doesn't matter how isolated I've kept myself and Whit over the years, how safe that made me feel, I'll never go back to that.

Even with this reporter causing trouble.

I'll gladly take him on because I've got a family who'll stand at my side when I do.

CAMI

My hip aches. I can't find any position that doesn't send pain shooting down my leg or up my spine. Shifting, I try to ease the discomfort. Except nothing I do does.

When I get my hands on Kenneth, I'm going to knock his fucking teeth out.

"Hey. You okay?"

I glance up at Beckett. "Yes." The word sounds like it's been ground into dust.

"Sounds like it," he says with a smirk. "Can I get you another drink?"

"No. You can get me out of here."

His eyebrows shoot up, his eyes wide and shocked for a moment before concern floods them. "How much pain are you in? Should I take you to the hospital?"

"No. I don't need a hospital. I need a hot bath and for all these people to take their concern somewhere else."

"Cami." His says my name with so much feeling that my eyes water.

Dammit.

"They're worried about you."

"I get that. I do. But it's..." I try to think of a word that won't make me seem ungrateful but can't. "Suffocating."

"No one's hovering." Beckett looks around and I follow his gaze.

He's right. No one has hovered. They send me smiles or cocked eyebrows on occasion and I smile to let them know I'm fine. Except I've been doing it for two hours.

I'm tired.

Sore.

Cranky.

And angry.

So fucking angry.

It's my own fault I'm siting here on a bruised butt. I should have known Kenneth was up to no good when I first spotted him. Instead, I let Whit lead the way outside and when he grabbed her arm...

Fury rose up so hard and fast I choked on it.

Her gasp of shock, the way she wrenched herself away had me acting before thinking. If I'd just taken a second to ground my feet instead of...

No. There had been no time to waste, at least that's what my instincts told me so I'd shouldered her behind me as she stepped back and put my hand out to shove Kenneth away.

Except I missed the step and my feet got tangled and when my hand landed on Kenneth's chest, he lost his footing too. Only he grabbed me for stability and because he was a few steps below, gravity took over and I was falling forward with nothing to break my fall.

Especially when that chicken-shit managed to keep upright and took off.

"Hey." Beckett's hand cradles my jaw and lifts my face until our eyes connect. "You can't hunt him down and kill him."

"Why not?" It doesn't even enter my head that he's able to read me. Hell, my murderous thoughts are probably written all over my face.

Beckett chuckles. "Well, for a start, there are at least six people in here, no, make that nine, who want to get in line before you."

I mentally count heads and realize he's counted every adult here. The fact he thinks Walker, Bran, Chase, and himself can be included alongside Mom and Dad, and my three best friends brings tears to my eyes. "Oh."

"So, how about I do as you asked?"

"Huh?" I sniff back the threatening tears.

"I'll get you out of here to somewhere you can have that hot bath in peace."

I look over at Mom and Dad. The first thing they said when they got here was they'd take me home with them after dinner. As much as their house has always been home, I don't want to go there.

I don't want to go to my apartment either.

"Where are you going to find that bath?" I ask quietly while my eyes remain on my parents.

"My house. Whit is staying here overnight. Chase and Natalie want to give her a distraction from what happened and promise to call if she wakes with a nightmare or can't sleep or whatever. My house will be empty." His gaze bores into mine. "Well, except for me."

An image of his newly fitted whirlpool tub pops into my head. "The tub in your bathroom?"

"Yes. It's perfect for sore muscles and bruises."

I see uncertainty, concern, a touch of anger, in his eyes and I know the later isn't directed at me but *for* me. The other two, well, he's obviously worried about me. Everyone is. The uncertainty is either about what my answer will be or having me alone in his house.

There's a small niggle of worry about being alone with him in my chest. The more I'm around Beckett, the more I like him, and if I let him care for me tonight, if I let him make sure I've got what I need, what I want, that like is going to slide deeper.

I don't know if I want that. I don't need the complication to our relationship if like tips over into more.

The physical attraction I feel for Beckett has been the abstract kind. He's hot, I'm not blind, except I think I've been in denial because the other men here, including Dad, are attractive and I readily admit that.

But those men don't have my nerves buzzing. Don't have my stomach swooping. And they certainly don't have my ovaries clenching when I see them with their kids or someone else's.

No. Beckett Higgison is the inspiration of those sensations.

"O-okay." I lick my lips. Swallow the lump in my throat. "Get me out of here."

He studies me for a moment, looking for what, I don't know, but eventually, he says, "Done," as he stands up straight.

I'm not sure what's more shocking. The speed in which we're in Beckett's car heading to his house or that no one—not even my parents—protested us leaving.

I saw Beckett have words with Dad and I know it was tense but they shook hands at the end and Dad gave me a light hug before ushering me into the front seat of Beckett's SUV.

Everyone had concerned looks on their faces and I understand why but I could do without the reminder of what happened this afternoon.

Beckett hit the button for the seat warmer when he started the car and the radiating heat helps soothe my hip a little. "Thank you."

"You're welcome." He takes his eyes off the road for a moment to shoot me a quick smile. "And thank you. For being there for Whit."

I scoff. "She didn't need me. I'm sure she would have gotten away and run back into the building."

"Yes. No doubt. I've taught her how to take care of herself. And I'm not thanking you for saving her. I'm thanking you for being there for her."

It takes me a moment to understand what he means. My

brain is a little fuzzy due to the pain I can't seem to get in front of with over the counter meds. His next words help.

"She's only had me to stand up for her since Mama Dot died."

I turn my head where it rests on the back of my seat. "She has all of us now."

"I know." The side of his mouth I can see curls up. "She's catching on to that quicker than I am."

"Kids adapt faster than adults."

"They do. And Whit is quicker than most kids her age."

"I've said it before but it bears repeating. She's a remarkable young woman. You should be proud of her and you."

"I am. Myself more so recently."

The hum that vibrates my throat could be agreement or censure. I've gotten to know the Higgisons over the last few weeks and what I've seen leads me to believe Beckett has a high standard of what he should be, as a hockey player, as a man, as Whitney's father, and he's always seen himself fall short in the latter.

Why he could think that is beyond me. She's a polite, bright, caring girl, and also brave. The way she stood up and admitted her mistake—or what she saw as one because of the fallout from it— shows she's not afraid of the hard stuff or owning up to being wrong.

"I think you're both remarkable."

The chuckle that rumbles through Beckett's chest and fills the cab is laced with disbelief.

"I do. You're one of the top players in the NHL and while getting to the top of that tier of athletes you raised a daughter basically on your own. That's remarkable, Beckett."

He shrugs. "If you say so."

"I do. And others would agree. Why don't you see yourself that way?"

It takes him a few minutes to answer and when he pulls into the garage at his house, I think he isn't going to. Except when he switches off the engine and waits for the roller door to close, he grips the wheel with white knuckles and stares straight ahead, the line of his jaw tense.

"I've made mistakes. Big ones. But the results of those is Whit, and she's never been, could never be, a mistake."

He pops his door as he unbuckles his belt and is out of the truck, striding around the front of it while I sit there and stare.

He's just given me another small glimpse into his life. A normal person might brush aside his words, think they're about becoming a teenage parent, but I'm not the average person.

I make my living reading between the lines. Ferreting out the finer details that make the articles I write more in-depth, more three dimensional.

I've been intrigued by Beckett and Whitney from the beginning, from the second Draper yelled his question about Beckett having a seventeen-year-old daughter I've been consciously and subconsciously rolling their story around my head.

I want to know everything.

And not for an article.

I want to know everything about Beckett because that like I've been acknowledging is definitely moving along into the more column.

I sit there so long, my mind spinning with the possibilities of the mistakes he referred to, that he comes back and pulls open my door.

"Need help getting out?" he asks with a frown.

"No. I've got it." To show him I have, I unhook my belt and twist to the side. It takes him a moment to step back and give me room to get out.

Once I've got my feet on the floor, he tips his head toward the door leading to the kitchen. "I'll go up and get the bath ready."

"Okay."

"Take your time. I'll find something of Whit's you can sleep in too." He turns to go before snapping back again to add, "And you can sleep in my bed."

The images his words conjure have me stiffening, from shock or arousal—a little of both. "I—"

"No, not with me! Shit!" He scrubs a hand over his face. "That's not what I meant."

Laughter bubbles up and I put a hand over my mouth to stop it. I don't know why I think this conversation is funny. But I'm tired, in pain, and honestly struggling to understand the emotions I feel around this man.

"Yeah, okay, laugh at me putting my foot in my mouth." He smiles at me. "Take your time coming upstairs and if the steps prove too difficult, give me a shout. Okay?"

He dips down so our eyes are level, his gaze locked on mine when I answer. "Yeah. Okay."

"I mean it, Cami, if you need help getting up the stairs, call out."

"I will. Promise." I don't want to but I'm not stupid and if it hurts too much to climb to the first floor I will let him help me. The last thing I need is to topple down another flight of stairs.

"All right then. See you upstairs." He leaves me without looking back until he opens the door to the house when he glances over his shoulder to say, "Don't worry about setting the alarm. I'll come back down and do that."

When he's out of sight, a rush of air deflates my lungs and drops my shoulders. The motion brings a small whimper with it. I hope the hot bath Beckett is providing gives me some relief because if it doesn't, I'm going to have to give in and head to the hospital or an all-night clinic to get something stronger than the over the counter meds I've been taking.

With slow, measured steps, I make my way inside. The single step up into the house pulls muscles and skin bruised from my fight with the concrete steps. The slipper-socks Natalie gave me help me shuffle my way to the staircase.

But when I look up, the steps appear to go on forever, and the thought of climbing them, of lifting my legs has me whimpering. Loudly.

Beckett appears at the top of the stairs, the frown on his face aimed my way. "You okay? What happened?"

He heads down, taking the steps two at a time, until he's right beside me.

"Cami?"

"It hurts." I can't keep the tears out of my voice. Or off my face.

And when Beckett scoops me up in his arms and cradles me against his chest, I can't hold back the sobs.

BECKETT

One thing I've learned about Cami Nelson is she isn't weak.

She's independent and capable and having her in my arms in the middle of a complete breakdown makes me want to find Kenneth Dupre and rip his fucking head off.

"Shh…" Lowering to the edge of my bed, I wiggle around with Cami in my lap and lean my back against the headboard. "It's okay. You're safe."

I murmur words I think will make her feel better except I know nothing I can say right now will do much good. All I can do is hold her until the worst of her tears pass.

The water still runs in the bathroom and luckily it takes a while for the tub to fill. Not to mention the special drain I had installed along with the tub in case of overflow.

"I'm sorry." The words are hiccuped into my chest where her face is pressed and the warmth of her breath sends a skitter of goosebumps over my skin.

"Nothing to be sorry about, Cam." I smooth a hand up and down her spine. "You're allowed the release. I can imagine the cocktail of emotions you went through and the adrenaline spike from something like that would knock the biggest guy on his ass."

"I want to knock Kenneth on his ass."

I chuckle. "You and me both. Plus everyone we left at Chase's house."

"Nat's."

"What?"

"It's Nat's house. I didn't even realize she'd moved Chase and his siblings in."

"Yeah, that's an interesting situation."

"Hmm..." Her face rubs against my shirt and I'm sure she sucks in a deep breath. "Do I hear water?"

"Yes. If you're ready for that hot bath, the tub should be full enough now."

"You left the water running?"

Her head tips back and the sight of her with mascara smudged under her eyes—trailing down her cheeks—spikes my anger at Kenneth once more.

"C'mon, let's get you in the bath and see if you can soak some of the day away."

"I'll settle for easing the pain in my hip."

"Your hip?" I ask as I move us off the bed.

"Yeah."

"I thought you landed on your butt." Which had me concerned about her spine but if she came down on her hip, she could have done damage to the joint, her pelvis, hell, she could have broken it.

"I think it was my hip and butt. Both hurt, but the hip is worse."

"Can I take a look? I've got some cream you can put on it if it's bruised. Once you're out of the bath."

"Thanks. If you've got some pain meds I can take before bed, that would be great too."

"I do."

I can tell how much pain she's in by the fact she doesn't protest me carrying her into the bathroom. When I lower her to her feet, she doesn't hide the pain she's in like she did earlier and I want to wrap my hands around that fucking reporter's neck.

Reining in my anger, I focus on what Cami needs. "Do you need help getting in?"

I have no idea how I'm going to see Cami naked and not react. She'll be the first naked woman I've seen up close in eighteen years.

Hell, who am I kidding. It'll be the first time I've ever seen a naked woman in the flesh. The secrecy of my relationship with Whit's mother meant rushed sex in places we could be discovered so the complete removal of clothes never happened.

I shouldn't be thinking about Cami in a sexual way, not when she's hurt and trusting me to take care of her, but I can't help the arousal I feel around her. Up 'til now I've ignored it, denied it. Even when I tried to dislike her, I couldn't hide from it.

I'd stuck my head in the sand with Whit's mother and look where that got me. I can't blame that debacle on Catrina in spite of how old I was, how old she was, I own up to my involvement. Plus the biggest mistake of my life gave me my greatest gift.

"Beckett?"

Pulled from my thoughts I meet Cami's gaze. "Sorry. Do you need help?"

"I think so. I don't think I can lift my leg high enough to get in the tub."

"Okay..." How can we do this without me putting my hands all over her? "Tell me what you need."

"Can you hold me still, take some of my weight off my left leg while I get my shirt off?"

"I can." Moving around behind her, I span her waist with my hands and lift. "That good?"

"Yes. Thanks."

"No problem."

We're quiet while she unbuttons her blouse and lets it fall from her shoulders. I don't know whether to help her out of it now or stay where I am. This isn't like the times I've had to care for Whit. Just last winter she had the flu so bad I had to help her shower after—

That's it!

"Cami, if you leave your underwear on I can stay here and make sure you're okay."

"Huh?"

"In the bath, I can help you get in the bath, take a look at your hip to see how bad the bruising is."

"Oh, okay, yeah." Her shoulders slump. "And maybe make sure I don't fall asleep once I get in there."

I feel better with a plan. I can concentrate on that and nothing else. "Can you undo your pants and push them down?"

"Yes."

"Get them down as far as you can and then I'll lift you up so you can try kicking them off with your good leg."

Before she starts on her pants, she pulls her arms from her shirt and drops it to the floor. There's bruising on her left side above her pants. It's almost to my hand and it takes everything I have to remain still and not swear at how much there is.

But when she undoes her pants and pushes them past her hips, there's no stopping the curses.

"Fucking hell I'm going to kill that motherfucker."

My words make Cami jolt and cry out when she puts her left leg down. If it wasn't for my strength she'd be on the floor.

"Shit! Sorry. I didn't mean to scare you."

"It's okay, I think I zoned out a little."

"Probably from the pain." I try to keep my grip gentle but the twitch in my fingers tells me I'm borderline in control. "Cam."

"Yeah."

"I think you should go to the hospital and get your hip x-rayed."

"It's not that bad. Bruising always makes things look worse than they are. It's not broken."

"Your bones might not be, but I'm worried about the muscles and ligaments around the joint."

"Honestly, Beckett, I bruise easily and I know I came down hard on my hip then my butt bounced on a few of the steps on the way to the bottom."

I swallow over the emotion clogging my throat. I want to avenge her and take care of her. It's hard to reconcile this woman I barely know pulls the same depth of care and protection from me that Whit does.

"I can't get them off."

Her words are laced with tears and I'm reminded I need to keep my head in the game. The most important thing right now is getting Cami in the tub to soothe some of her pain. And I need to get the cream the trainers make sure we have a supply of from my hockey bag.

"Let me see if I can do it with my foot. Okay, if I step on them then lift you up?"

"Don't worry about ruining them. Just get them off."

I do as asked and in less than a minute I've got a semi-naked Cami over the tub edge. "I'll lower you slowly, let me know if the water's too hot."

The more I look at her bruises the more I wish I could go back in time and not be late today. If only I'd been there when she and Whit came out of the school.

Hell, if I'd been there, I would have seen that motherfucker and made him leave before they ever laid eyes on him.

"It's okay."

Her words bring me out of my head. Again. And as she sinks deeper, bends her knees with a groan to go down on her butt, I shake my head to clear the thoughts of murder floating in and out.

When she's waist deep, my hands and forearms under the water I ask, "You okay for me to let go?" I'm still holding some of her weight and I'm worried putting pressure on her hip, the back left flank of her butt and thigh, will cause her more pain.

"Yes," she says as she leans to the right, her legs floating slightly in the water in front of her. "I'm going to try lying all the way down. The tub is big enough."

"It is." I loosen my grip and slide my hands up her side, watching carefully in case she slips under. She's almost on her back when I straighten. "If you're all right on your own, I'll grab the cream I mentioned and pain meds."

"I'm okay." She tips her head back and looks up at me. "Thank you. You don't have to do this. I know I put you on the spot when I asked you to get me out of there."

"I don't need your thanks. And you didn't put me on the spot. I would have offered to take care of you anyway. You were there for Whit."

The smile she gives me is sweet, not like the grimaces I've seen in the last few hours. "Whitney is a great kid. I'd do anything for her."

Her words are laced with pain and genuine affection, and I want to pull her closer and hold her tight.

Except that's not the type of relationship we have.

Or do we?

I haven't a clue. All I know is she pushes buttons and twists things inside me I've been unaware of before meeting her.

Before I got to know her I didn't trust her, wanted to hate her, wanted to keep her away from me and Whit, and yet she's proven to be an ally in my need to protect my daughter.

"I'll go get..."

"Go. I'm good."

Leaving the bathroom is hard, something I never considered it would be. And the need to rush back to Cami has me taking the stairs two and three at a time, before running to the utility room and checking the door to the garage is locked.

My hockey bag isn't on the shelf where I usually leave it and I curse when I remember it's still in the back of my truck. Unlocking the door I just locked, I yank it open and run around to the far side of the truck to pull my gear bag out.

"Fuck!" I need to dump my stuff in the machine. The ziplock bag I put my clothes in works to contain the stink for a few hours but any more than that and I may as well leave everything out in the open.

Taking the time to sort my gear, I make sure the washer is on before relocking the door to the garage and pocketing the cream for Cami's bruises.

I make quick work of checking the doors and windows in the rest of the house. Satisfied the house is locked up tight, I head back upstairs.

For a second when I walk into the bathroom, I think Cami is asleep and about to slip beneath the water and drown, but her quiet voice dispels that fear.

"It's good. Doesn't hurt as much in here."

"I've got the cream. It'll soothe some of the ache too, and I've got some heat patches we can put on before you crawl into bed."

I keep my eyes on her face because it took a split second to see the underwear she's got on does nothing to conceal her from view now the material is wet.

"Are you ready to get out?" Shit! I forgot to get her something to put on. "Wait. I need to grab something from Whit's—"

"One of your shirts will work. I don't know if I can stand anything around my waist, there's some bruising there and when I prodded at it, it hurt, so sleep shorts won't work."

Her eyes are still closed, and her face has lost some of the tension from earlier.

My eyes immediately go to the area she's talking about and I can't seem to pull my gaze away as I say, "Oh, I didn't think of that."

Conflicting emotions war inside me.

Arousal, because she's sexy as fuck lying there in underwear that hides nothing.

Fear, because the bruising is bad and I worry there's internal damage.

Anger, because I want to choke the life out of Kenneth Dupre for ever putting a hand on her.

Fuck that. I want to strangle the motherfucker for daring to breathe in her presence.

"Beckett."

Her voice has my eyes darting to her face where they're captured by her glittery dark sapphire gaze.

"I'm okay. It looks bad, I know that, but it's not as bad as it seems."

"I..." My throat works through the emotion clogging it. "It's looks so bad. And I think it's gotten worse in the last few minutes."

"Probably." Her smile is small and the corners of her lips tremble with pain and exhaustion. "I expect it'll be worse tomorrow."

"I think you should see someone in the morning just to be sure there's no internal damage."

"I think that's overkill but if I'm in as much pain as I am tonight, I'll go just to get some heavy duty pain meds."

"Fuck!" Spinning around, I yank open the top drawer of my vanity. "Where are they?" I mutter as I frantically search through the mess but I don't see the little bottle of pain meds I usually keep in the bathroom.

It's then I remember using the last two a few days ago when I forgot to hydrate well enough during training and came home with a headache.

"I need to go downstairs to get the pain killers."

"Help me out first. I'll dry off while you get them."

The water behind me splashes and when I turn around it's to find Cami on her feet. "Shit. Don't move. What if you slip?"

The laugh she lets loose sounds brittle with weariness and I can see her eyelids are droopy.

Snatching up a towel, I sling it around her shoulders before carefully palming her waist and lifting her out of the tub. "You okay to stand now?"

"Yes. The hot water helped. A lot."

"I'll grab a shirt then get the meds."

"Okay."

Leaving the bathroom again delivers a tug to return I'm getting used to. Cami Nelson may have started out as a woman I didn't want anything to do with but since the day we met she's slowly wormed her way under my skin.

The question is, how deep has she gotten?

CAMI

A moan slips up my throat as I roll over and press into the heat next to me. I vaguely recognize the scent filling my nose but I'm too tired to figure out what it is.

Besides, the heat does wonders for the ache in my hip.

There's a whispered sshh... and I'm pulled in closer to the heat source. The smile on my face follows me back to sleep.

A cry bursts from my throat as pain lances through my pelvis and down my leg.

"Fuck! Sorry." Strong hands move me around and settle me on my other side. "That better?"

"Hmm..." I can't form words, my brain is too busy trying to work out where I am and why I hurt so badly.

"Cam? Are you okay?"

Beckett.

Memories come rushing in.

We're at his house.

In his bed.

My eyes pop open only to find the room dark. "What time is it?"

"Just after five. Do you need more pain meds?"

"Yeah, I think so." The throbbing in my hip matches the one in my head. "I've got a headache now too," I murmur.

"You haven't had enough fluids. Your body is trying to repair itself. You'll need to stay hydrated to make that easier."

"Can I have a glass of water?"

"Hang on, there's one on the bedside but don't move. I'll get it."

The bed dips when Beckett gets out and I wonder when we ended up in bed together. I'm still groggy from sleep and pain and while I can remember where I am, what happened, the finer details are hazy.

"Here. Let me help you sit up and hold the glass."

"I'm not a child," I mutter.

"No, you're definitely not. But you are injured and sore and you've been moaning in your sleep for the last couple of hours."

"Oh."

I feel chastised when I've done nothing wrong. Although his reasons for helping make sense and I let him guide me upright.

The water isn't cold, but it's cool enough to soothe my dry throat. When I've had my fill I lean back against the hand cradling the back of my head. "Thanks. I'm good now."

"Not quite." I hear a pop and then he says, "Hold out your hand."

When I do he shakes two pills into my palm then quick as I can blink, he puts the bottle of pills on the side table and picks up the glass of water again, pressing it against my lips, urging me to drink.

"I need to put the pills in my mouth first."

"Oh, sorry. Whit has problems taking meds so I taught her to take a mouthful of water first, then tip her head back and drop them to the back of her throat. Makes swallowing them easier when they're right where they need to go."

I'm not sure I'm following what he says but I take a drink then tip my head back.

"Now open your mouth and drop the pills in," Beckett instructs while placing his fingers beneath my chin to keep my head back.

Doing as I'm told I'm surprised at how easy it is to take the meds. Not that I have trouble doing it the usual way, but still, his trick is ingenious.

"Want more water before you go back to sleep? You've only had half a glass."

My stomach feels rumbly. I know it's because I didn't eat much dinner at Nat and Chase's, and I've been popping pills like candy since we left Whitney's school.

What I want, although not comfortable asking for, is toast. If I'd gone home with Mom and Dad, it wouldn't be an issue. I'd just get up and go make myself some but I'm in Beckett's house, under his care, and I don't want to be more of a burden than I already am.

"What?" He points a finger at my face and circles it around. "What's that look?"

"Nothing."

"Oh, it's something." He places the glass back on the bedside table before leaning over me, one hand planted in the bedding beside my thigh. "Tell me. Now."

He uses what I'm sure is his dad voice and I have to fight the smile my mouth wants to make.

I'm not his child, he doesn't need to care for me the way he is, and while I like it—probably too much—I'm determined to take care of myself.

We have a stare off for at least a minute before the low rumble of my stomach makes me give in. "I'm hungry."

"What do you want? If I've got it, you can have it; if not, I'll see if I can get it."

"Toast."

"Toast? You want toast?"

Nodding, I press a hand to my stomach when it rumbles loudly. "Yeah, some plain toast."

"Plain toast." The look he gives me is hard to decipher.

"If you—"

"Of course I can get you toast. I'm shocked it's what you asked for, that's all."

"What else would I want?"

"Well, Whit asks for homemade chicken noodle soup or mashed potatoes."

"Mashed potatoes?"

"Yeah, it's her comfort food. Mama Dot used to make it when Whit was little and had tonsillitis what seemed like every other week." He shrugs. "I guess for her, a bowl of mashed potatoes is a bowl of love."

"I'm the same with toast. When I first went to live with Dad and Mom, it was all I could eat because it was all I'd ever had to eat."

Rolling my lips into my mouth I lower my head. I hadn't meant to reveal that piece of information. I've never told anyone about the years I lived with my biological mother.

Even Dad doesn't know the extent of the neglect.

"There's a story there but as you need to rest and you won't do that well without something in your belly, I'll leave it alone for now."

My past isn't a secret. Hell, most of it was played out in the media like some kind of freak show before Dad put a stop to it. Anyone could find out the details if they dug far enough. "Thanks."

"We all have a past we don't talk about." He pushes off the bed and stands. "Want to eat the toast in bed or down in the kitchen?"

The thought of moving has me cringing but then I think about how stiff I'll be in the morning and figure getting up and moving around now might help alleviate that. "Kitchen."

"All right, let me find the slippers you wore home."

He's heading for the bathroom before I register what he said and once I do, I'm surprised by the way his words make me feel.

Comfort. Warmth. Contentment.

All things I associate with Mom and Dad.

Things I should not be feeling while lying in Beckett's bed.

I don't know if it's gratitude or genuine feelings sparking the emotions his words evoked. Either way, I need to put the brakes on them.

I can't get comfortable here. Beckett has barely turned the corner of disliking me and I'm sure if I hadn't gotten between Whitney and Kenneth, he wouldn't be as accommodating.

"Come on. Let's get you that toast so we can get a few more hours of sleep before the day begins."

"Don't you need to get to training?" I ask as he helps me up and out of bed.

"No."

I was right. I'm stiff as hell and it hurts like a bitch. Biting the inside of my cheek I try to keep my whimpers to a minimum.

"And Chase and Natalie are taking care of Whitney for me." Beckett slips an arm around my waist lightly and urges me toward the door. "I can carry you again if this is too much."

I guess the tension in my body and the groans I'm unsuccessful at hiding are what prompts his offer. Except I'm determined to make it on my own. At least down to the kitchen. Getting back up here might be a different story.

"I'm good. Need to get things circulating."

"Hmm..." The sound isn't agreement and I don't want to think about it being censure. Whatever it is, he doesn't comment further and even moderates his steps to match my slower ones.

I feel like an invalid. And I suppose I am at the moment. I've never been the best patient. Comes from my foundation years being devoid of care, of my tears and hurts going ignored unless I required a trip to the doctor or hospital.

It takes a good ten minutes, but I'm finally lowering myself onto a stool at Beckett's kitchen island. I'm exhausted from the effort it took to get here without crying. I might still cry.

"Take a deep breath, Cam. You're breathing too fast." Beckett's hand rests between my shoulder blades. "Suck in nice and slow and let it out the same way. Take your time."

"The pain meds haven't kicked in yet," is my excuse.

"No, probably not. And if you weren't so stubborn I could have carried you down here and saved you the pain."

"I prefer determined," I mutter as I lower my forehead to rest on the counter.

"Don't go to sleep there."

"No chance of that. Every inch of me aches with the stabs of a thousand needles."

"That's kind of graphic."

"But true." I groan, rocking my head on the hard surface while I try to work through the discomfort walking down here produced.

"Maybe another hot bath would help? You can sleep later."

"I have to go home."

"No, you don't. We've got over twenty-four hours before we leave for Miami and the season opener. You can rest here until you need to pack."

"How do you know I'm going?" I haven't lifted my head so my words are a little muffled by my hair and the counter.

"Everyone is going."

He's right. Anyone who wants to attend has a free flight and seat for the game. And those that don't have seats in the arena have them in the team hotel because Nat has booked out the whole place.

Every room, every suite, even the function rooms which are where she's having big screens and buffets of food set up.

And after the game, win or lose, the players will return to the hotel to spend time with those who made the trip.

It's crazy to go to this extent but I get why. To build a team from scratch and have it be a winning one, you need to reward every single person who has a hand in making it happen.

"One or two pieces?"

Tipping up my head, I rest my chin where my brow was and ponder the question, try to gauge how hungry I am. If I ask for one and I'm still hungry, that will be more work for Beckett and keep us out of bed longer. If I say two and can't eat them...

"It can't be that hard a decision," he says with a smirk.

"Two."

He drops two slices of bread in the toaster then turns and leans on the edge of the counter behind him, his hands gripping the edge on either side of his thighs. "Talk to me."

"About?"

"Anything. You. Your job. Rogue sportswear. The Rogues. Whatever."

"We're the same age." Why I blurted that out, I don't know.

"Are we?"

"Yeah, you're thirty-three. Right?"

"Yes. Thirty-four in December."

"So you're older than me by a few months."

"Oh? When's your birthday?"

"May twenty-first."

He cocks his head. "You seem unsure of that."

I shrug. "Kind of am. Dad had to have records searched to find out because my biological mother birthed me at home and didn't register me."

"Your biological...you're adopted?"

"No. Dad is my dad. Mom is my step-mom because my birth mother refused to sign over rights for her to adopt me." I sigh. "It's a long, long, crazy story that I might tell you about some time."

"When did you move in with your dad?"

"I was eight when the courts awarded him custody."

"And you've lived with him since?"

"Yes."

"Thanks for sharing that with me."

Shrugging again, I look away.

Beckett's next words have me turning back to look at him. "Whitney thinks her mother died before she was two, and she did, but I've never told her how her mother died."

"I'm sure it's hard for you to talk about." I slowly sit up. It feels like I should be upright for this conversation.

"Not the way you'd think."

"Oh?"

"Whitney's mother was my high school counselor."

He leaves the words hanging. And my sleepy pain-numbed brain takes a full minute to understand the importance of his words.

My eyes pop wide and my mouth drops open.

"Yeah, that's a sordid scandal if ever there was one."

"But, but... Holy shit, Beckett. Tell me the woman went to jail!" The fury rolling through my pain-ravaged muscles annihilates every other emotion except the need to find the woman who took advantage of him when he was just a kid.

"She did." He swallows. "And she died there."

BECKETT

I don't know why I told Cami about Whit's mother. I've never told anyone other than Mama Dot, the policeman that interviewed me, and the judge.

People know of course. Most of the police force in the town I went to high school in. And then there were the kids I went to school with. They had to speculate I was the one involved when Catrina Hooper was arrested and marched out of the school, because I disappeared the same day.

"I'm not a victim."

Cami's eyes widen further and indignation floods her face. "You most certainly are!"

"No, I'm not. I get that she took advantage of a kid, but I was mature beyond my years due to living with a crack-whore most of my life. I was in love with her."

"Bullshit!" Cami pushes to her feet. The fire in her eyes blazing at me. "At that age you don't know what love is. I can imagine exactly how it happened. She showed you attention and you soaked it up because you didn't have it."

"I'm not a victim." The phrase is stuck on a loop in my head.

"Not..." Her head cocks to the side and she studies me. "No.

You're right. You're not a victim. You're a survivor. You're a miracle. And your daughter is tribute to that."

"I…" She rounds the counter and walks right up to me until her slippers are brushing the tips of my toes.

She's a good bit shorter than me, maybe five inches or so, which means our height difference isn't that bad. I still have to tip my head down and she has to tip hers up to make eye contact. "I want to hug you."

"O-kay."

Her arms are around me, squeezing tight as she turns her head and presses her cheek against my shoulder. "I want to say sorry. Sorry that that happened to you, and I wish it hadn't but then there would be no Whitney and that would be more of a tragedy than how she was conceived."

"She's the silver lining in the biggest mistake of my life. Which is why it wasn't really a mistake."

I slip my arms around her back and pull her a little closer. I don't want to hold her too tight, don't want to press on any of the fifty million bruises dotting her side and back.

With my chin resting on her head I say, "I've never told anyone. Not since the trial, and I only ever told the story three times."

"I don't know what to say."

"Nothing to say. It is what it is."

"Will you ever tell Whitney?"

"Yes. When she's older. I thought maybe after she finishes college but recently I've been contemplating telling her on her eighteenth birthday."

"When she's legally an adult."

"Yes."

"I won't tell anyone."

"Didn't think you would."

"But I think maybe you should tell Nat."

My head jerks up and my arms loosen. "What? Why?"

She holds on tight but tips her face up to look at me. "Don't get angry. First let me ask you a question."

I can't work out what she's thinking and while my gut is screaming "shut this shit down and end the conversation" I have to give her the benefit of the doubt because she's proven to be on our side time and time again.

With a hard swallow, I say, "Go ahead."

"Is this the reason you kept yourself and Whitney out of the public eye?"

"Yes. And no. It was hard raising a kid on my own. I had Mama Dot but I wanted to take care of my daughter, so I did the bulk of the work. I went to school, then straight home to Whit. Once I hit the NHL I did the same. Went to work, came straight home to her."

"Is it possible for someone to find out about her mother?"

"No. My name was suppressed, and the case files sealed. The names on Whit's birth certificate aren't real."

"What do you mean they aren't real?"

"I changed my name the day Whit was born. And the name in the mother's section is a fake one the court made up to help keep our identities a secret."

"Your name isn't Beckett Higgison?"

"Not my birth name, no. It's the name I took so we could have a future without the cloud of our past hanging over us."

"I won't ask where you got your name from or what your birth name is, but I will ask again. Is it possible someone could find out who you both are? If they dig far enough?"

"I hope not, but I suppose if they knew where to look or someone gave them something to go on."

"All right. Well, for now I think we can table the telling Nat thing but you should think about it. I can, with your permission, hire someone to bury the info about your real identity where no one will ever find it, but I'll have to use the same people we use for KAW and Nat isn't the only one who will hear about it if I do.

Oakley and Blake will as well. And I can't imagine either of them keeping the information from the men they're married to."

I can see the gears in her head spinning. It's remarkable the way I'm getting to know her tells. "What are you thinking?"

"I don't think we should do anything until after Whitney's birthday and you tell her, if that's still your plan."

"At this point it is."

"Okay, we wait until you've told her then we can ask her what she wants to do. If she wants me to see about burying any connection between you and your past that might still be there."

"I'm scared to tell her. Scared of what she'll think of me. Of the mother she's never known, who never wanted her."

"How did you manage to get custody of her?"

"I found out Catrina was pregnant when I overheard her making an appointment for an abortion. We argued, she told me it had nothing to do with me and I should forget I heard anything."

"Except you couldn't."

"No. I tried to talk her out of it for a few days and when I realized it wasn't possible, when I realized I was the latest in a long line of teenagers she'd slept with, I told Mama Dot and she took me straight to the police station. Catrina was arrested the next morning and the courts stopped her from aborting Whit."

"She went through with the pregnancy because she had no choice."

"Yes. Whit was born in the local hospital under police guard and handed straight to me seven months after I overheard that phone call."

"God, Beckett." Her arms tighten around my waist. "I can't begin to imagine what you went through, how you didn't just cope but thrived."

"I don't remember a lot of it. I knew I needed to set us both up and I was good at hockey. Really good. I was already getting noticed and Mama Dot talked to me about the best way to make sure the two of us would be safe."

"Money."

"Yes. Money. It's why I went straight from high school to the NHL."

"In Canada."

"We moved there the day Whit was born. We had everything lined up, ready. Mama Dot's house packed up and a place in Edmonton where I enrolled in the local high school to finish my schooling, but the goal was, from before Whit was in my arms, to make the NHL."

"You really are a miracle."

"No. I'm just a man who did what he had to in order to protect his child."

"I understand your anger at me that first night now."

"I couldn't see past your job. Sometimes still can't. I'm trusting you to keep this to yourself, Cami."

She pulls from my arms and steps back; the shock on her face has me wishing I hadn't voiced my concern. Before I can apologize, she's poking me in the chest with her finger.

"If you think for one hot second I'd ever breathe a word of this to anyone, never mind put it in an article, you're a dumbass!"

With that she spins away and stomps from the room, which is a feat considering she could barely walk a few minutes ago.

Behind me the toast pops and I grin. Cami may think this conversation is over, but I promised her toast.

And I should probably deliver it with an apology. Quickly plating the toast, I swipe some butter over each piece and grab jars of strawberry jelly and peanut butter just in case she wants something else on them.

When I get back to my bedroom, I find her sitting up in bed, back to my headboard, arms crossed, an angry scowl on her face.

"I would *never* tell anyone what you just told me." Her words are fierce, hard like the headboard behind her.

"I know. I didn't mean to imply you would." I sigh. "It's hard to say why I said what I did. I mean I know why, but again, I can't rule out there's a piece of me that meant the words the way you took them."

"So you think I'm going to what? Just blurt your secret out to someone? Write it up in the paper?"

"No. But I won't deny the fear I feel now that somebody other than myself knows who I really am. I went to a lot of effort to wipe out the past so that Whit could have the best life she could without the dark cloud of how she was conceived hanging over her head."

"I understand that. And maybe I over-reacted a little, but, Beckett, you have to know I'd never share what you shared with me in confidence. You don't know the full story of how I came to live with my dad and if you did, you'd know I'm the last person to put an adult, never mind a child, through the scandal revealing your true identity would be."

"Okay. I guess we have to accept this isn't a normal situation and our emotions, mine more than yours, are fully invested and tangled in a way that makes both of us a bit over-reactive."

"Over-reactive? Is that a word?" The small smile curving her lips has me hoping we can move past this little misunderstanding.

I shrug. "It felt right."

"Is that my toast?"

"Yes." I hold out the plate until she takes it, then offer the two jars. "I wasn't sure if you wanted either of these."

"I'll have some of the peanut butter." The smile curling her lips now is more of a smirk. "Do I use my finger to put it on?"

"Shit. Sorry. I'll go get—"

"It's fine. I can eat it plain but let me get out of bed."

"Why?"

"Because you don't want me leaving crumbs in here."

"Cam, I can say with all honesty, crumbs in my bed are not a problem. Whit and I used to do breakfast in bed every chance we had before we moved here."

"That might be so, but I'm not going to ruin these nice sheets when I'm planning to crawl back under them and sleep for as long as the outside world will let me."

"How's the hip?" I ask when I see her grimace as she slips to the floor beside the bed and leans her back against it.

"Okay. I think the meds have kicked in and the march up the stairs loosened things up," she says sheepishly.

"Do you want more of that cream before you go back to sleep?"

"If you can spare some. There wasn't much in the jar."

"I can get more from one of the trainers tomorrow."

"Are you excited?"

"About the game?" The subject change is unexpected. I thought we'd continue talking about my past. "Um, yeah, I guess. Maybe more anticipating."

"Think you can keep the stre—"

"Don't say it!" I lunge forward and press a hand over her mouth.

"What?" Her eyes are wide and her voice muffled against my palm but I can hear her clearly enough.

"Don't jinx us by asking that out loud. Actually, don't even think about it." I lower my hand and settle in beside her.

"Oooo...kay, sure." She eyes me sideways as she takes a bite of her toast. "Thanks for this."

"You always talk with your mouth full?" My question conjures images of Cami's mouth filled with something else and I have to suck in a breath; the visceral reaction my body has to my imagination has my heart racing and my groin pulsing. I'm glad I'd already taken a seat on the floor so I can lift the leg closest to her to hide the tent rising in my shorts.

I watch her swallow her bite and wonder when my libido decided to come back onboard after years of being dormant.

I've gone without sex for years and not once has it been a problem. A few weeks ago, when I first laid eyes on Cami Nelson it never entered my mind that it might become one.

"Sorry. I'm not usually this much of a slob but now that you've put this in front of me, I'm starving."

"I can make you something else. Eggs?" It would be good to get out of the room. Take a breath of air not laced with the scent of Cami. But she's shaking her head, dashing my hopes of escaping and getting my dick under control in private.

"This is enough."

She finishes the first piece and starts on the second and I can't seem to pull my gaze off her. It's not until she's almost done with that slice that she speaks again.

"You're staring."

"Sorry, sorry." I force my gaze up to meet hers. "I didn't mean to make you uncomfortable."

"You're not. Just wondered if you knew you were watching me eat and if maybe that means you're hungry too."

"No. I'm not hungry." My gaze drops to her mouth again.

At least I'm not hungry for food.

And being hungry for Cami Nelson is something I'm not sure I'm ready for.

CAMI

Beckett hasn't let me go home since he pulled into his garage last night. Nat turned up with some clothes and toiletries from my apartment first thing this morning and when I raised an eyebrow at her she gave me a look I didn't want to argue with.

It wasn't until a few hours later, when Detectives Clark and Anders came knocking, that I understood my best friend's gruff delivery.

Someone broke into my apartment during the night.

And it wasn't Kenneth Dupre because he was being entertained by the Baton Rouge Police Department at the time it happened.

Although he did give the police an idea of who might be behind the break-in just by telling them who paid him to get the scoop on Whitney Higgison.

Herman Draper.

I can't believe he's still hanging around after all these weeks. Surely some other celebrity has done something scandalous he could be digging up dirt on.

"Hey."

Glancing away from my stare-down with the squirrel making

itself a home in the big tree outside Beckett's family room window, I find the man holding me hostage.

Okay, I'm not really a prisoner but when I suggested I get out of his hair by going to Mom and Dad's, the look I got had me zipping my lips and retreating to this comfy couch.

"Are you hungry?"

"No. We just had lunch."

"If you want something, just ask."

"I want to get out of your hair."

"You're not in my hair."

"Beckett!"

"Okay, fine. Everyone wants you to stay here."

Sitting up, I twist around to face him. "Who's everyone?"

"Natalie, Oakley, Blake, your dad."

"Dad? When did you talk to my dad?"

"This morning. After the detectives left."

"So you're all pow-wowing and deciding what's best for me like I'm a child?"

"No. We just want you to rest so you won't be in as much pain."

"I can do that at Dad's."

"Yeah, you could, but no one is home there."

"Ah." And the light bulb goes off. "I need a babysitter now?"

"Not a babysitter, just someone who can help you if you need it."

"I don't need it. I've been a mooch on you long enough—"

"You are not mooching," he all but shouts. With a sigh, he rakes his fingers through his hair. "Fine. *I* want you to stay here. *I* need to see you're okay and I can't do that if you go to your dad's."

"Oh. Well."

I can't think of what to say to that. We've barely spoken since we woke up this morning. The conversation we had before we went back to sleep weighed heavily on each of our minds in the light of day.

Well, I assume it's weighing on Beckett, because it definitely felt like it was taking up a lot of space inside *my* head and it wasn't my secret being revealed.

"Chase is dropping Whit off in about fifteen minutes."

"Is it that late?" I don't have my watch on or my phone to know what time it is, not that I've cared about it before now, but I guess it is getting late in the day.

"They had a half-day today so Natalie picked her and the twins up and took them to the practice rink to wait for Chase to finish."

I pause for a minute pondering my best friend playing driver to a bunch of teenagers. "Who has the baby?"

Beckett grins, the sight of it making my belly quiver, and I have to look away for a moment.

"Rumor has it the equipment staff rigged up some kind of sled and the players have been taking turns towing her and Drew Lattimer Watts around the rink."

I laugh at the images playing in my head. "I bet that was Branton's idea."

"Probably. Although Chase seems to be a big kid most of the time so he might have thought of it."

"I can't believe he gave up college and hockey to help raise his younger siblings."

"He's brave, that's for sure. And he got that extra time with his mom."

"It's sad. All of them losing their parents like that."

"Yeah, I thought I had it rough. But at least I didn't start with loving parents and have them taken away within months of each other."

"I'm not sure I'd look at it that way, everyone deserves to be loved by parents, birth of otherwise. I'd take that over eliminating world hunger any day of the week. But life doesn't work like that, and we all have our traumas to deal with."

"I think Chase and his sisters will be okay."

"Me too." I smile. "Especially now they've been brought into the Rogues family."

"I didn't understand what Blake meant when she first spoke to me about joining the team, about how they didn't just want to build a winning team but a family we could all rely on to have our backs. She was so adamant that I be prepared to support whoever needed it."

His forehead wrinkles and his eyes go unfocused.

"I never thought I'd experience what having a large family meant. It's just me and Whit, and unless she decides she wants a handful of children we'll always be a small family."

"Family isn't blood. You should know that. Didn't Mama Dot take care of you and Whitney?"

"Yes."

"That's family. Caring for each other and having each other's back. It's what we built when we started Rogue sportswear, it's what we're building with the Rogues."

"You've done it. We're not even six months in and you've got that tightly woven family unit. It's why we're playing so well, why we're winning."

"You're winning because you all have skills."

"Yes, that too, but I'm not playing with a teammate, I'm playing with family. And that makes me want to play better. For them, as much as for me."

"Dad!"

"That was quick." Beckett frowns and looks at his watch. "Fifteen means ten apparently."

"Dad!"

"In the family room," Beckett calls over his shoulder. "Why that girl can't just come looking is beyond me."

I smile because I know I used to do the same when I was younger. Hell, I'm pretty sure I still do it now when I go home.

"Hey!"

"Whitbee." Beckett holds one arm out. "Come give me a hug."

With a roll of her eyes, Whitney walks over and delivers the requested cuddle. She surprises me by letting go of her dad and bending over to give me one too.

"How are you feeling?" she asks, a frown marring her pretty face. "You look a little pale."

"I'm fine. Tired. I don't think I slept very well even though I slept if that makes sense."

"It does." Turning to Beckett, she asks, "Can we order pizza for dinner?"

"I pulled a tray of lasagna out of the freezer."

"Oh, that works. Can we make garlic bread?"

"Sure. Go check we have what we need and if not, I can duck out and get it while you stay here with Cami."

"I don't need a babysitter!"

Beckett grins at me. "It's not you I'm referring to being babysat."

"Oh." My indignation leaves like the air from a popped balloon.

"I also don't need a babysitter, but I'll stay with Cami if you have to go to the shop. Let me go check what we have."

Whitney is out of the room before I can blink. It's always surprising how quick kids move, how much energy they have, even when you're prepared for it.

"Did she seem off to you?" Beckett asks, his frown aimed at the doorway Whitney disappeared through.

"Ah...no. Why?"

"I don't know. I can't put my finger on it but something..."

"She's probably still out of sorts after yesterday. And don't forget there was the thing with her car. The drama around her post revealing her existence to the world. A lot has happened in a few weeks."

"I guess." Shaking his head, he turns back to me. "You're probably right. With the move down here, the new school, the pre-season and now the regular season starting. It is a lot at once. Hopefully these few days away will be good for her."

"I was planning to work while we're there but now…" I shrug. "I might need to see if Deb can come with us."

"Give her a call. Even if you feel up to working, she'll be able to help and you won't have to carry anything, you can get her to do it."

"True." Looking around I try to remember where I left my phone.

"It's upstairs. In the bedroom with your bag."

"Ah, right."

Pushing up, I get almost upright when Beckett strolls out of the room tossing, "I'll get it," over his shoulder as he goes.

I can't help the growl that rumbles in my throat. I'm getting tired of being treated like an invalid. Yes, I'm hurt. Yes, the bruises look bad. And yes, I'm slow to move, my muscles stiff from the beating they took courtesy of stone steps.

I get all that. But I'm still capable of doing things and it'll help me recover if I move.

"He treating you like you're spun glass?"

My gaze goes to the doorway. With a sigh, I continue upwards, using the arm of the chair to steady myself until I'm sure I'll stay upright. "Yes. He is."

"That's normal."

I arch an eyebrow Whitney's way. "Oh? How so?"

"He takes care of those he loves. You should have seen him with Mama Dot. And whenever I'm sick it's like his world is ending. He can't do enough to help me feel better. I'm pretty sure he sleeps on the floor in my room. Except I don't know that he actually sleeps."

Her shrug is subtle, but her words hit me like a sledgehammer.

Beckett doesn't love me. He feels guilty I got hurt trying to protect his daughter.

"I'm sure what you say is true, but in my case it's the fact I took a tumble saving you. Although, I'm fairly sure you'd have saved yourself if I hadn't been there."

"I don't know. He seemed determined. And after getting up close with him yesterday, I realized he's been following me around the last few weeks."

My muscles tense, pain shooting in every direction, and I suck in a breath. "Following you? Have you told your dad? The police?"

"I told the detectives yesterday." She looks over her shoulder quickly before continuing. "And no, I haven't told Dad because he'll lose his shit when he finds out."

Yes, he will. Of that I'm certain, but now I know and I don't like liars, and keeping something like this from her father feels like a lie.

"You're going to tell him, aren't you?"

"Ah, well." She looks at me sheepishly. "Not if you tell him."

Whitney blows out a breath and drops her chin when I don't reply.

"Fine. I'll tell him after dinner."

"Tell me what?" Beckett asks. Skirting around Whitney, he brings me my phone. "You've got a few missed calls."

"Thanks"

Turning, he crosses his arms and glares at Whitney. "Tell me what?"

"The guy from yesterday has been hanging around. I've seen him a few times and yes, I told the detectives."

Beckett's body vibrates with what I can only assume is rage. "Kenneth Dupre has been following you?"

"Yes, I think so, but until yesterday he didn't get anywhere near me."

"Are you sure?"

"Yes, Dad." She folds her arms in a perfect imitation of her father and glares right back. "I wouldn't lie to you about something important."

"But I'm only just hearing about it now?"

"I didn't have a chance before you left with Cami last night."

"You could have called."

"Why? It wouldn't make any difference telling you now or then." With a shake of her head, she turns to leave the room. "We don't need anything from the shop. I'll get started on the garlic bread."

"Whit!"

"Leave it."

Beckett spins to face me. "What?"

"Leave it. She's right. Telling you last night wouldn't have made a difference."

"It's like she's keeping things from me. She's never done that before."

I know the look on my face has to telegraph my sheer incredulity at his statement. The man who's keeping a huge secret from his daughter has the audacity to complain about her delay in telling him she put some things together recently.

"She didn't realize she was being followed until yesterday when Kenneth tried to grab her. She *couldn't* have told you before that." I take a step closer. "And people who live in glass houses shouldn't throw stones."

"What the hell does that mean?"

"She isn't the only one keeping things to herself because she thinks it's the best thing to do." Brushing past him, I head in the direction Whitney went. "I'll help Whitney with dinner."

"I'll—"

"We don't need help."

The growl behind me shows his frustration and to be honest, he's not the only one feeling that way.

I hate it when people act hypocritically.

I hate it even more when they act that way and they're too dumb to see they're doing it.

BECKETT

I've always liked silence. My own company. Whether that's because it's what I grew up with and was used to or my nature, I don't know.

But the silence that has hung in the air in my house the last few hours has been deafening.

The two females sharing the space have been uncharacteristically quiet. We've prepared dinner. Eaten dinner. Cleaned up after dinner.

Even those were done in silence.

I'm a little shocked. I've heard about teenagers giving their parents the silent treatment but I've never been subjected to it.

Until today.

It makes me wonder what's going on with Whit. I sensed something earlier, even asked Cami if she noticed but after Whit told me about her suspicions of being followed, I thought that was it.

Realizing she's seen the man who attacked her and Cami yesterday multiple times in recent weeks must be playing on her mind. It has to be scary. It sure as hell is for me because he could have cornered Whit at any one of those times and no one would have been there to help her.

And I all but yelled at her for not telling me.

I don't know if I should apologize or let her work her way out of her feelings on her own.

Except I can't stand that she won't even look at me. Can't stand getting the cold shoulder.

And it's not only Whit I'm getting it from.

Although at least Cami will look at me, even if it's only to shoot me dirty looks I can't decipher.

Whit didn't even say goodnight when she headed upstairs to bed.

At least I think she's gone to bed. Hard to tell when she's managed to move around the house without a sound while awake.

Honestly, it's a skill I didn't know she possessed. Her silent movements and cold shoulder would be admirable if I wasn't on the receiving end of them.

With a sigh, I turn to Cami. "I get that you're mad at me, that Whit is mad at me, but I can't stand this quiet. Talk to me. Tell me what you think I did wrong?"

"What I think you did wrong?" The look on her face tells me I've fucked up again.

"Sorry. I didn't mean it like that." Scrubbing a hand over my face I suck in a deep breath and blow it out. "I don't like fighting with Whit and this doesn't really feel like a fight. Well, not our usual kind anyway."

Cami remains tight lipped.

"And I hate being at odds with you too."

"Isn't that how we started? At odds? There's nothing new happening between us."

Her words bring me up short.

Yes, I didn't like her to begin with, but it wasn't personal, not really, and since then I've found myself somehow tethered to this woman I barely know. She's still pretty much a stranger and yet I told her my deepest darkest secret.

"What you need to do is worry about patching things up with Whitney." Cami's shoulders hunch as she wraps her arms around her waist. "I hate conflict. I lived it every day for the first eight years of my life. I avoid it at all costs now."

My gaze is glued to her and I hold my breath, wait for her to say more.

"I think you need to apologize to Whitney. I think you both overreacted to the situation. Maybe it was because of yesterday. Fear and concern can make things seem worse than they are. Maybe it's because I'm here, in your space. Whatever it is, she didn't do anything wrong, didn't lie, and didn't really keep anything from you."

As soon as she says those last words I know what ticked her off earlier. "But I'm keeping something from her."

"Yes."

"Fuck!" I'm a dick. I'm moving before I think. "I'll be back. I need to talk to Whit."

Taking the stairs two at a time I'm in front of my daughter's closed bedroom door before I stop dead in my tracks and stare at the barrier Whit has put between us.

It's rare for Whit to close her bedroom door. I don't think there's more than a dozen times I've seen it. When she was little, she liked me to leave the light on in the hallway and her door cracked a couple of inches.

She's never slammed it in a fit of rage because she doesn't have a temper like that. And the only reason I know slamming doors are a teenage girl thing is from TV.

From everything I know, Whit has never been the average teenager.

Faced with a shut door I'm unsure how to proceed. Normally I'd rap my knuckles on the doorframe and poke my head inside. But this? This requires a knock and patience.

I have to tap my knuckles on the wood and wait to see if I'm allowed in.

What if she's locked it?

Dropping my gaze to the door handle, I stare at it.

Does it even have a lock?

Sound behind me has me turning to find Cami coming up the stairs, her movements stiff and slow. I'm torn between going to help her and knocking on the door in front of me.

"Don't use me as an excuse to chicken out."

Cami's quiet voice makes me jolt. I wasn't prepared for her to speak. I definitely wasn't prepared to be called out.

With a deep breath, and a stretch of my neck, I turn back to Whit's door and knock.

It takes so long for a response that Cami has time to disappear into my room and I'm on the verge of knocking again. But then the door swings open and Whit stands before me, her face devoid of emotion.

I can't remember ever seeing my daughter with a blank face. She's usually animated; even sick, she's gushing with emotion. This straight-faced girl has me taking a step back.

"Um, hey, can I come in?"

Her gaze moves behind me but I don't turn to see what she's looking at. I keep my eyes locked on Whit's face in hope of seeing something other than this unemotional version of her.

When her gaze lands on me again, she stares for so long my muscles spasm with the urge to move. With half an eye roll and a gust of air, she says, "Sure. Come in."

Turning, she walks to her bed and climbs on, slipping under the covers in spite of still being in her clothes.

"Can we talk?" I pull the chair from her desk over beside the bed and take a seat. When she doesn't answer me but continues to look at me with those emotionless eyes I had no idea she'd mastered, I blow out a breath and lean forward, my forearms on my thighs, hands loose even though I want to clench them. "I'm sorry."

My words don't get me so much as a twitch.

"I wasn't angry at you. I was angry at the situation and my lack of control over it. Before, when it was just us and the world didn't know about you, I didn't have to worry about this kind of thing. We both flew under the radar and I liked that. I had control of that."

Swallowing, I keep my eyes on hers and hope she can see, as well as hear, the truth of what I'm saying.

"I love you more than anything in this world, Whitbee, and if anything happened to you. If someone hurt you because of me..." I hang my head for a second before meeting her gaze, my eyes wet with the emotion the thoughts in my head evoke. "It would destroy me."

She's quiet, but I can see she's thinking about what I've said. And that's all I can ask. As long as she hears me, as long as I'm truthful with my own thoughts and feelings, she has to understand that all I want is for her to be safe.

"I didn't keep it from you on purpose and I thought the detectives would tell you anyway."

"They didn't."

"I get that. Now."

"I'm sorry I accused you of hiding it from me."

"It's okay. I know things are emotional right now. With Cami getting hurt trying to protect me..." she tips her head to the side. "Why did she do that? She doesn't really know me."

"Because that's the type of person she is. If it had been someone other than you, she'd have stepped in to help."

"I guess, but you should have seen the look on her face, Dad. And when she threw her laptop at him." A small smile tips up the sides of her mouth. "She threw it like a frisbee. It skimmed his head because he was already turning to run away but it was the coolest thing to see it fly past him."

An answering smirk curls my lips as a vision of what she describes pops into my head. "I bet."

"Do you think we could see if the school security system recorded it?"

My smile widens. "I think you might need to ask someone else about that. Maybe Natalie."

"Can I?"

"I don't see why not. I wouldn't mind watching Cami fighting back. Although I'm not sure I want to see him grab you. Maybe we can get them to give us from the point after that?"

"He didn't hurt me. I saw him move before he touched me so I was already twisting away like I learned in those self-defense lessons you made me take."

"I didn't make you take those, you asked to go!"

She grins and the vise encircling my chest loosens. "I know."

"Are we good? Do I need to say sorry again?"

"We're good."

"No extra sorry necessary?"

"No. And I'm sorry for not making sure I told you earlier."

"We both could have handled things differently and we will in the future. Or at least try." It's a promise I make to her and me.

"Can I ask you something?"

"You can ask me anything."

"Is Cami your girlfriend?"

"What? No." I jackknife upright. "What gave you that idea?"

"Well, you kind of freaked out about her being hurt yesterday and then you brought her home to take care of her..." She shrugs and I have to admit, her observations are spot on. Which makes her question legitimate.

"Huh. I did do all that, didn't I?"

"Yes. And she's still here." Her hand comes up when I open my mouth. "I'm not complaining. I like her. I like spending time with her."

"Well, that's good, because you're spending the next few days together."

"What? Why? I thought I was coming to the game!" She's up on her knees, leaning toward me. "I want to be at the game. I don't want to stay—"

"Whoa. Hold on." I've got both hands up to stop her words. "You are coming to the game. That hasn't changed. I only meant that I'd like to ask you to stick close to Cami when I'm not with you."

"Oh." She lowers to her heels and smiles. "I can do that. Do you think she'll let me help her take video to use in her interviews?"

"You can ask."

"I was talking to the videographer she brought to the barbecue the other week and I think I want to do something in the media. Not be a reporter or anything like that, but film making."

The concern wrinkling her brow has me sitting straight. "You can do whatever you want to. But I thought you wanted to do a business degree."

We talked a bit about what she wanted but her recent comments about sticking close to me, possibly doing college online, have me wondering if she's had a complete change of mind.

"You talked about going to school in New York at one point," I remind her.

Nodding, she smiles. "I did. But the closer the time comes, the less I want to do that, and I haven't applied to any colleges, Dad."

"What? I thought we'd filled out a bunch of applications before we moved here."

"We did." She tips her head toward her desk. "They're in the top drawer."

I glance over my shoulder. "You don't want to send them in?"

"No." The firmness of her voice has me turning back to look at her. "I want time off. I want to take a year to think about what I want."

"But—"

"I won't be doing nothing. I'm thinking of asking Natalie if she'll let me be an unpaid, or low-paid, intern at the Rogues. I want to learn everything about the team from how the arena is run to coaching the players to managing the franchise."

"Really?" She's never shown much interest in hockey other than it's what I do for a job. Her deeper interest now seems odd to me.

"Yes. It's been fun watching these last few weeks and I've seen a bit of what happens behind the scenes since hanging out with the twins because Natalie is around them a lot. Plus I did some research on how KAW got the franchise. All the bad press they got for getting it. It's fascinating."

"Okay, well, if it's what you want, go for it. You know I'll support you any way I can."

"So you're okay with me not going away to college?"

I smile at the way she braces for my answer. "I'm fine with that if you have a plan. You know I didn't go to college. I barely scraped through high school."

"But you had a skill, one you could turn into a career. There's nothing wrong with not having a degree, Dad."

"I know. I just want you to have everything you want and every opportunity I didn't."

"You give me that. And I've learned something during these last few months, particularly in recent weeks."

"Oh, what's that?"

"*We're* the most important thing we can ever have. Our family, the Rogues family."

"How did you get so wise?"

It seems we've discovered the same thing at the same time because her words are true. All the money in the world can't compare to the support of family.

"I had a very wise man raise me."

When she launches herself at me, I wrap my arms around her and pull her close.

The love that flows through my veins for this kid always surprises me. She's everything to me and tonight has shown me that she's no longer a kid.

She's a young woman.

A young woman I'm proud of.

A young woman I'm proud to have had a hand in raising.

A young woman who deserves the truth.

CAMI

We're in the final minute of game one in the regular season and the excitement in the room is palpable.

I'm up in the visiting owner's suite of the Miami Steam's arena, while Nat and Oakley are downstairs waiting to join the team after the end of game horn sounds.

I've been taking video all night from the suite while Deb has roamed the arena doing the same. Even Whitney has taken some footage while watching her dad play like the star he is.

Beckett Higgison might be in the older bracket of professional hockey players but he's no less skilled, no slower or less aggressive than the younger men on the ice.

He's been instrumental in getting the Rogues the five-two score illuminated on the Jumbotron hanging from the middle of Miami's arena.

As the seconds tick down, a hush falls over the room and nobody moves. I'm sure no one breathes. I certainly don't.

My eyes are glued to the ice, waiting with bated breath for that horn to signal the end of the game.

From the corner of my eye, I see Whitney move up against the glass, her head moving back and forth as she follows the puck and the men chasing it, and for some reason I lift my phone and hit record.

We're down to a couple of seconds when her hand comes up and covers her mouth and I watch the anticipation and joy explode on her face as the crowd in the arena and the room around me goes wild.

A split second before the end of game horn blasts, the goal buzzer goes off.

Phone still aimed at Whitney, I turn my head to see what all the excitement is about.

As if to prove my thoughts about him true, Beckett has scored another goal.

His third of the game.

Hats fly over the glass onto the ice and I move my phone to take in the scene below.

It doesn't matter that this isn't our home ice, our home crowd, hockey fans the country over know how to celebrate a hat trick.

It's crazy, the pandemonium that follows the end of the first game of the season. Win or lose, it's the beginning of every team's run for the Cup.

And the Rogues have kept their undefeated status of pre-season and marched into their first NHL regular season with their heads held high.

I might not have been instrumental in putting the team together, might not be involved in everyday management or train-ing, but a swell of pride rises in my chest anyway and has my eyes watering.

"They did it!" Dad claps a hand on my back and I almost drop my phone.

Juggling it, I hit stop on the video and turn to throw my arms around him. "They did!"

"If this isn't a poked tongue at the league, I don't know what is," Pa says, his voice loud enough to carry over the cheering. "I'm taking Micky down to the locker room. Anyone else want to head down with us?"

Whitney comes to a bouncing stop beside us. "Me! Yes! Me!" She turns to go but quickly spins back, her eyes meeting mine. "Do you think it would be okay if I videoed everyone waiting for the team?"

"Sure, just make sure they know you're doing it and okay with being recorded."

"It'll only be the players' families and Rogue staff down there. Oakley said Nat vetoed the press or anyone else," Pa adds.

"She can do that at another team's arena?" Whitney asks. "Wow. That's some serious power."

"That woman has never let anyone stop her getting what she wants," Dad says, one arm still around my shoulder. "I'd love to see her as president. She'd kick ass."

Laughing, I bump his hip with mine. "Don't give her any ideas."

"Nat isn't going anywhere. She finally has what she's always wanted." Pa's words seem innocuous enough but there's a smile on his face and an underlying hint of something I can't quite put my finger on. Turning, he hooks his arm through Whitney's. "See you down there or back at the hotel. I'll take care of this one until her dad comes out."

Nodding, I watch them go, collecting others on their way to the door. By the time Pa leaves, he's got a trail of kids and adults following him.

"Jimmy is in his element here. I haven't seen him this happy since before Nora died."

I have to agree with Dad. The Rogues, Oakley's marriage to Walker, and the arrival of Micky, have made Pa a very happy man. Tipping my head up, I ask, "Are you heading down now?"

"I thought I'd stick with you. See if you need anything."

"I'm good, Dad. You can go down if you want. I just need to make sure everything is okay here, nothing left behind—"

"I'm on that." Trevor stops next to us. "I've got enough hands to help too; just take care of your things and you're good."

"Are you sure?"

He looks at me like I've lost my mind.

"Right, right. Stupid question." Smiling, I turn to Dad. "All right. Let's go congratulate the team before we hit the hotel and we lose our chance."

"We can catch up with Mom—she's down there already."

"She is?" I glance around the suite and realize we're the only ones left. "Wow. It cleared out quick."

"Most went down with Jimmy but some headed out before that."

"Oh."

Dad slips his arm through mine and urges me toward the door. "So, talk to me about Beckett and Whitney."

"What about them?"

"You threw yourself and your laptop at Kenneth Dupre." He cocks an eyebrow at me.

"And?"

"Cam."

He gives me the look he's always given me when he wants me to talk. It worked when I was younger. It's not so good now I'm older, but I've always confided in Dad or Mom so I find myself caving.

"I didn't think about it. He grabbed for Whitney and I couldn't let him get away with that."

"That's all it is? You protecting a child?"

"She's not really a child and she'd pretty much saved herself by twisting away, but something clicked in my head, and I couldn't not do something."

"There are a few similarities between you and Whitney."

I nod. There are. But then again, we're completely different too. Whitney's mother was a predator of a different kind to mine.

"I'm here if you need to talk." He gives my arm a squeeze with his. "About anything."

I hear the underlying question and answer him right away. "I haven't heard from her."

"Hmm..."

"Yeah. I don't know if that's a good thing or not either."

"You mind if I get someone to see where Andrea is?"

"Of course not. You have as much right to be sure she isn't going to crawl out of the woodwork as I do."

"Less than you. Far less than you."

"I don't think so. She lost the power to hurt me a long time ago. She's a nuisance more than anything now."

"Still, it's better to know if we should prepare for anything she might come up with."

"True. But you don't need to worry about me. I can take care of myself."

Dad eyes me sideways and chuckles. "You proved that a few days ago when you single handedly scared off Kenneth Dupre."

"I don't know if I scared him off as much as he knew he wasn't going to get what he wanted and cut his losses."

"Ms. Nelson?"

Looking up I find a security guard in front of us. "Yes."

"If you'll follow me." At my raised eyebrow he explains, "I'm to escort you to the locker room."

"We don't need an escort."

"Not usually, no, but with the press being held back from both teams, things are a little contentious through the public areas and we have to traverse a small section of that to reach the private elevators to the basement levels."

"Oh. Okay. Thanks." I offer the man a smile in the hope of lightening his dour expression. It doesn't work but my smile remains all the same.

Dad leans closer to whisper in my ear, "He takes his job seriously."

Tipping my head slightly and talking quietly out the side of my mouth I say, "Ray probably put the fear of god in him."

"Ray does that without trying."

"He does." I grin. "It's why Nat hired him."

"You mean convinced him to work with the Rogues org exclusively."

"Same thing."

Dad chuckles as we leave the deserted hallway leading to the private suites and enter the chaotic melee that is the concourse between this side of the arena and the other.

"Wow. He wasn't kidding." Dad's arm unlocks from mine so he can wrap it around my shoulders and tug me tight against his side. "Might have needed more than one guard."

"We'll be fine. Just keep your head up and eyes to the front."

"I know how to deal with a room full of executives, I can deal with this."

"Sorry. I forgot I was raised by a shark."

"Two sharks. Don't discount your mom's abilities."

Someone slams into my back and pain stabs through my right side, making me stumble forward. Dad's arm barely keeps me upright, but somehow, I manage to stay on my feet.

I must have cried out because the guard turns back, his eyes narrowing on something—or someone—behind me. Next thing I know, he's at my side, him and Dad flanking me, as we all but run toward the door that will give us access to the private elevators.

The guard waves a card over a sensor before shoving the door open. Rushing through into the corridor one the other side, the noise and chaos instantly silences when the door snaps shut behind us.

"I'm sorry. I'll radio the security room to have them review footage and have that reporter removed from the arena. At the very least stopped from entering the press conference."

"Reporter?"

"He had a press pass around his neck."

I look at Dad. "Did you see him?"

"No." Dad's frown digs deep grooves into the flesh around his mouth and across his forehead. "I was too busy keeping you from falling when you pitched forward."

"Oh, okay, I'm sure it was an accident." I glance back at the door. "It was a madhouse out there."

When I turn back, both men are frowning at me and I don't know why, but it gets my hackles up. Instead of commenting and dragging our delay out further, I try for a reassuring smile.

"We should get moving. We'll miss everyone before they head in to the press room or back to the hotel."

Neither man moves right away and I'm on the verge of saying something else when Dad offers me a smile and looks at the guard.

"Lead the way. We've got a team to congratulate."

I'm so caught up in my head thinking about what I want to take video of when we reach the team that I'm not paying attention to where the guard is leading us. But I'm brought up short by Ray Denim's booming voice bouncing off the walls around us.

"What did he put in your bag?"

"Huh?"

"Your bag? What did he put in it?"

"I have no idea who or what you're talking about."

"Herman Draper put something in your bag when he shoved you from behind."

It takes me a moment to work out what Ray is saying, but when I do it's like my bag is on fire. I can't get it off my shoulder fast enough.

The thud it makes when it hits the floor echoes around me and I stare at it with horror.

Ray's the first to move. Crouching, he yanks the sides apart and begins taking things out one at a time. Nothing he removes is unfamiliar, and as each item is put on the floor next to my bag my impatience grows until I can't stand it anymore.

With a grunt of frustration, I sink to my knees and grab my bag from Ray. He doesn't get time to protest before I tip it upside down and shake, emptying the remaining contents out.

Tossing the bag to the side, I run my hands through everything, spreading it out so I can find what we're looking for.

I don't see it at first. It's not until I sweep my gaze over the pens, notebooks, flash drives and other miscellaneous handbag stuff like tissues and lip balm, for a second time that I see the foreign object.

"I don't wear lipstick." I sit back on my heels, the need to distance myself from the silver tube I've never seen before making my skin crawl.

"What?" Ray's gaze meets mine.

"Lipstick. I don't wear it," I repeat, pointing at the tube that isn't mine.

"Ah, okay." He doesn't touch it or anything else. "Everything else yours?"

I nod slowly, my head feeling too heavy, my thoughts a little sluggish. "Yes."

"Take another look. Be sure."

I do as he asks. But that sluggish feeling has moved to my eyes and it takes me a while to process everything on the floor. When I get to the last item, I see nothing I haven't put in my bag myself except the lipstick tube.

"I'm sure." A wave of dizziness makes me put a hand on the ground for stability. "It's the only thing."

"What's going on?"

Beckett's voice pulls my gaze up. He's towering over me, and it takes a minute for me to realize he's in a suit. It's not the first time I've seen him in one, but for some reason it's the first time I've noticed how good he looks in one. "Wow."

"Cam? You okay?" He grabs a handful of each trouser leg and tugs up as his knees widen and bend so he can lower into a crouch beside me. "Cam?"

"I..." What was the question?

"She's fine."

My gaze moves to Ray and I have to put a second hand on the floor to keep my balance. When I look back at Beckett his gaze is trained on me, his face distorted by a frown.

"Cam?"

"Yeah... I'm okay. Someone. Outside." Another wave of dizziness makes my head so fuzzy my thoughts scatter, and it takes me a minute to get the rest of my words out. "Apparently put something in my bag."

"Apparently?"

I nod but stop when the dizzy sensation makes everything spin and my stomach roll. "I didn't..." Why can't I think straight? "Camera. Caught."

"You caught it on camera?"

Looking back at the things scattered on the floor I murmur, "No," because I'm not sure what we're talking about anymore and I can't find my phone...

"The incident was caught by arena security?" I don't think Beckett is talking to me anymore but I try to focus on him anyway even though it's proving really hard to tip my head up. "You know who it was?"

"Yes. We're searching for him now."

Ray's voice is more growl than words and it takes all my effort to lift my head to look at the Rogues' head of security.

When my skull proves too heavy for my neck, I let gravity lower my head, my blurry eyes meeting Beckett's on the way. He's looking at me funny but my brain isn't working right and I can't find words or summon a smile. It's all I can do to stay upright.

I try to shake my head to clear it, except the motion is slow and only makes the dizzy sensation worse.

My head grows heavier and my vision starts to sparkle, blacken around the edges, sounds muffling like I'm submerged under water...

Closing my eyes, the last thing I hear is Beckett's panicked voice.

"Cam!"

BECKETT

"Cam!"

I manage to get my hands on Cami's shoulders just in time to stop her from face planting on the floor. With a hard yank, I pull her to me and topple back onto my ass. Looking down I see the woman in my lap is out cold.

"What the fuck?"

There's activity around me but all I can do is shift until Cami is across my lap, cradled in my arms against my chest. Happy she's comfortable, I look up.

"What the fuck happened?"

"I don't know. Someone is getting the team doctor now." Ray Denim crouches beside me. "Can you see anywhere she's hurt? The shove was hard enough to make her stumble—"

"What shove? Where?"

"He shoved her forward when he dropped something in her bag."

"How did he shove her? Where was the contact? Shoulder to shoulder? Hand on shoulder?"

"Can't tell from the footage but it was from behind."

"So he pushed her in the back?"

"It had to be her right side." Cami's father moves in front of us. "I was on her left and when she pitched forward, it was across me. Can you lean her toward me, maybe we can see something to indicate why she's out?"

"Could she have just fainted?" Whit asks.

Glancing up I find my daughter staring down at me, worry creasing her brow. "I don't know, she was fine, seemed a little distracted maybe, but then she just went out."

"Clear the way!" Natalie comes charging down the corridor behind Whit, the concern on her face matching everyone else's. "All right, we don't need everyone hanging around, step back and let the doctor do his job."

His job is taking care of hockey players, and while I've always been grateful to have a team doctor, in this moment it feels like a lifeline. Until he asks something I can't do.

"Lay her down on the floor so I can examine her."

"I'm not putting her on the floor!"

"I need to examine her."

With my gaze locked on his, I grit out between clenched teeth, "I'm not putting her on the floor."

"Check her eyes, I'll take her pulse."

I look to the woman who's been with the team, shadowing Dr. Kerns, for less than a week and nod. "What she said. Do that."

There's a quick standoff but the Natalie in full GM mode puts a stop to it.

"Do what you can. The EMTs are on their way with a gurney."

It takes seconds for them to come up with nothing. Cami's pulse is normal, her eyes equal and responsive, and her dad confirms she didn't actually fall, just stumbled, so we're not looking for a head injury.

"I think she's been drugged."

My gaze darts to the woman now taking her blood pressure. "What? Why? How?"

I'm not the only one who speaks; in fact the questions are

flying from every direction, but the woman keeps her gaze on mine.

"Everything indicates she's sedated. Can you tell me what happened?"

"No, I—"

"Here." Ray holds out his phone. "This is the clearest video we have of the incident. The other camera angles don't pick up as much detail as this one, but I can show you those as well."

We all lean in for a closer look and as the clip rolls, my muscles get tighter and tighter until the woman next to me shouts.

"Stop. Replay that bit."

I have no idea what she saw to prompt her outburst but I'm not about to argue. Cami hasn't moved since I pulled her into my arms and if it wasn't for the fact I can see her chest rising and falling I'd be yelling for someone to do something.

Ray replays the last few seconds twice before the woman asks if he can play it in slow motion. It takes him far too long for him to work out how to do it and when he does, I find myself looking away.

I can't watch it again.

"There! See that?" Her exclamation brings my gaze back to the phone where she's pointing at the screen. "He's got a syringe in his hand. Just before he gets close. He's hidden it well the rest of the time."

"Damn. How'd you spot that?" Ray murmurs while replaying the film again.

With a shrug, she says, "I see them in my sleep since I started med school."

"You think he used it on her?" Ray asks, still frowning at his phone.

"Yes." Her gaze moves to Dr. Kerns. "She appears sedated to me."

Dr. Kerns nods. "I agree with Dr. Wendall's assessment."

"Do you think it would be okay to examine her right side?"

The woman, who's apparently a doctor, asks. "See if I can find a puncture wound?"

I open my mouth to say yes and instantly shut it. I can't make that decision. I have no right to make it.

"Yes. Do it," Natalie commands. "Let's clear everyone from the corridor first. The EMTs are still a few minutes out. There was some sort of brawl outside the arena and they're all attending to fans with various injuries."

Putting her words to action with her usual GM force, Natalie has the corridor reduced to me on the floor with Cami in my lap, Dr. Kerns and Dr.Wendall, and Cami's mom, in less than a minute.

I have no idea when Cami's mom arrived, or where her father went, and I don't have time to voice my questions before the Rogues GM is giving orders again.

"Do what you need to," Natalie directs.

"I'm not putting her on the floor."

"You don't have to. If you can turn her to expose her right side, I can lift her shirt and check her. From the video I think he may have gotten her around the waist area, possibly right above her hip," Dr. Wendall explains.

It's easy to move Cami—she weighs less than my hockey bag full of gear. Once I have her rolled to her left, her front turned toward me, I'm comforted by her even breathing, the rise and fall of her chest against my stomach.

"How will you—" Air sucks through my teeth. "Fuck."

"Yeah. There's no doubt he got her with the syringe," Dr. Kerns says, the frown dragging his mouth down one I've never seen. "The question is what was in it."

"I'm thinking a sedative. Something not too dangerous. Her pressure is still one-ten over seventy."

"What do you think it was?" I ask. The thought of Cami being injected with anything makes me feel physically sick and I have to swallow the bile rising in my throat.

"Hard to say. Could be a number of different drugs. Off the top of my head, I don't know what's available here in Florida."

"And we can't rule out he brought whatever he used with him from out of state," Dr. Kerns adds.

"True, but—"

"Are any of them dangerous?" I interrupt.

"Yes and no. It depends on what drug he used and the dosage."

Dr. Wendall lowers Cami's shirt. "I don't think the syringe he had could hold enough to be dangerous."

"Even though she's small?" I look at the woman in my arms. She might be tall but there isn't an ounce of fat on her anywhere.

"At a guess, and at this point that's what we're doing, I'd say she'll be out a few hours at most." The conviction in Dr. Wendall's voice gives me no relief. Because her words are true. Right now we're all guessing.

"EMTs are coming in now." Natalie crouches beside me. "You want to stand up and put her on the gurney?"

"Yes." I'm not sure I can bring myself to let Cami go, except if I don't, we can't get her to the hospital and the care she needs. "What will happen now?" My question is directed at no one in particular.

"We get her to the hospital where they'll take some blood, run a few tests, keep an eye on her until she wakes up," Dr. Kerns explains as he gets on one side of me to help steady me as I get to my feet. "They'll probably want to keep her overnight, depending on when she wakes and what they find in her system."

Looking at Natalie, I ask, "Can we get them to release her into Dr. Kerns's care once they run tests?"

"What are you thinking?"

"We're out of here first thing. If they keep her overnight, they won't release her in time for her to travel home with us. Unless someone can stay here."

"Either way we'll work it out, right, Dana?" Natalie speaks to Cami's mom for the first time since I noticed her.

"Yes. As soon as we hear what the doctors at the hospital say."

The words don't reassure me. I want to stay with Cami, but I know her mom or dad should do that. "You'll let me know—"

"Why don't you go with her to the hospital?" Cami's mom puts her hand on my arm. "Fenton and I will take care of Whitney."

"Oh, you don't want—"

"I do," she interrupts. "And I'm sure Fenton does too, but it might be better if you go because no offense, Beckett, but you're less likely to be recognized than either of us."

She's giving me a silent message, one I can't decipher, but understand. "Okay, if you're sure."

"I am." Turning to Natalie she asks, "Can we get her to the hospital without the media finding out?"

"I'll make it happen."

"What do you need us to do to help?"

"Nothing. Oakley is dealing with the press right—"

"Shit. I was supposed—"

Natalie holds up her hand. "You don't have to do anything. And before you ask about everyone wanting to interview you because of your hat trick, we're going to take a leaf out of Cami's book and release an interview with you and Whitney."

"Whit?"

"Yes. I'm going to bring her back in now, get her to ask you some questions."

"But." I glance down at the woman in my arms before returning my gaze to the Rogues GM.

"Or, we can do something else…"

I can tell Natalie's mind is spinning with possibilities. Her eyes light up a second before she snaps her fingers.

"Let's do another conversation with a Rogue tomorrow, once Cami is better, about tonight's game. The rest of the team can cover for you for now. I can even release a statement saying we'll be airing a special episode of Conversations with a Rogue tomorrow night."

"Maybe get Whitney to talk like you first suggested."

I look at Cami's mom. "Like when Cami interviewed us before?"

"Yes. I think it would make your no-show at the team press conference less of an issue, especially if we play up the father-daughter angle, and if we've managed to keep Cami's visit to the hospital quiet, it will help bury it further."

"I can help with that."

We all turn to find Ray striding toward us. If I hadn't already met the man, knew he was on our side, I'd be running. His whole demeanor screams *man on a mission*, and I'd hate to be his target.

"What have you got?" Natalie crosses her arms, her feet shoulder-width apart, her posture telegraphing ready to defend. She's in full GM mode.

"It was your basic sleeping pills ground down and liquified."

"Sleeping pills? Name?" Dr. Kerns steps forward and demands.

"Zolpidem."

"How'd he liquify them?" Dr. Wendall asks, her voice a little less abrupt.

"Sterile water."

"Thank god the man's not a complete idiot," Dr. Wendall mutters.

"How do you know all this?" I ask Ray.

"On a hunch I contacted the detectives in Baton Rouge, got them to question Dupre. They put a bit of pressure on him, made it sound as though the victim of Draper's plan was an underage girl."

"Jesus. And he believed that?"

Ray shrugs. "Must have because he was singing like a canary about Draper trying to give him the syringe to use on Whitney the other day."

"Are you sure? Can we trust what this guy says?"

"I think so. He's got nothing to lose now; he's already in deep shit. Plus I don't think Draper has the connections to get anything else. Or the money."

"What else did you find on Draper?" Natalie demands like she knows Ray has more information.

"Amos found a connection to Kristina Bancroft."

"Walker's ex?" The incredulity in Natalie's voice has me tightening my hold on Cami.

Ray confirms with a nod. "Amos and I are working on finding the details. On a good note, I have a backdoor into Blaywood Private Hospital. We can get Cami there within the hour and they'll put a rush on her test results so we can get her out before anyone figures out who she is."

"Okay. Thanks. Can you coordinate that and stay with Beckett and Cami until they return to Baton Rouge?" Natalie questions.

"Of course."

"We'll also need someone to cover Whitney, Dana, and Fenton."

"Mr. Barnes has his own security team, but I can brief them and send a couple of guys as backup if needed."

"All right." With a clap of her hands, Natalie gets everyone's attention. "Dr. Kerns and Dr. Wendall, keep your phones on, we may need one of you to accompany Cami back home. Dana, find Whitney and Fenton, and do whatever you need to do to get Whitney home tonight."

"Tonight?" I'm not sure I want Whit going home without me but the idea of leaving the woman in my arms...

"Yes. We need to offer the media as little as we can. Control the narrative as Cami would say."

"I'll get your number from Whitney and text you so you can keep us updated on Cam," Dana says.

"Okay. And thanks for taking care of my daughter."

"Of course. It's only fair. You're taking care of mine." She offers a smile before turning to leave.

"On that note," Natalie begins. "Ray, do I need to bring the

EMTs in or do you want to do whatever to get Cami to Blaywood?"

"Up to you. As long as Dr. Kerns says she's good to travel, I can drive the three of us to Blaywood, which will cut down on the number of people who know something happened."

"Dr. Kerns?"

"I'll check her again, but I think that should be fine."

"I can do it. Can travel with them too, make it look less suspicious. Just two couples out for the night," Dr. Wendall offers.

Ray eyes the young woman, a small smile curling his lips. "That's good."

"I'm comfortable with that if you all are." Dr. Kerns's gaze moves over everyone.

With no objections, and a plan in place, Ray ushers Dr. Wendall and myself, Cami still in my arms, away from the exit.

"We're taking the south exit from the arena," he explains. "My men have already cleared the path of people and there's an SUV waiting for us outside the door."

"Should I ask how you've got a back way into Blaywood?"

Ray laughs. "Nothing nefarious. I know the head of trauma. Went through the service with him years ago."

"And you kept in contact?"

"I pulled him out of a situation once."

"One you can't give any details of."

"Oh, I can give you details. Just didn't think you'd want them."

"My mind is currently running on two tracks. Worry about my daughter and worry about Cami. A distraction might be nice."

"Sure. I can do that. Traveling through a village in Afghanistan we took some fire that scattered us. What we didn't know was we were targeted for our medic."

"The head of trauma."

"Yep. Anyway, they obviously had eyes on us for a while because they knew who he was before they started shooting," Ray continues as he leads us through the bowels of Miami's arena. "Turned out to be a small group of insurgents with a wounded— aka dying—leader. When Duce couldn't save him, they put a gun to his head. But we'd gotten there by then. The locals were not happy to have a group of terrorists hiding out in their village and basically walked us right up to the front door of the house they were holed up in."

"And you went in and pulled him out before the gun at his head went off."

"Not quite."

"But—"

"Duce lost part of his left cheek and ear. The reason he ended up head of trauma at Blaywood."

"He owes you."

"I don't see it that way. He put a plug in a bullet hole in my arm at one point. Same with one in my thigh. He also pulled a piece of shrapnel out of my ass."

His words have me distracted enough I don't notice how far we've come until he pushes open a door to the outside.

"Let's get her in the backseat, strap her in with you beside her, rest her head on your shoulder so it looks like she's asleep or had too much to drink on our night out." He's grinning at me when he pulls open the back door of the SUV.

"Sounds good."

It doesn't take us long to get situated and on the road. But it isn't until we're directed into an exam room by a man who looks more like an underground fighter than a doctor that I feel some relief.

After a quick check of vitals and a small blood draw, we're asked if we'd like anything to eat or drink while we wait and directed where we can find both. All free of charge. I make a mental note to find out how to make a donation to the hospital.

Three hours later, Cami still hasn't stirred and the doctor confirms she was given Zolpidem. Not enough to be dangerous, but she'll be sleeping until tomorrow and should have minimal side effects.

More relief loosens my muscles but I'm not completely relaxed yet.

"All right, let's get back to Baton Rouge." Ray holds out his hand to his old friend. "Thanks, Duce. I owe you."

"Anytime, Sunshine."

Duce grins but Ray just rolls his eyes and mutters, "Whatever, asshole."

It isn't until the private jet leaves the ground on its way to Baton Rouge that I feel the last of the tension drain from my body.

CAMI

Rolling over, I moan as sore muscles pull and a dull pain thrums in my hip. Softness beneath me offers comfort, but with the way my body aches it gives little relief.

"Cam?"

The whisper of my name has a smile pulling at my lips and I try to open my eyes but my lids are stuck and when I attempt to move my arm so I can rub the sleep from them it's too hard. Like my limb is weighed down.

A grumble of frustration vibrates in my throat and the bed dips beside me.

"Shh… You're safe."

Safe? Why would I not be safe…

Warm pressure gliding over my head has my thoughts scattering.

Sinking into the soothing warmth engulfing me I take my time to catalogue the rest of my body, to wonder why I feel so groggy.

Was I in an accident?

I can't recall where I am. Or who I'm with. But the sense of security I get from the presence, from the scent filling my nose, the timbre of the voice, puts me at ease.

I know the smell. I recognize the voice.

Except neither are trigging knowledge of who they belong to; it's right there, I just can't grab it...

I should be panicking, I should be moving away, forcing my eyes open and figuring out where I am. Why I'm in pain.

"Is she waking up yet?"

The light feminine voice flips a switch and the panic I couldn't quite muster before screams through my veins and explodes into motion.

I'm upright, pushing through the comfort of a moment ago into muscle tightening anxiety.

Swaying on my feet, my eyes wide, I swivel my head in search of the threat. "Whitney!"

"Whoa." Large hands grip my shoulders. "Easy, Cam."

Twisting away, I swing around, and pounding pain shoots through the back of my skull.

Arms up ready to defend, I lock eyes with a set of light brown ones. Recognition slams into me and my lungs and body deflate when I realize where I am.

Who I'm with.

"Beckett?"

"Hey. You're okay. You're safe."

"I..." Why does he keep saying that? Glancing around, I see I'm in his bedroom. Was in his bed. Again? "When..."

Shaking my head, I try to clear the fog from my brain. Movement catches my eye and I turn to see Whitney hovering in the doorway as though afraid to enter the room.

I step toward her. "Are you okay?"

My question has her eyebrows shooting up her forehead. "Um, yeah." Her gaze darts over my shoulder before coming back to me. "Are you?"

"Of course. Why wouldn't I be?"

"Cam."

Beckett's voice pulls my gaze back to him and I see he's moved closer, has a hand held out.

"Come sit down."

His soft voice, the concern written all over his face, has me taking a step away. "Why? What's going on? Why am I here... When did I get here?"

The last thing I remember is...

"The game." A smile stretches my lips. "We won the game."

"Yeah, we did." His smile doesn't hold the joy I expect.

"Then..." I tip my head, eyes going to the ceiling like what I want to know will be written on it, and try to remember what happened after the game.

Did I get drunk at the post-game celebration?

"Come sit. Have some water."

His gentleness, the careful movements he's making toward me have me stepping back again and anger rolling through me. "What the fuck is going on?"

"Please, Cam, come sit down before you fall down, and I'll explain what we know so far."

I'm not frightened of Beckett. I'm scared of what he's going to tell me. In spite of my fear, I let him take my hand and guide me back to his bed.

"Here." Whitney appears in front of me, a glass of water held out. "Do you have a headache? I can get you some pain meds if you need but they said if you can put up with it you should try. At least until the Zolpidem is completely out of your system."

"Zolpidem?" My eyes move to Beckett.

"It's a drug used to treat insomnia."

"Why the hell did I take a sleeping pill?"

"Drink some water and I'll explain."

His words don't ease my mind, they only make me more confused. But what can I do other than what he's asking?

I know neither of them would hurt me and their concern is genuine, if confusing.

When I lower to the edge of Beckett's bed and take the glass from Whitney, both of them breathe a sigh of relief and sit on either side of me.

Their actions are not making me feel any better and after a couple of sips I brace myself and demand, "Tell me."

"What do you remember?" Beckett asks.

"We won the game."

"After the game. Do you remember anything from after the game?"

I think about it, because the longer I sit here the more my brain seems to clear. "You got a hat trick." At his nod, I continue. "Nat banned the media from the locker room."

"She did."

"I was with Dad"—air rushes through my teeth and into my lungs as memories flash through my head. "Someone pushed me. Put something in my bag."

"Draper. But he didn't just push you. He injected you with Zolpidem and what he put in your bag was a tracking device."

That explains the sleeping pill. But the other... "A tracking device?"

"We're not sure why he did that, but Ray speculates his intention was to follow you until the Zolpidem took effect."

"Why?"

"We don't know that either."

Bringing a hand up, I rub my forehead. "I feel weird."

"You will for a little bit until the Zolpidem leaves your system. The doctor said to keep your fluids up to help flush it through." He accompanies his words with a hand on the glass urging it back to my mouth. "Food will help too. I'll make you some toast. Unless you feel up to eating something else."

"I can make it." Whitney pushes to her feet and looks down at me. "I'll make whatever you want."

"Toast is good." I don't want them to fuss over me more than necessary and at that thought, another pops up. "Why am I here? Why didn't I go home?"

"Your apartment is a crime scene."

"My apartment..." More memories surface and I'm not liking most of them.

"And your mom and dad decided staying here would be better because we can be here with you all the time. Not that you need a babysitter."

"Seems like I do lately," I mumble.

I can't believe my life is turning into a soap opera again. I thought I'd put that behind me years ago. The idea of going through the drama Andrea made my life makes my skin crawl, makes me feel dirty.

"Can I take a shower?"

"Of course." Beckett jumps to his feet. "Let me help you."

He's gone, striding toward the bathroom before I can protest. I hate that he's being forced to look after me a second time. But I can't deny the feeling his attention gives me.

I like it.

I want it.

"I'll wait until you finish to make your toast."

I glance up at Whitney. "Are you okay?"

The smile she gives me is filled with relief. "Yes. I'm fine."

I can't peg what her expression is. And I don't have to because her next words spell it out for me.

"I'm so glad you're okay. I wanted to cry when I saw you passed out in Dad's arms. And I knew, just *knew*, it had something to do with me, but no one is saying that. Except everything started when I made that post at the beginning of pre-season. If I hadn't done that, you wouldn't have gotten hurt. Twice! And Dad wouldn't be freaking out about keeping us both safe."

There's a lot to unpack in her words but I go with reassuring her about her dad's behavior first. "He's not freaking out. He's just being careful."

"Oh no, he's definitely freaking out." Her gaze moves to the bathroom door before coming back to me. "I know him and he might not be showing it, but he's scared. I wasn't there, but I bet when you fell into his lap out cold you took years off his life."

She's right. It had to have freaked him out. I don't remember it. Can't remember anything clearly past being in the owner's suite at the end of the game. And honestly, that's a little scary.

I'll have to look up the side effects of Zolpidem. See if memory loss is one of them.

"All right. The water is warm and I've laid a fresh towel out close to the shower. Do you need help getting in?" Beckett strolls back into the bedroom, a frown on his face. "How's your hip?"

"It's fine." It's not, but I don't want to impose any more than I have.

"Right. I'll go get the cream and the heat pads ready."

"I don't nee—"

Beckett holds up a hand. "I saw the bruises again last night when we got home and got you into bed. I'll get the cream and the heat pads, and you'll use both."

"Uh oh, that's his Dad voice. Better do what he says." Whitney grins at me.

"Fine." Emotions war inside me. I feel equally determined to take care of myself and yet strangely comforted by Beckett's brand of looking out for me. Pushing to my feet, I ask, "Where's my bag?"

"In the closet." Beckett points over his shoulder. "What do you need? I'll get it."

"I need the whole thing. It's got my toiletries and clothes in there. Wait. My bag is here?" So much of the last... "What time is it? What *day* is it?"

"You've been asleep about fourteen hours."

"Oh." Why does it feel like more of my life is missing from my memory?

"And Whit helped your mom pack up your hotel room and brought your stuff home."

If Whitney helped Mom, why am I here and not at home?

So many questions and not enough answers. I want to shake my head and rattle all the missing memories lose, but I don't think that will help the dull pain at the back of my skull.

"I'll put your bag in the bathroom. Do you need Whit to help you with anything?"

"No. I think I'm okay."

"I'll stay here so you can call out if you need me." Whitney lowers herself back to the bed.

"You don't need to do that."

"I know I don't have to." She smiles at me and I know I'm not going to win this argument, and to be honest I don't have the energy to fight it.

"Okay. I'm getting in the shower." I head for the bathroom only for Beckett to overtake me, my bag in his hand.

Once he places it on the floor, he opens it up and asks, "What do you need? I'll put it on the vanity so it's within easy reach."

"Beckett." I wait for him to look at me. "I'm not an invalid. I can bend down and get whatever I need."

"You've got a headache. Bending down repeatedly won't help it."

I don't recall confirming I have a headache.

"You get a crease, right here"—he presses a finger to the skin at the top of my nose—"when you're in pain."

"It could be my hip."

Beckett nods. "It could. But you're walking without a limp now so it's not your hip and the doctor said you might wake with a headache."

"I feel out of touch. Confused."

"That could be the remnants of the sleep med or the lack of memory. The last time you were awake, we were outside the visitors' locker room in the Miami arena. Now you're here."

What he says makes sense and while I get how I got here doesn't really matter, I want to *know* it. I need to put all the pieces together. I hate the out of control feeling I have right now. It too reminiscent of a past I put behind me long ago.

"Will you tell me everything that happened?"

"Of course." He points at my bag. "Tell me what you need out of here and I'll let you get that shower."

"My pjs and toiletries bag."

He quickly has a pile on the counter. "That's it?"

"Yeah."

"Call out to Whit if you need help."

"I won't need—"

"Cam. Don't push yourself. There's no shame in asking for help in a situation like this."

I know he's right. But when your formative years are spent taking care of yourself because no one else cares enough to do it, your natural instinct is to do it on your own.

It took years before I let Dad and Mom look after me. Years of hiding every bump or bruise or illness because I didn't trust they'd help if I told them.

"Stop overthinking this and hop in the shower. The hot water should help clear your head and ease any aches remaining from the other day."

I force a smile. "It's hard to stop my mind from spinning. Although I'll try because you're right. I have a headache and all this thinking is only making it worse."

"I'll put together something more substantial than toast and make you a protein shake. Your body is still in repair mode from the fall and now this." He shakes his head. "You've been through the wringer. Food, fluid, and rest for you for the next couple of days."

"I should go—"

"Don't start that again. I want you here. I *need* you here."

Beckett doesn't give me time to comment on his words before he leaves the room and closes the door behind him.

As much as I want to ponder what he said, why he said it, the relief the steaming shower offers is my priority. Pulling my shampoo and conditioner from my bag, I strip out of the shirt Beckett must have put on me at some point and hop under the warm spray.

The moan that leaves me is loud and I'm not surprised when Whitney knocks on the door.

"Cami? Are you okay?"

"Yeah. I'm fine."

"You'd tell me if you weren't, right?"

I smile. She's so perceptive. Normally I'd say yes and not mean it, but I can't lie to Whitney. "I'm a little shaky. But I think if I sit on the floor, I can wash my hair."

"Oh, screw that!"

The next thing I know, Whitney is not only in the bathroom, she's in the shower with me. Her clothes are soaked in seconds and I'm so weak and muddled that I don't protest when she helps me sit on the floor and grabs the handheld shower head and switches the water flow to it.

"Tilt your head back so I can wet your hair, then pass me the shampoo."

What strength I had on first waking is quickly draining away and I have to admit I'd never have been able to do this on my own. I'm not even sure if I'll be able to stand once she's done.

"Thank you."

"You took care of me. More than once. It's only fair I take care of you in return."

"Hmm..." The warm water, the press of her fingers through my hair, the care she's showing me, it all makes me want to cry.

I'm not an emotional person. Not prone to tears. But right now I'm helpless to stop them from falling.

"It's okay. We'll take care of you."

Whitney's words make the tears flow faster and neither of us says another word while she finishes washing my hair.

And when she's satisfied I'm clean, she helps me stand and dries me off and dresses me like a child before helping me back to Beckett's bed.

BECKETT

"She asleep again?" I lean against the doorframe and watch Whit as she sits on the edge of my bed and stares at Cami.

"Yeah. I think showering wore her out." She doesn't take her eyes off Cami when she asks, "You think she'll still want to hang around us when she works out it's all my fault?"

"What?" Pushing off the doorway, I stride over to my bed. "None of this is your fault. Why would you even think that?"

Glancing up, her tear-filled eyes meet mine. "Everything started when I posted that picture."

"Oh, Whitbee. No. This is not on you. And Cami does not blame you for what happened to her."

"How do you know?"

"Because that's not who she is."

"I don't want her to hate me."

The quiver of her bottom lip has me reaching out and tugging her to her feet. Pulling her into me, I press her face to my chest like I did when she was little. "Shh..."

She lets me hold her and I'm relieved when her tears don't come. I hate it when she cries. It guts me. When she sniffs loudly and pushes away, I let her go but frame her face so she's forced to look at me.

"This is not your fault. And Cami would never blame you for something someone else did."

"I feel so bad, Dad. I had to help her wash her hair and get dressed and she's so still now."

The fear in her eyes amplifies my own and my next words are as much a reassurance for her as they are me.

"That's probably the Zolpidem still affecting her." With everything in me I wish the words to be true.

"When will it stop? I don't like seeing her like this. I want the Cami who threw her laptop at that reporter."

"You and me both, baby, but her body needs time to recover from her fall and the drug, and we need to give her that."

"Can I stay in here with her until she wakes up again?"

"If that's what you want to do."

"I think one of us should be with her until she's better."

Whit's need to care for Cami matches mine, making it easy for me to go along with her request. "I agree. Although I don't think she's in any danger. She's just sleeping."

"I still want to stay with her. I can bring my laptop in and work on my English assignment."

"Okay. Go get what you need and when you're back, I'll head downstairs and make us something to eat. Or order in. I'm not sure what we have in the fridge." Hell, I can't remember the last time I shopped for groceries.

"Can you see if we have everything to make chicken noodle soup? I think she'd like that."

Studying Whit, I realize Cami isn't the only one who could do with some homemade soup. "Yeah, I can do that. And if we don't have what I need, I'll go to the shop."

"Should we wake her up when the food is ready or let her sleep?"

"I think it's best if we let her sleep. Let her body do what it needs to, to recover." An idea hits me and I smile. "How about a picnic? I can bring our food up here and we can put a blanket on the floor while we keep an eye on her."

I need to take care of both of them. Whit is scared and needs reassurance Cami is going to be okay, and if letting her stay in my room until Cami wakes is what does that, then I'm going to do everything I can to make it happen.

Pressing a kiss to her forehead I let go of her face and nudge her toward the door. "Go get your laptop. I'll clean up the bathroom before I head downstairs."

"Thanks, Dad."

"For?"

"Humoring me."

"I'm not humoring you."

"If you say so."

"I'm not. Letting you stay in here with Cami eases my own fears so if I'm humoring you, you're humoring me."

She frowns, her gaze going back to Cami and before she speaks, I know I've chosen the wrong words. "You're worried?"

"No. Not worried. I know she's going to be fine, but, like when you're sick, I want to be near her so if she needs something I'm there to get it for her."

The smile she shoots me is full of adult knowledge and scarier than having a drugged Cami sleeping in my bed. "Like me, huh?"

"Go." I put my hands on her shoulders, turn her and push her toward the door. "Get your laptop."

With a laugh she leaves the room and I shake my head. Whit has never known me to care for anyone besides her and Mama Dot, and while I'm not in a relationship with Cami, I'm invested.

Invested in a way I've never been before.

The feelings I have for her are nothing like the ones I had at fifteen. And for the first time in a long time, I understand why people called me a victim. I've never felt like one but when I look at it now, I see it.

My gaze moves over Cami.

She's curled on her side, and I have to move to see if her chest is rising and falling. Rationally I know she's going to be fine but it doesn't stop my brain from spinning worst-case scenarios.

And as I stand here watching her breathe, I have to admit I'm falling for this woman.

Sexual attraction aside, I like her. Even if I'm not comfortable with her job—I admire her independence and strength even though circumstances have required she relinquish both in recent days.

I want her in my life, want to be in hers. In what capacity I'm not sure. I've never been in a relationship.

Hell, I haven't had sex since before Whit was born, not even a one-night stand.

It's not like I haven't had the opportunity. But I've never been interested in any of the puck bunnies who throw themselves at players. Never felt like I was missing out when I looked at other players with their partners.

Having Whit has always been enough.

Until now.

Now I want to see where this thing between Cami and me can go. I want to explore the emotions she makes me feel. Want to see if I still know how to please a woman, if I remember how to make a woman com—

"I'm back." Whit gives me a quizzical look when she sees me standing next to the bed watching Cami like a creeper. "Did you tidy the bathroom?"

"Ah, no." I scrub a hand down my face. "I'll do it now."

"Don't bother. I can do it." She puts her laptop on the far side of the bed and checks on her patient, making sure Cami is tucked beneath the covers. "Can you bring up some more water? This is warm now."

Taking the glass from her, I smile. "Sure."

"And if you go to the shop, can you get a couple of energy drinks? I think they might help her when she wakes up."

"There's some in the gym fridge."

"Oh, can you move them to the kitchen?"

"Sure."

"Don't worry about the water. I'll let you know when she's awake so it's nice and cold."

"Anything else?" I ask, struggling to contain my amusement.

"No." Whit glances around the room before leaning over to tug the covers up again. "I think that's it."

I'm grinning as I walk out of my room.

Witnessing Whit take care of Cami doesn't just put a smile on my face. It warms my heart to know I've raised a child who's compassionate. I might not have seen it before Cami pointed it out, but I should be proud of myself.

I was still a kid myself when Whit was born, but I've been a good parent in spite of my age and not growing up with decent—never mind good—role models as examples.

Mama Dot came into my life when I was fourteen and while she was a great influence, a wonderful guide, she held more of a grandmotherly role, for both of us.

The majority of my parenting has been done on instinct. And a deep knowledge of what a parent *shouldn't* be.

The day they handed me a squealing, slippery baby, I vowed to love her and protect her with everything I had.

Knowing I did that, seeing the results through Cami's eyes, has me understanding why she thinks I need to tell Whit about her mother.

My daughter is strong enough to deal with the circumstances of her birth. Mature enough to handle the scandalous way she entered the world.

And if for some reason she's not, I'll be there for her. I'll remind her I love her more than I can ever explain.

There's an urgency inside me to tell Whit about her mother now, one that has never been there before. Over the years I avoid thinking about Catrina at all. Except Whit has the right to know her, to make her own judgment of the woman who birthed her.

I can't tarnish my daughter's opinion with my own. I need to allow her to make up her own mind and the only way to do that is to give her the truth.

After checking the pantry and fridge and finding we have what I need to make a pot of chicken noodle soup, I set out to get it on the stove quickly.

Years of practice making Whit's favorite comfort food means it only takes minutes to have a large saucepan bubbling away, the delicious scent filling the kitchen. With our dinner dealt with, I head for my home office.

I'm not really sure what I'm looking for when I unlock the filing cabinet and pull out the folder holding the paperwork from the trial, my name change, and Whit's birth.

She's seen her birth certificate. Has no reason to believe anything on it is untrue, and while her name and mine are real, mine hasn't always been Beckett Higgison.

Flicking through the papers, I find my official name change document and lay it on the desk.

Staring at my birth name, I feel no connection to it. I ceased being Gregory Becks the day I became a father. Nothing before that day means anything to me. Whit's birthday is as much mine as it is hers.

Should I start with that?

If I show her this, she'll want to know why I changed my name the day she was born. Nothing in the court files has my name on it. Birth name or legal name. There's nothing to tell her the court transcripts or newspaper articles are about us.

I have no idea how to go about revealing the circumstances of her birth. All I know is I have to tell her.

She'll be eighteen on December tenth.

I've got two months to work out how to reveal the truth.

"Dad!"

Whit's shout and the sound of her feet pounding down the stairs has me scrambling to shove everything back in the folder. Opening the bottom drawer of my desk, I drop it in and slam the drawer shut as I rush around the desk then across the room.

I'm almost at the door when she skids to a stop in the doorway. The smile on her face has the anxiety squeezing my chest releasing and my legs slowing.

"She's awake!" She bounces on the balls of her feet. "And she's normal."

I have to laugh. "Normal?"

"Yeah, she's not spacey and she remembers everything including passing out."

"Oh. Well, the soup should simmer for another half hour, but we could eat it now."

"I'll get her a bowl." She's spinning on her heel before I can stop her.

With another laugh I follow her to the kitchen. "I thought we were going to have a picnic upstairs."

"We don't have to now. She's coming down after she brushes her teeth."

Why Cami needs to brush her teeth before we eat is a mystery but if she says she feels well enough to come downstairs to have dinner, I'm not going to argue.

Except the thought of her possibly getting dizzy on the stairs and falling has me turning around.

"I'll make sure she's okay on the stairs."

"I'll set the dining table. I don't want her sitting on a high stool at the breakfast bar even though she says—and looks—like she's fine."

Whit's words have me grinning as I race up the stairs. I really have done a good job raising her. And while I hope she'll understand the secret I've kept about her mother, I know she's mature enough to deal with it, even if she's mad at me to begin with.

"Hey." Cami's voice has my stride faltering.

"Oh, hey." I frown at her. "Why are you dressed in that?"

"I need to get out of your hair. I've taken up too much of your time."

"What?" I take a step closer, my frown turning into an angry scowl. "No."

"No?"

"Yes. No, as in no, you are not going anywhere. And the last thing you've done is take up too much of my time."

"But—"

"Cam." Stepping so close I feel the heat from her body, I lower my head and bend my knees a little, bringing my face in line with hers. "You. Are. Not. Going. Anywhere."

Her eyes dart back and forth between mine and I can almost hear her mind working, scrambling to come up with another argument.

In a desperate attempt to silence any words she might be about to say, I do something I've never done before.

I crush my mouth to hers.

The gasp she lets out allows me to slip my tongue between her lips, to explore her heat, taste her flavor.

Instinct has me wrapping my arms around her waist, pulling her closer, pressing her breasts to my chest.

Her mouth is wet heat and mint, her body warm and soft.

And the moan that fills the space around us could be mine or hers.

I don't know.

The only thing I'm certain of is I don't want to stop.

If we do, I want to start all over again.

With a growl, I pull her impossibly close and lift.

Another rumble in my chest pushes me forward until I press her back to the wall.

I lean into her, eat at her mouth.

It's raw and lacks finesse, but it's the most electric contact I've ever experienced.

So electric my dick aches, the throb beating deep, pounding through muscle and bone, drowning out everything except the need to be closer.

Drowning out everything except Cam.

CAMI

Beckett kisses as though his life depends on it—as if mine does.

As though if he doesn't seal his mouth to mine we'll die.

It's rough, the thrust of his tongue, the press of his lips, but it's the most genuine kiss I've ever had.

There's no mistaking this man wants me.

It wouldn't be any clearer if he took out a billboard advertisement or it flashed on the Jumbotron at the arena the next Rogues home game.

His mouth on mine trips a switch I had no idea existed and no desire to turn back off.

My hands find his head, my fingers twisting in his hair, as fire races through my veins. It pulses hot and frenzied, snapping every cell to attention, tightening and tightening and tightening something so deep in my belly it really does feel like I'll die if he stops.

When he lifts me from the floor, it's automatic for me to raise my legs, to wrap them around his hips and squeeze so there's not even air between us.

The hard length of his cock presses against my throbbing clit and I'm helpless to stop from grinding against him.

It's not enough.

I want to feel his skin on mind.

Feel his heat singe my slick core.

Feel every inch of his hardness inside me, filling me up, taking me over.

With a groan, I pull my mouth from his.

"Beckett." His name is a plea. A curse. A demand.

"I know," he murmurs into the curve of my jaw as his mouth moves downward. "Jesus. Cam."

He shudders against me and I can't stop myself from demanding more. "Fuck me."

The sound he makes is guttural, a primitive cry that could be agreement or objection. Whatever it is, it has my fingers clawing at his shirt, scraping at his skin.

"Beckett," I moan, the need racing through me restricting my breath.

He mumbles something I can't understand before sealing his mouth to mine once more.

Hot and wet, this kiss is no less frenzied or more practiced. It's raw and hungry and matches the craving taking me over.

A rock of my hips has us both groaning, the sounds swallowed down. When Beckett matches my actions, thrusts against me, I can only whimper in need.

I want this man inside me.

I want his skin against mine.

I want—

"Dad? Is Cami okay?"

The shout from below has us yanking apart. Harsh breaths saw in and out of both of us and the lust filled gaze locked on mine delivers relief as well as frustration.

"Shit." He drops his forehead to mine. "I'm sorry. Give me a second."

"Dad?" Whitney's voice is closer.

Beckett clears his throat as he lifts his head and turns to the side and calls out, "Cami's fine. We'll be down in a second."

Breath still ragged, our eyes locked again, we don't say a word for what feels like an eternity but is probably only a few seconds.

When I unhook my legs, he slowly lowers me to my feet and holds my waist until I'm steady. I have to stifle a groan of disappointment when his hands leave me.

"I'm sorry. I shouldn't have—"

I press a hand to his mouth. "Don't say it."

He arches an eyebrow.

"There's nothing to be sorry for." The last thing I want is for him to regret delivering the best kiss of my life.

Long fingers wrap around my wrist and lift my hand away from his lips. "I've never forced myself on a woman before."

The sound that comes out of my mouth is one of disbelief. "Did I fight you off? No. Did I actively participate in that mind blowing lip-lock? Yes."

"I still shouldn't have—"

"Shouldn't have stopped?" I nod. "Agreed. But your teenage daughter is downstairs and as much as I want to keep doing what we were doing, see what else we can do, I think we need to shelve this *discussion* for later. Preferably when Whitney is not in the house."

I'm not a prude but the thought of kissing Beckett again, at the idea of taking the kiss to the place I'm pretty sure it was headed, while Whitney is in the house leaves me feeling icky.

"I've never been with a guy who had children. I'm not sure how to handle that. Not that I think we're together." Shit. Am I presuming here? I don't think this is just sex, but I can't be sure and before now, Beckett hasn't shown any signs of wanting me.

"I can hear your brain working."

With a shrug, I say, "It does that a lot."

"I've noticed." He scrubs a hand down his face. "I don't know the protocol here because I've never been with anyone."

His confession shocks both of us if his wide eyes and my slack jaw are an indication. "But..."

"Whit's mom, yes, kind of. But no one else."

"Oh." So this is just sex. The disappointment that rolls through me threatens to take out my knees.

"Wait. That's not what I meant." He ducks his head so our eyes are level. "I've never dated. Never had a one-night stand."

When his words register, when what he's saying makes sense, my jaw goes slack again and if there were flies around, I'd be catching them. "*Never?*"

He shakes his head. "No."

"You haven't had…"

"Not since before Whit was born."

I'm not sure what shocks me more. The confession, the fact he's been celibate for eighteen years, or that he wants to break that streak with me.

"Dad!"

"Shit. We need to get downstairs or she'll come up here." He reaches for my hand and weaves his fingers through mine as though he has the right, as though he's been doing it for years. "But this *discussion* isn't over. If you're okay with it, I'd like to kiss you again."

I can't help the bark of laughter that bursts free. "Sorry. Not laughing at you."

"Oh." He tugs on my hand and gets us moving out of the bedroom. "What are you laughing at?"

"I'm not sure I'd call what just happened a kiss."

"No?"

"No. There was more to it."

The smile he shoots my way is blinding. "So you wouldn't mind doing it again? With me?"

His voice wobbles on the last two words and I'm shocked again.

How this man, so confident on the ice, can be insecure off it, boggles my mind. Except now I know some of his history, I understand it.

Squeezing his hand, I reassure him. "I more than don't mind. In fact I'd be very disappointed if you didn't kiss me again."

"Good. Okay. Good."

Laughing, I let him lead the way downstairs. We're not all the way down when the most delicious smell has my stomach rumbling loudly.

Pressing my free hand to my belly, I send a sheepish smile Beckett's way. "Guess I'm hungry."

"You haven't eaten since yesterday." He glances at the watch on his wrist. "Almost twenty-four hours."

"Really? What time is it?" I feel like I've slept for days but I can't have been out that long. My hair's still damp from my earlier shower.

"Five. PM."

"Wow. Okay, yeah, close to twenty-four hours. No wonder my belly feels hollow."

"The doctor said you might have a bit of nausea when you woke. I made soup though, so that should be gentle on your system."

"Soup?"

"Chicken noodle."

"Does it taste as good as it smells?"

"Yes!" Whitney races over to us as we reach the last step. "Here. This way."

Whitney grabs my hand and pulls me away from her father, tows me into the dining room where the table has been set for three.

"Sit down." She urges me into a chair already pulled out from the table. "I'll get the soup. Dad, get drinks. I brought a couple of the energy ones from the gym fridge up for Cami. Get her one of those as well as some ice water. I'll just have ice water." Directions given, Whitney leaves the room.

I tip my head up and smile at Beckett. "She usually give orders?"

"No, but she's been really worried about you." He bends over and brings his face close to mine. "She insisted on sitting with you when you fell asleep after your shower."

"Oh." I frown in the direction Whitney went. "I hate that."

"Don't. She's a lot like me, keeps to herself a lot so doesn't have a heap of friends. Her concern shows she's chosen you as one."

"Hmm... I'm sure you weren't happy about that."

"In the beginning, no, but then I wasn't taking into account who you are. Just saw your job and decided you couldn't be trusted."

"Probably didn't help that I was involved in the whole Draper incident."

Beckett blows out a breath. "Probably. Doesn't mean I don't owe you an apology."

"I think you've apologized enough."

"I haven't at all."

"Beckett, as much as I love words and they're how I make a living, I'm a firm believer in actions speaking louder than words and you've done nothing but show me you're sorry in the last few days."

"Huh."

"Dad, where are our drinks?" Whitney asks as she comes back, her hands gripping a large steaming pot.

"Sorry, on it now." Beckett shoots me a grin and a wink before he heads off.

"This is the best soup." Whitney places the pot on a folded towel between the three placemats. "I'll serve you just in case you're a little shaky. It's not one of the side effects of Zolpidem but you haven't eaten in a day so..."

Arching an eyebrow, I study her. "And you know this how?"

"I looked it up online. Dad told me what the doctor said but I needed more than that, so I did some research."

"I think not eating has drained me of energy and I'm glad you're happy to serve me."

Her gaze meets mine. "You're in luck because Dad's chicken noodle soup is the perfect thing to build your strength back up."

"It smells good."

"Tastes good too." She slowly spoons the fragrant liquid into a bowl. "I'll give you half a bowl first. You can have more if you feel up to it."

I press a hand to my rumbling tummy. "I'll definitely be having more."

"Don't make yourself sick. I can always heat up more later."

"Whitney."

Her eyes meet mine again. "Yeah?"

"I'm okay. I'm hungry, a little drained of energy, but other than that I feel completely normal."

"Are you sure?"

"Yes." Reaching out, I put a hand on her arm when she places my bowl in front of me. "I'm fine."

A sob catches in her throat before she blurts out, "It's all my fault."

"No." I push to my feet. Take the ladle from her hand and put it back in the pot. With both her hands in mine, I make sure I have her undivided attention. "None of what has happened is your fault."

"But the reporter the other day, and the one yesterday, they wanted to talk to me."

"That doesn't make any of it your fault."

"Dad said you wouldn't blame me."

"He's right, I don't. But I understand why you might feel as though you're to blame for everything. I've been there. In your shoes. When I was younger, my biological mother wasn't very nice to me and I was convinced it was my fault. That because I wasn't a good girl, she treated me the way she did."

"That's...were you bad?"

"No. But it didn't stop me from thinking I should be better. It took a lot of years and a lot of therapy to break that mindset. Don't fall into it. We can only control our own actions. If you had pushed me down the stairs or stabbed me with Zolpidem, then yes, it would definitely be your fault. But you didn't. Two very unscrupulous men did."

She studies me for a moment, checking to see if I'm speaking the truth no doubt, before saying, "I won't be upset if you decide not to let me stay with you when Dad has away games."

Her words have me jolting. "Oh, Whitney." Pulling her in, I wrap my arms around her. "This only makes me want to stay with you more."

"Oh."

She's almost the same height as me, maybe a little taller, I can't be sure because I'm not wearing shoes and she's got a pair of sneakers on, but our cheeks are lined up and my jaw brushes her shoulder.

Holding her tight, I will her to believe my words. I'm not worried if she doesn't. Like I said to Beckett. Actions speak louder than words. I'll just show her what has happened in the last few days has no effect on the way I feel about her.

And I'm beginning to suspect I'm falling for Whitney Higgison as deeply as I think I'm falling for her father.

BECKETT

I'm losing my mind. Not once in eighteen years has going without sex been an issue for me.

Not even as a teenager—when hormones are at their highest—was I consumed with the thought of sex the way I have been in the last twelve hours.

It's all I've thought about.

I don't remember wanting it this sharply when I was having sex either.

When I was with Whit's mom she always initiated, always took the lead, gave directions, and with the lust scorching my veins since I kissed Cam last night, I know I never truly desired Catrina physically.

The sensations and emotions I've experienced with Cam are real in a way they never were with Whit's mom even though I thought I was in love with her.

I'm sure I should see a therapist, probably look into it for Whit as well as myself, especially in the future when I tell her about her mom.

Meeting Cami, developing feelings for her, emotional and physical, has shone a light on my previous relationship like nothing else ever has.

It was all a lie.

To an extent I knew that, accepted Catrina didn't love me the way I loved her, but now...

Now I know I didn't love her at all. I loved the attention, the validation her perceived affection gave me. For someone starved of that for most of my life, it was addicting.

Except it was all fake.

From the moment she singled me out and offered to pay for my lunch, to the last time we were together only hours before I heard her make the appointment to abort our baby. All of it an act to suit her own needs.

And while I thought I understood why I was referred to as a victim, in the last twelve hours I've come to accept I was one.

I was preyed upon by a woman who'd gotten away with it before. A woman who would have done it again if I hadn't wanted to protect my child.

A child who's now a young woman and about to leave me alone in the house with the woman I can't stop thinking about having sex with.

"Are you sure it's okay?" Whit asks as she shoves a sweater in her bag.

"Yes, of course." I've never wanted to push Whit away before, but right now I'm on the verge of shoving her out the door.

Her gaze flickers over mine. "You're not worried about me?"

"Always. But I trust Chase and Natalie to look after you and I know you aren't stupid. You won't put yourself in a dangerous situation and if you find yourself in one, you'll do everything you can to get out of it."

"Huh." Whit tilts her head and studies me like I'm a puzzle to be solved.

For a second I wonder if she can see right through me, if she can see the reason I'm letting her out of my sight so soon after the incidents with Kenneth Dupre and Herman Draper is so I can be alone with Cami.

The doorbell interrupts her scrutiny and with a smile and

quick kiss to my cheek, she dashes for the door. "If you need me to come home, just call."

"I won't."

"But if you do, I'm okay with it."

"Whitbee, go, enjoy the day and I'll see you tonight."

"Will you tell Cami I said goodbye?" she tosses over her shoulder.

"Of course."

"And make sure she takes it easy. I know she seemed normal last night, but she still needs to rest," she tells me like I've never taken care of anyone before.

"Whit?"

With her hand on the front door, she looks back at me. "Yeah?"

"I've taken care of you multiple times over the years, I think I can handle making sure Cami doesn't overdo it today."

With a sheepish grin, she says, "Yeah, okay. I just feel bad that I get to have fun today and you two are stuck inside the house."

If only she knew the fun I plan to have while stuck inside this house.

On second thought, no, I don't ever want to think of her knowing the very adult fun you can have inside all day.

"We'll be fine. Go before they leave without you."

"Okay. See ya."

She's out the door before the last word is out of her mouth. With a chuckle, I check the door is shut and the lock engaged before I set the alarm.

The new security system is another reason I want Cam here. I know her father probably has one that rivals mine but *knowing* she's safe and *seeing* she's safe are two different things.

Satisfied no one is getting in without my knowledge, I head for the kitchen. Time to make some breakfast. I've been up a few hours, spent an hour of that in the gym and taken a shower.

Two showers.

Cold showers.

One at five when I woke sporting the biggest morning erection of my life beside a sound asleep Cam. And the second after an hour of physically punishing my body in various ways failed to extinguish the heat burning through me.

I've never experienced lust.

Sex has never been something I wanted or needed.

Until now.

Until Cami.

It's almost like my libido has been in hibernation and now that it's emerged from its dormant state, it's ravenous.

Just the thought of Cam has fire blazing along my nerves, stripping the endings bare and leaving them raw—oversensitive.

Last night when she went to bed, I breathed a sigh of relief only to discover my mistake a few hours later when I joined her in my bedroom.

Where she or I would sleep never came up in conversation. And with us having slept in the same bed a couple of times now, I didn't think twice about climbing the stairs to my room.

I didn't think twice until I crawled under the covers and Cam wiggled her way across the mattress and wrapped herself around me.

I've never slept with a woman before her. Never seen one naked.

I may as well be a virgin.

With my lack of experience, I should be nervous about pursuing a relationship with Cam but all I feel is excitement, pleasure, rightness.

How can someone I barely know feel so right?

And why does it feel like I know her?

I can't get a handle on the feelings Cam inspires.

Caution and fear should take precedence except they're not. In fact, they're nowhere near what's rolling around inside me.

"Hey."

Spinning around, I find Cam, hair rumpled, my t-shirt brushing the tops of her thighs, standing a few feet away, and the hard-on I've spent most of the morning trying to tame is back with a vengeance.

I don't think, just react.

Hands on her waist, I lift her onto the counter and step between her legs.

Mouth and hands on her, I barely give either of us time to breathe.

I'm rough, reckless, ravenous.

I'm not holding back. I can't.

The desire I feel, the fire burning bright, is marrow deep and if I don't quench my thirst, it will take us both down in a blaze so hot there will be nothing left but ashes.

Her hands are on my head, her fingers tangled in my hair, tugging as though she's trying to keep me close.

She needn't worry. I'm not going anywhere until we've doused the flames burning my bones, licking at my skin.

I might not know from experience what to do, but I know what I want to do.

And it's not Cam on my kitchen counter.

"Fuck." Tearing my mouth from hers, I gasp for breath, my whole body vibrating with need. "We have to move this to the bedroom."

She looks at me like I'm crazy. "I'm good here." To prove her point she uses her grip on my hair to yank me closer again.

"I haven't had sex in eighteen years. I'm not breaking that run by fucking you on my kitchen counter," I growl as I pull her against me and lift. "I want you in my bed. Spread out so I can touch every inch of you."

"Oh, okay." Her fingers slip from my hair as she lowers her arms and wraps them around my neck. "I'm good with that too."

Turning with her in my arms, I head for the stairs only to be brought up short when she leans back.

"Wait. Wait? Eighteen years?" She looks at me incredulously. "You were serious about that? I thought—"

"I'd never lie about something like that."

"No." She shakes her head. "You wouldn't lie about that."

"If you don't want to do this..." I can't believe I'm saying this, giving her time to rethink her decision, but we can't keep going if she's not fully onboard. I'd never force myself on anyone.

"Beckett, you cannot honestly believe I would want to stop after that kiss. After last night's kiss."

"I... Well." I shrug. "I might not be any good at this."

"Oh, you're plenty good at this and we've barely started. Take me wherever you want as long as it means you'll kiss me again."

"I hope you'll let me do more than kiss you."

"Beckett, you better do more than kiss me. I want you to fuck me."

My dick throbs and it's all I can do to keep us on track. Laughing, I get us moving again and when I reach the stairs, I take them two at a time.

"Pretty sure I'm going to embarrass myself the second I get inside you, especially when you say things like that. But I need to make it worth it for you before we get to that."

"But—"

"Yeah, I'm practically a virgin. Doesn't mean I don't know how to make it good for you."

"You already have."

"Not enough. I'd prefer to strip you out of my shirt and indulge everything I can think of but never done."

"I'm sure you did a lot with..."

"No. And that's another ugly story I'd rather not get into right now. I want us to be the only two people in my bed when I get you there."

"We will be."

"Good. Because I've got a lifetime of sexual exploration to do."

As we reach my bedroom door, Cam whispers, "Stop."

Not about to do anything she's not up for, I stop. "What?" I lower my voice to match hers.

"Where's Whitney?"

"Out."

"Out?"

"Yes, out. For the day. With Chase and Natalie and the kids," I explain.

"Oh. When did she leave?"

"About five minutes ago. She said to say goodbye."

"And she'll be gone all day?"

"Cam."

"We have the house to ourselves?"

"Yes. Now can we—" The look she gives me, the curve of her mouth, has me losing all thoughts.

The smile curling her lips is the sexiest thing I've ever seen. Then again, it could be because she's in my arms and I know what we're going to spend the day doing that's making me think that.

"What are you thinking?" I ask when she continues to smile at me.

"How do you feel about a bubble bath?"

Frowning, I ask, "Hip still hurting?"

"No. My hip is fine." To demonstrate she squeezes my waist with her legs. "I've always fantasized about having sex in a big tub overflowing with bubbles like the one in your bathroom."

"You're never done it?" Why does the thought of sharing a first with Cam have a burst of satisfaction filling my chest and my cock twitching?

"Nope. Never dated a guy with one big enough." She rocks against me. "Not big enough in more ways than one."

"As much as I'd like to experience that with you, and we will before the end of the day, I need you on my bed. I want to explore every inch of you, find every spot that makes you shiver, every spot that makes you sigh. I want to learn everything that pleases you, how you taste, what your skin smells like, how soft it is."

"This is sounding very one-sided."

I move into the bedroom. "It is. Because I'm going to embarrass myself in two seconds once I get inside you or if you touch me."

"I doubt that."

I chuckle. "You'll see."

"Yes, we will."

I'm not sure how, but it sounds like I've laid down a challenge. I'm up for anything with this woman. If she needs me to prove I'm on a very short fuse, I will.

But first I'm going to light her fuse and send her soaring.

CAMI

"Stop." Panting, I grip Beckett's hair tighter. "Please. Beckett. I can't."

"One more. Please," he speaks against my slick folds and sends another wave of pleasure so sharp it hurts rolling through me.

I've come three times, my pussy so sensitive even his breath feels too much. I'm right there. On the edge of spiraling out of control. Again.

A lick later, a thrust and press of fingers and I'm screaming through another orgasm so pleasurable it's blinding.

"There. Right there is where I want you."

I have no idea when he moved from between my legs, but his face is in mine, his forehead resting against me as he raises my leg and drives himself inside me.

"Beck!"

"Fuck. Cam."

Neither of us moves. He's buried deeper than anyone before. Stretching me in ways I'm not used to.

I knew he was bigger than any other guy but knowing and feeling can't be compared.

Nothing could have prepared me for Beckett fucking me. And he hasn't even moved yet.

"Cam?"

"Mmm..."

"I need."

"Take it. Take whatever you need." The urge to give this man everything he's never had outweighs any discomfort I might feel being impaled on his impressive cock.

He hasn't let me touch him, hasn't let me explore his body the way he did mine but I'm okay with that. I'm okay to give him this first time.

"I don't want to hurt you."

"You can't."

"I could. I can't hold—"

"Don't hold back!" Wrapping my legs around his back, I lock my ankles and use them as leverage to move underneath him.

"Cam."

"Fuck me, Beck."

"I don't want—"

"You do. Take me. Fuck me. I'm yours." The last two words feel like a vow. A promise. One I'm incapable of examining when Beckett pulls his hips back then punches them forward again.

Air rushes from my lungs as he sets a rhythm so fast, so hard, the headboard bangs the wall in an accompanying beat.

"Fuck. Dammit. I knew it," Beckett pants into my neck where he's tucked his face. "Fuck!"

His hips stutter, the plunge of his cock short and rapid before he arches back and drives himself deep with a guttural cry of triumph.

Every pulse of his release bathes me in warmth and I'm wondering why I'm not concerned we forgot protection.

I'm not on anything. Haven't been in years, but even when I was, I *never* let a man inside me without a condom.

Except Beckett is different.

He's been different from the start of whatever this is. And it's looking like love.

"We didn't use anything." He opens his eyes, his gaze boring into mine. "My come is leaking out of you."

I don't know why his words make me laugh but they do. And as my stomach muscles contract, more come is pushed out.

Beckett's head lowers, his gaze moving to where our bodies are still pressed together. "I can't decide if that's the hottest thing ever or disgusting."

"Well, considering you're still hard inside me, I'm going to say the first?"

"Yeah." He nods. "Yeah." His head rises and the smile on his face could only be described as cocky. "Yeah. It's hot as fuck and I want to fuck you again."

"I'm not that sure you stopped the first time." I clench around him.

"Hmm…maybe it's your turn to take over."

His words are confusing for all of a second because in that breath of time he slides his hands under me and rolls.

How he manages to keep us connected as he reverses our positions I don't know. But staring down at him, seeing the satisfied, predatory look in his eyes has my insides clenching of their own accord.

"Your turn to fuck me, Cam." He punctuates his words with upward thrusts of his hips, each one grinding my sensitive clit into the base of his cock.

"Oh." Leaning forward, I splay my hands on his chest and push up with my thighs.

It isn't long before I'm bouncing on his cock fast and furious. And if I roll my pelvis a certain way, I stroke my clit with each plunge down.

"I want to suck your tit."

Beckett's words make me falter. Snap my gaze to his. "Do whatever you want."

"No. I need to ask."

He doesn't say it but I know he's referring to Whitney's

mother. And that small intrusion of his past as my pace slowing until I stop completely.

Bending over I bring my forehead down to rest on his. "You don't need to ask me. I give you permission to do what you want but I promise, if I don't like something you do, or it hurts, I will tell you."

"I'd hate myself if I hurt you."

"You'd never do it on purpose."

"That's not comforting."

"It's life. But intent is important. You would never set out to hurt me."

"No. I wouldn't."

"And I promise to never set out to hurt you either."

"I don't know what we're doing."

"Pretty sure we're having sex."

"That's not what I mean."

With a sigh, I push up and look down at the concern in Beckett's eyes. "I know."

"Do you? Know what we're doing?"

"No. Not completely."

"I can't help worrying I'll fuck up somehow."

"We'll both fuck up, Beck. It's life. Nobody is perfect. We'll make mistakes but I will never intentionally hurt you the way she did. I won't lie to you about what's happening or how I feel. I don't know the full story, don't need to know to understand whatever we do, wherever we go from here, it has to be transparent."

"I think I'm falling for you."

I grin. "Yeah?"

When he nods, I lower my lips to his.

"Good. Because I think I'm falling for you too."

I don't give him time to say more. I kiss him deep and rock my hips in slow rolls.

It's lazy and luscious, the kiss and the sex.

And for now I'll ignore the little voice in my head that says this isn't sex. It's making love. We're not ready for that. We've barely moved past Beckett's initial dislike of me.

"Harder."

Beckett's command is accompanied with his hands on my waist guiding my movements. It's hard to deny this man anything and I have to wonder if it will always be that way or if it's because this is new. Newer for him than me, but still.

The flush of new emotions can make you do things you wouldn't normally and I don't want to fall into that category.

I want us to be real.

I want us to be building on the friendship we've found ourselves developing.

I want us to be more than a flash and burn.

He's been celibate for most of his life, and I haven't exactly been hopping from bed to bed. This could be nothing more than an itch getting scratched.

"Stop thinking." In a reverse of his earlier move, Beckett turns us and stares down at me. "Just feel. Feel how good we are."

Tilting my hips with his hands, he rocks in and out in slow deliberate thrusts designed to keep my attention. Deep and hard and filling, every plunge of his cock inside me lights a spark that travels along my nerves and ignites a flame.

"Yeah, that's it." His pace picks up. "Like that. Take all of me."

I can't talk, can only stare into his gaze and watch the way his emotions flicker through the light brown rim around pupils blown so wide his eyes appear bottomless, alive with possibilities I've never imagined.

"I want you with me." His words are double-edged and we both know it. But again, I'm helpless to deny this man anything.

"I am."

"What do you need?"

"You. I just need you."

"You have me." He pushes harder. Drives deeper. "You have all of me."

I'm not sure if it's his words, or the way he hits my clit with every down thrust, that has me riding the edge once more.

He's wringing me tighter and tighter with each stroke of his hard cock through my swollen flesh and when he tips my hips, brings his knees up, and changes the angle, I sail right over that edge.

"Beck!" My body clamps tight. From head to toes, muscles contract so tight it's almost painful as pleasure surges through me.

"Fuck! Cam!"

Following me over, Beckett crushes me beneath him as his body lets go. It's a weight I'll gladly bear. A comfort and satisfaction in knowing I did that. I took this masculine, capable man and brought him to his knees.

We stay that way, Beckett like a weighted blanket on top of me for long moments before he lifts his head and smiles.

"How about that bath now? It's seems we're both a little sticky."

"I think we need to change the sheets first."

"Nah, we can do that later. Or not. I figure we'll just mess them up again. Come to think of it. There probably isn't any point taking a bath either. I'm only going to want to get you dirty again."

"We can't spend all day having sex."

He looks affronted. "Why not?"

"Well, we, um..."

"See, no logical reasons we can't do this for the rest of the day. You won't do it with Whit in the house so I need to make the most of the time she isn't here."

Before I can say a word, he rolls us over and lift me off him. The loss of his heat inside me is sharp and shocking but I don't have time to focus on it long because he has us out of bed and heading for the bedroom door, me over his shoulder.

"Beckett! What the hell?"

"I want to revisit earlier."

"Earlier?" I have no idea what he's talking about and being upside down isn't helping my mind work it out.

"Yeah, earlier when I said I didn't want to fuck you on my kitchen counter."

"You want to have that conversation again?" My brain is obviously overflowing with blood because I still can't work out what he's doing.

"Yep." His hand comes down on my bare ass, making me yelp. "I want to fuck you on it now."

"Now? But we just—"

Another slap to my ass has me sucking in a breath. "Hush, woman. I'm thinking about other places in the house I can fuck you before my daughter comes home and cock-blocks me."

"I... Um." Yeah, I have no words. I think he's serious. And if he is, I'll be lucky if I can walk this evening.

"You promised to tell me if you didn't like something or I hurt you."

His soft words have me relaxing. "I did. I will."

"I won't be mad if you don't want to do this."

"Beck, the only time I'll get mad is if you wind me up and leave me hanging. Although, sometimes that can be fun."

Delayed gratification has never really been my thing but the few times I've done it have been enjoyable. And Beckett admitted to his limited experience. He might enjoy it.

I add it to a mental list of things to suggest we try in the future.

"All right. Fucking on the kitchen counter now. Bubble bath after that."

Smiling, I hold onto his naked hips as he moves through the house. "Can I use scented bubbles?"

"Are there any other kind?"

His question is genuine and I remember his limited experience and exposure to adult females. "Yeah, you can get them in all sorts of scents. I had one that was fresh snow scented last Christmas."

"I only have whatever Whit bought when I had the tub installed."

"Let's worry about it later. Right now, I think you mentioned counter sex."

"I did." With a shrug of his shoulder, he has me upright and my ass on the cold counter. "But first. I'm hungry."

Disappointment floods me. "Oh."

Laughter booms through the room. "You should see your face."

I know I'm pouting and I shouldn't be ready for sex again already but I am.

"When I say hungry..." He grips my knees and shoves them wide. "I meant for you."

In the next second Beckett is on his knees, his face buried in my crotch, tongue thrusting deep inside me.

I don't have time to catch my breath. The man is a fast learner, he already knows his way around my pussy, and it takes little time for me to be crying out and convulsing with a bone-shaking orgasm.

When I can finally breathe again, when my brain is working enough to form words, I voice a question I asked earlier. "Can I suck your cock now?"

Climbing to his feet, one large hand wrapped around the cock I'm dying to taste, he contemplates my question.

"Come on. It's only fair. You've had your mouth on me all morning."

"Can I hold your head and fuck your face?"

Jesus. We've gone from zero to a thousand in seconds. I shouldn't be surprised. He may have been celibate but he's not asexual. And I can't stop myself from giving him what he wants.

"If that's what you want to do, then yes. You can fuck my face."

The grin that tilts his lips is little-boy cheeky and in total opposition to his next words.

"On your knees."

BECKETT

Going without sleep and dragging ass never felt so good.

In the weeks since Cam and I moved our relationship from sort-of-friends to lovers to whatever level comes next, I've spent every spare moment I can inside her.

We've managed the occasional night alone in the house but most of the time we're finding minutes for a quickie, or an hour if we're lucky.

And usually it's me forgoing my day naps that give us those hours.

She spends most nights at my house and even though Whit and I set up a guest room, I'm sure my daughter is well aware Cam doesn't sleep in the new bed we bought.

The arrangement has worked out for all of us. Cam works from home, which means she's there when Whit gets home from school if I'm not and neither of them are out where Draper or Dupre can get to them more than necessary.

The two men are the only dark spots in our lives.

Not even the couple of games the Rogues lost have dampened my mood. The fact they were close games, with goals scored in the dying seconds to clinch the win for the other teams, helps soften the blow.

None of us feels like losers.

"Hey."

Glancing up I see Chase coming toward me. "Hey, what's up?"

"The twins messaged to say they're staying at school longer because Whitney has something on."

"Whit does?" I wrack my brain to recall her schedule. I can't remember anything but I know if I needed to pick her up Cam would have told me. Sent me a gentle reminder a few hours before. It's another thing I'm more than happy with.

Cam has embraced my daughter as much as she has me. So much so, they team up against me when it's time to choose what to watch on movie night or what we're making for dinner.

We might not have talked about it, or publicized our relationship, but we're partners in every way that counts.

And Cam is the closest thing to a mother Whit has ever had. The bond between them is as solid as the one I feel between me and Cam.

I can't imagine our lives without her now.

"You okay?"

Focusing back on Chase, I smile. "Yeah, sorry. Just thinking."

"You thinking about coming out?"

"*What?*"

"Oh, come on, we all know you and Cami are together."

"Oh. That coming out. For a second, I thought... Never mind. Yes. We're together but we're taking it slow because of everything that's happened."

"Nothing has lately though, right? Those reporters haven't given you any more trouble?"

"No. Not that I'm aware of." His frown has me asking, "Do you know something?"

"No. Not really."

"What kind of answer is that."

Chase shrugs. "Whitney's been acting a little off according to the twins. I figured it was because of you and Cami but she loves Cami so I don't think that's it."

"She does love her, and the feeling is reciprocated, but it could be that making Whit a *little off*. A lot has changed in her life recently. First the move down here, the new school, and then the media thing, plus Cam."

Damn. I need to check in with Whit. I've let my relationship with Cam take over most of my thoughts and time.

"Thanks for the heads up. I'll talk to Whit tonight, see if I can get to the bottom of it."

"I'm sure it's nothing. The twins are still adjusting to being here too, and Whitney is the only friend they have."

"They haven't made others?"

"No. But that's not unusual for them. They have each other and rarely let anyone else into their circle. It's why I'm always so happy to have Whitney over and to be honest, I may have pushed that friendship more than I should. They're a few years younger than Whitney, she might not be the best choice for helping pull them out of their bubble."

"How are you doing? Not just with the move here, playing in the NHL. How are you and the girls doing?"

"We're okay. Gem helps a lot."

Chase's reference to the Rogues GM always makes me think there's more to their relationship, but from what I've seen it really is just a boss helping one of her employees. There aren't any longing glances or small touches, nothing to indicate they're more.

If there is a deeper relationship between them, they hide it better than me and Cam. Another thing to remember to talk about later.

First I need to make sure Whit is okay with me seeing Cam—with her basically living with us. And now I think about it, I'm sure that's what Chase's sisters are picking up on.

"Thanks for telling me what the twins said. I'll let you know how my talk with Whit goes so you can ease their minds."

"Thanks." Chase looks around the deserted Rogues gym. "You starting or finishing?"

"Finishing." Disappointment flashes across his face. "But I can stick around and spot you if you're doing weights."

"Nah, it's okay. Now that I don't have to get the twins, I'm going to get a half-hour run in before I have to leave to pick up Candace from daycare."

"Okay, I'll message you later about Whit. See you tomorrow at morning skate."

"Yep." He pops in earbuds. "See ya later."

I watch him a moment wondering if there was more to him seeking me out before shaking my head and heading out.

I'm through the building and almost to my car when Natalie calls my name. Turning around, I see her coming toward me at a fast clip and marvel at how she manages to do that in the heels she always wears.

"Beckett. I'm glad I caught you. Can you come to my office for a minute?"

"Ah, sure. Is something wrong?"

The way she looks around as though someone might be listening has my instincts rising.

"Natalie?"

"We should talk in my office."

Before I can argue, she's power walking back the way she came and I've got no choice except to follow.

Between the players' parking lot and her office she remains tight-lipped, and the further we go, the angrier I get.

I don't like secrecy, I had enough of it with Catrina, and no, it doesn't escape me that Cam and I have been carrying on behind closed doors too.

The more my thoughts spiral, the more angry I get at the position I've put myself in. Again.

Is it the only way I know how to be with someone? Behind closed doors?

"Beckett." Oakley's voice has my head snapping around. "Ray is finding them both."

"Finding them?" My gaze flies to Natalie. "What the hell is going on?"

"Sit down and I'll explain what I know."

"No. Talk. Now." Crossing my arms, I brace for whatever she's about to tell me.

"I received a call a few moments ago regarding Whitney's mother."

Her words make no sense. "Whit's mother?"

"Yes. Catrina Hooper."

If a person can spontaneously combust without actually blowing up, I do it.

"What the fuck!"

"Please, Beckett. Take a seat." Oakley places her hand on my arm and I shake her off before rounding on her.

"What the fuck did Cam tell you?" I get right in her face, but like the badass she's shown herself to be, Oakley James Alcott doesn't back away even when a two-hundred-fifty pound man hovers over her.

"Cami has told us nothing."

"Bullshit! She's the only one who knows the truth!"

Fuck. I grab my head. What have I done?

"I trusted her!"

"Beckett! I won't ask you again to sit down but if you don't calm the hell down, I'll get Dr. Kerns up here to give you something to calm your ass down."

Natalie's raised voice snaps me out of angry outburst. Then again, the sudden fear for Whit might have done that.

"Whitney!" Spinning on my heel I find the door barred by one of the men on the Rogues security team.

"She's fine. We know where she is and two of our men are retrieving her right now."

"Retrieving her? She's not a dog!"

"No, she's not, and I apologize for the terminology, but I'm not used to speaking to clients." The man's sheepish expression deflates some of my anger but does nothing to relieve my fear.

"Where is she? Whit?"

"She's at school. I'm told she had an appointment with the school counselor."

Just the mention of the position has a violent shudder rippling down my spine. I don't recall Whit mentioning seeing the school's counselor. I know she's spoken with the careers advisor but counselor?

Turning back to the room I find Oakley and Natalie waiting for me. The sympathetic looks on their faces has my anger reducing further.

"Sorry. I..."

How do I explain my outburst without revealing my secret? Hell, if they know Whit's mother's name they probably understand my reaction. With the initial rush of anger and panic subsiding I'm able to think more clearly.

Even if I could get past the guy at the door I need to know what's happening before I go charging out in defense of my daughter. Doing as originally asked, I walk over to Natalie's desk and take one of the visitor seats in front of it.

Elbows on knees, head bowed because I can't look at anyone when I hear what they say, I ask, "Tell me about the call."

"It was Fenton Barnes. He wanted to know what I knew about Whitney's mother, Catrina Hooper. I, of course, know nothing and told him so. He then told me to find you and lock you down, he'd get Cami and Whitney here."

"I don't understand." Rubbing my hands over my head doesn't bring me any clarity.

"Neither do we, but from your reaction this isn't a simple neglectful mother story," Oakley adds as she joins me in a chair in front of the GM's desk. "And I really don't understand you lashing out at Cami about whatever this is."

Fuck! Cam was right. I need to tell Natalie and I may as well tell Oakley and Blake while I'm at it.

"Is Coach Watts around? I'd rather only talk about this once."

"She's on her way up." At Natalie's words, the door behind us swings open and slams into the back of the security guy making him grunt.

"Oops. Sorry." Coach Watts slips inside. "What's going on? Bran just called and said there was some exclusive story being aired tonight about Beckett. Something about a sordid affair and stealing his daughter from her mother."

I'm so shocked by her words I can't speak.

Everyone else seems to have been affected the same, because for long seconds nobody speaks.

"Okay, this is obviously news..." Coach is pulling her phone from her pocket. "Let me call Bran back and get more details."

"What show? I don't need anything but the name of the show," Natalie demands as she too picks up her phone to make a call.

I don't hear either conversation. I'm still stuck on Coach Watt's words.

Something about a sordid affair and stealing his daughter from her mother.

It's kind of true. I did have a sordid affair. And in a way, I stole my daughter, but not from her mother. I stole her from the jaws of death.

"Beckett!" Oakley snaps her fingers in front of my face. "Snap out of it. What are we dealing with? We can't fight it if we don't know what it is."

"I. Whit." I swallow. Hard. "She's everything to me."

"We get that. It's why whatever the hell we're dealing with *will* be dealt with. Now explain."

"No one knows except Cam." Swallowing again, I force the next words out. "Not even Whit knows."

"That I understand. What I don't know is what no one knows."

Eyes on Oakley, I open my mouth but can't get the words past the lump in my throat.

"Here. Drink this." Natalie shoves a tumbler of amber liquid in front of me. "I know you don't drink alcohol during the season but two mouthfuls won't hurt. Drink."

I've never been a drinker. Didn't have the access or money as a teen and once Whit came into my life, I had no time to indulge even if I wanted to. And that hasn't changed as she's gotten older.

But maybe a drink will help. Taking the glass I down the two fingers in one go.

The burn feels good going down and better when it settles in my churning gut. Handing back the empty glass I start at the beginning.

"My mother was a drug addict. By the time I was thirteen, I was in and out of foster care so many times I'm sure the doors never closed behind me. At thirteen she was found dead in a gutter and I went to live with Mama Dot. She was the first woman to care for me."

I take a deep breath before going on.

"The second woman was my high school counselor. Catrina Hooper."

The breath Natalie sucks in tells me she understands where I'm going but I can't stop now or I'll never start again.

"The year I turned fifteen, Ms. Hooper became Catrina. I can't even remember the moment it stepped over the line and at the time I didn't believe that it had. Now, as an adult, and after talking with Cam, I see that line was a trench so wide it should never have been spanned. But I'm not sorry about what happened or how it fell apart because without any of it there is no Whitney."

"She's Whitney's mother."

"Yes. A twenty-eight year old high school counselor gave birth to my daughter five days after I turned sixteen."

"And Whitney doesn't know?"

I look at Oakley. "Why would I tell a child that?"

Oakley waves her hand. "Ignore that question, it was the dumbest thing to ever come out my mouth."

"Catrina was arrested and jailed before Whit was born and I

changed my name to give us both a clean slate and a chance to have a future without the stigma of her mother's actions hanging over us."

"You were just a kid." Blake crouches beside my chair. "I can't imagine dealing with Drew as a sixteen-year-old. Bex, you and Whitney are a miracle, you know that right?"

"Someone pointed it out recently."

"Cami."

I glance at Natalie. "Yes. Cam."

"It really is a miracle you are where you are, that Whitney is the amazing kid she is," Oakley adds with a shake of her head. "It could have turned out so different for the two of you."

"I know. But from the moment they placed my daughter in my arms, I knew I'd do anything and everything to secure her future. To make sure she got every opportunity possible. To make sure her life was the best it could be. To make sure she didn't have to fight to survive every day like I did."

"You did more than give that to Whitney, Beckett. You gave it to yourself too."

We all turn at the sound of Cam's voice.

Tears stream down her face, the lines marked by her makeup.

"I can't stop it from airing. Dad and I have been going round and round for over an hour. They won't pull it from the lineup." A sob rips through her chest and I'm on my feet, heading her way when she says words that remind me why I fell for this woman. "I can't protect her from this."

Pulling her into my arms, I hold her tight and offer no words because there aren't any. Neither of us can protect Whit from what's about to happen, what we can do is tell her before it becomes public knowledge.

CAMI

"Where's Whit? Is she here yet?"

I don't know who Beck is talking to but I guess it's the guy who tried to stop me from getting in to Nat's office until he recognized me.

"They're pulling into the underground dock area now."

"Is there media outside the arena?" Nat asks, her GM hat firmly in place.

"No, but Ray thought it was better to be safe than sorry. They have Chase Hawkins's sisters as well."

"Good. I'll let him know I have them here."

"He was heading to pick up Candace after a run." Beck's voice rumbles in his chest beneath my ear.

"I know. I'll message him the change of plans."

It's hard to reconcile my friend in a maternal role, but that's what Nat is to Chase's sisters. Or maybe it's more of a big sister role. Kind of like my relationship with Whitney.

"You need to tell her." I tip my head back to look up at Beck, I can't bring myself to let him go yet. "She needs to hear it from you."

"I will. But I want you with me."

"I think it might be better if it's just you two first. I'll be there for her after. You too. You know that, but this is about the two of you before it's about the three of us."

I hate sending him off to do this on his own, hate not being about to offer Whitney my support while she hears this news but I don't think it's my place, even if I'm entrenched in their lives now.

They were a family first. And what she's about to learn doesn't involve me.

"Okay. If you think that's best." Beck's gaze goes over my head. "Is there a room I can use to speak to Whit privately?"

"Sure, how about the owner's suite, Cami can wait out—"

The door bursts open, Whitney barreling in, tears streaming down her face, and I know it has to be almost a replay of my own entry.

"Whit." "Whitney."

Beck and I speak and move as one, both of us heading for the teenager crying her eyes out.

She's a blubbering mess when Beck pulls her into him, her words inaudible as she sobs around them.

It takes a few minutes for her to calm down and during that time Nat does what Nat does best and directs everyone else out of the room. When the door closes quietly behind them, I glance up at Beck and indicate my intention to leave with a tip of my head.

The shake of his has me frowning and staying in place.

"Whitbee, baby, I need you to listen to me. I need to tell you something—"

"I know," Whitney wails. "It was me! I told her and she told *them!*"

Beck's confused gaze meets mine but I'm no help. I haven't a clue what she's talking about.

"Told who what, baby?" Beck asks.

"The counselor. At school. She's not supposed to tell anyone what we talk about."

I feel Beck go rigid. And if my mind is putting together the pieces correctly, then father and daughter have now both been betrayed by the same authoritative position.

"Whitney, what did you tell the counselor?" The coldness in Beck's voice sends a shiver down my spine.

"Who you really are. Who I think my mom was." The sobs overtake her again and my gaze locks with Beck's.

"I thought it was you," he murmurs over the top of Whitney's head. "When Natalie first asked me about Catrina, I instantly blamed you."

His words send a shaft of pain through my chest so sharp I take a step back.

"It was knee-jerk. I know, in my head, my heart, you'd *never* do that."

I hear his words, the sincerity in them, but it isn't enough to snuff out the hurt they inflict. "You thought I'd told the media. That I'd revealed your secret to the world..."

"No. Not really. I was panicking, not thinking."

I hold up a hand. The calmness that comes over me is numbing.

"I'll leave you two alone. Talk to Whitney, get everything straightened out with her. You have an hour at the most to make a decision on what to do about the segment that's going live tonight. If you want to get in front of it, you need to do it sooner than later."

I don't know how I walk out without breaking down. Don't know where I'm going or what I'll do, I just know I need to get away from Beckett.

Oakley, Natalie, and Blake meet me in the hallway and one look at my face telegraphs my need for privacy. Oakley, the best of best friends, grabs my arm and pulls me toward her office.

Once enclosed in the quiet room with the three people who know more about me than anyone else, I let my emotions free.

It was already an emotional afternoon, the call from Dad, the hunt and barter to get the segment on Beckett and Whitney trashed, the fear for Whitney, now Beckett's confession.

I've been a tearful mess for the last hour at least and with the ache in my chest, the hollow feeling in my belly, I doubt the tears will stop any time soon.

"What do you need other than tissues?" Nat asks.

"N-n-nothing."

All I just need is to let it out.

Let go of the hurt the man I love inflicted with a few words, with his first instinctual reaction to a situation he had every right to react to.

I have to believe instinct and habit collided. That his words are true and he doesn't believe I'd ever reveal information about him or Whitney to the media. To anyone.

"He was panicking. He knew it wasn't you," Oakley explains. "He's just used to going it alone with Whitney, you're one of the first people in his life to protect her the way he does. He doesn't expect it."

Oakley's insight offers some relief. I know she's right and once I get over the hurt, get the emotions of today behind me, I'll be able to look at it more clearly.

Until then I'm going to have a good cry—something I've rarely done—and purge all the pain.

"I know." I sniff back a sob. "I just need."

"To cry." Blake wraps her arm around me. "You cry until you can't anymore and we'll be right here with you."

"Th-thanks."

I don't know how long I sit with my best friends to either side of me when Nat pushes a bunch of tissues into my hand. "I need to go out there. I have to check on things and get others in place. Let the rest of the entire org know we're on a media blackout."

"Okay."

"Do you have a plan to deal with this?"

Glancing up, I look at her.

She smiles. "I know you. You were running scenarios in your head from the moment you found out what was happening."

Nodding, I use the tissues to wipe my face. "Give me a

minute. But basically I think we should do what we did when Whitney outed herself. Share their story first."

"As much as necessary for the vultures to leave them alone."

"Yes."

"I'll get the owner's suite set up for it. Can you get it aired?"

"Dad's on his way. He's got every station he owns on alert. I think he's planning to blast it as far as he can the second it's recorded."

"Smart."

"I was going to ask but he beat me to it when he offered." Blowing my nose to clear the clog from my voice, I watch Nat tap away at her phone with a frown on her face.

"I need to get out there. One of the guards says someone in the media is trying to get in—"

"Oh!" I bounce to my feet. "It might be Deb. I called her."

Laughing, Nat says, "It's not Deb. I'm pretty sure it's your dad."

"They won't let him in?"

"I told them to lock the place down." She grins. "This is the reason I worked so hard to convince Ray to work exclusively with the Rogues."

"I need to clean up." I glance at Oakley. "Can I use the—"

"Don't even ask, woman. You own the team, the executive restroom is for all of us to use whenever we need." She looks at my clothes. "I might have something for you to wear. You can't interview them in that."

"I wasn't planning—"

"I want you to do it."

Beck's voice has me spinning to face the door. "Beckett—"

"If we're going on camera, Whit and I want you across from us."

"But—"

"No buts. We want you with us. We're okay with telling the world our story if you're beside us."

"Beck." My gaze moves to the young woman behind him, and I can't keep my emotions from my voice or my eyes. "Whitney."

In a second she's across the room in my arms, and the tears I thought had stopped return for another round.

"I'm so sorry."

"Shh…it's okay," I soothe her while my watery gaze locks on her father.

"I didn't mean—"

"I know, Whitney. And it's okay. You should have been able to talk to the school counselor without worry."

The scoff-laugh she emits put a smile on my face. "Yeah, except my history proves they can't be trusted."

"Don't label all of them by the actions of a few." Beck tips his chin in acknowledgment of my subtle dig of his initial reaction to me months ago.

"I found a folder in Dad's desk. It had everything about what Dad went through. The court documents don't have his name on it, but it wasn't hard to put it all together and work out who he was, who I am."

"And you needed a sounding board to process it."

"Yes."

"I understand why you did what you did but I'm going to tell you something I want you to remember in the future. My mom is a lawyer, you hire her for a dime and you can tell her anything you want and she'll never repeat it to anyone. She's a vault."

"But—"

Pulling back, I bring my hands up to frame her face. "No. Listen to me. She's your person. No matter when, no matter what, she's who you go to."

"She's right, Whitney."

We turn to find Mom and Dad have joined us.

Turning to Beckett, Mom asks, "You give her an allowance?"

"Yes."

"Can she get an advance on next months?"

"Ah…"

Holding out her hand, Mom demands, "Give me a dime."

"I don't have—"

"I do." Whitney pulls free of my hold and rummages in her pocket. "Here. It's all I've got."

Mom accepts the dollar bill and offers her hand to Whitney. "Consider me on retainer as your legal counsel."

"I've my own lawyer?"

"Shake her hand, young lady, because you're going to need someone to direct all the inquiries that are bound to head your way after today," Dad says.

His words have my gaze darting to Beck. "You should have someone too."

"Dana, you up for another client?"

"Speaking of that." Nat steps forward. "I've got something I want to talk to you about, Dana."

"Uh-oh, looks like my wife is about to work for the Rogues."

Oakley slips her arm through Dad's. "We do like to keep it in the family."

"I hate to break this love-fest up but we've got things to do." Blake grabs my hand. "First, we need to get everyone cleaned up so we don't look like we've been dragged across the ice and forced to talk about how Bex and Whitney are a miracle born from a deplorable situation."

"I wouldn't call it deplorable," Beck objects.

"Maybe not but what it was doesn't matter. What matters is where the two of you are now."

Blake's words are true and give me an idea.

"What if we talk more about the steps you took in order to give yourself and Whitney the best life? We can talk about Mama Dot and her hand in getting you through those first years, the joy of making the NHL at nineteen and knowing you were reaching the goals you set to give your daughter the life she deserves."

"Gloss over Catrina's part?" Beck asks.

"Yes. We can add small details. Enough for those interested in more to be able to find it."

"They can look it up themselves."

"Exactly."

"Can we do some kind of disclaimer that we won't be answering any other questions after this interview?"

"I think so, but you'll get them regardless."

"I figured." Beck takes a deep breath. "Okay, let's get this done so we can go home."

The hand he holds out proves the same as everything else about Beck, impossible for me to resist.

Using my hand to pull me in, he wraps his arms around me and presses his face into the side of my hair where he murmurs, "And by home, I mean our home. I know this isn't the right place or time, but I realized something when you left us in Natalie's office. Something I need you to know. I love you."

"Beck."

"I don't know when it happened, it feels like it's always been there, but watching you walk away and not knowing if you'd come back is something I never want to see again."

"I was coming back."

"I couldn't be sure of that. I want to be sure of that. I know this is quick and possibly reckless, but I want to marry you. I want to come home to you and Whit and any other kids we have."

Jerking back I lock my gaze on his. "You want more kids?"

"Yeah, I loved having Whit. And my biggest regret is not having more, giving her siblings."

"You... I..." Blinking rapidly, I try to stop the tears from falling. Again. "I don't know what to say."

He grins. "Say yes."

"Yes?"

He arches an eyebrow.

"Yes to all of it. Marriage. Coming home to us. Babies." The last word comes out a squeak. *Oh shit.* Closing my eyes I try to remember the last time...

Holy shit!

"Ah, Beck, can we go somewhere else to talk for a second?"

He eyes me before grabbing my hand and tugging me toward the door. "Give us a minute."

With no explanation to those around us, we leave and head down the hall to Nat's office. Once inside, Beck closes and locks the door behind us.

Turning me to face him, he grabs both my hands and locks his eyes with mine. "Tell me."

"I think I might be pregnant."

"You"—he shakes his head. "Come again?"

"I'm not a crier and I've done nothing but cry today and now that I'm thinking about it and you mentioned babies and the last few weeks, I've noticed certain pants don't fit but I can't be sure."

"Cam. Take a breath." Bringing our joined hands to his chest, he lowers his forehead to mine. "If you are, I'll be thrilled. If you aren't and you want to be, we'll try to make it happen."

"I don't know what I want. I've honestly never thought about kids until just now."

"Okay. And how do you feel about it now you are thinking about it?"

"Excited?"

"Is that a question?"

"I..." Taking a deep breath I try to pull my thoughts together. "It would be a little piece of you and me."

"He or she would."

"Would you really be okay doing it again?"

"I love Whit, loved it when she was little too. I miss those days and I'm not old, I won't be working after this contract so—"

"What?"

With a smile he explains. "When I signed the deal to play for the Rogues, I knew it would be my last years in the NHL. I'm retiring when my contract is up."

"Does Nat know that?" I whisper.

"No. Why are we whispering?" he asks in an equally quiet voice.

"In case she's listening." I look around. "She's probably got cameras in here too."

A burst of laughter shakes Beck's chest. "You know I've never laughed with a woman the way I do you."

"Whitney is a woman," I point out.

"Whit's my kid, laughing with her is a given. But you..." He shakes his head. "You give me something I've never had before."

"What?"

"A life."

"You've always had a life, Beck. You've had a successful career and raised a daughter."

"Yeah, I had a life, but with you, Whit and I are finally living it."

EPILOGUE

BECKETT

Less than a minute until the end of the third period and Vegas pulls their goalie.

It's a good move when we're tied up in the final game of the series and I'm surprised Coach Alcott hasn't done the same.

Then again, Chase has proved almost impossible to get past all season and if anyone can keep us from conceding a goal, it's him.

This is our last chance to make it to the Cup and I'm pulling hard on every ounce of energy I have left to make sure we fight right up to the final horn.

Vegas moves into our end, their extra man giving them an advantage, but fuck if we're letting them use it.

Bran gets his stick on a puck edge and sends it out of the huddle against the boards in my direction and I'm pretty sure I don't breathe when Caron, Vegas's top scorer, gets between it and me.

But we aren't giving up that easy even if my legs feel like they're about to give out and I'm positive Bran and Mikel feel the same.

A cheer shakes the arena when every player on the ice forms a huddle in front of the goal. Chase is at the back, guarding his goal like a troll guards his bridge. He'll eat any fucker alive who dares to cross the line.

Sticks are flying, poking at skates and feet and empty space.

No one seems to be able to get to the puck and the mash of players and equipment looks like a bunch of newbies let loose on the ice for the first time. None of us appear to have a clue what we're doing.

A gap opens up to my left, the space right in front of the net open wide except for Chase holding position.

There's a flash of black right before Chase pulls his stick back and sweeps it over the ice. The noise is barely a blip, but I hear it.

Blade on puck.

And the flash of black speeds away toward the other end of the rink.

Head up, my gaze locks on Chase but he's staring down the ice. Turning to see what has him focused so hard, I freeze.

Everything seems to go in slow motion after that. The players are still hunting around beside me for a puck that isn't there.

Chase straightens, his gaze locked firmly on Vegas's goal, and I move beside him.

The noise of the arena muffles, drones in my ears like the buzz of a thousand bees, but I don't take my eyes off the same thing Chase is looking at.

The puck.

What feels like a lifetime but is milli-seconds, I watch history in the making.

The puck, traveling at a speed my eyes can barely keep up with, whips down center ice, straight and true, sliding right over the goal line into the back of the net.

Chase's clearing shot is a goal.

Our goalie scored the game winning goal!

Pandemonium erupts around us.

Players, fans, officials.

It's a cacophony of noise that threatens to raise the roof.

"Holy fudge sticks!" Chase's shout swivels my head and I launch myself at him.

"We're playing for the Cup," I yell in his ear as I take us both to the ice. Bran jumps on next, followed by Mikel, Tasman, and Gannon.

More bodies pile on and it's then I realize the whole team is off the bench and on the ice. We're a pile of Rogues in front of our goal, the hero of the day lying at the bottom.

Chase's gaze is on me, his eyes wide in shock and I grab his mask, give it a shake.

"We're going to the Cup!"

"Holy fudge sticks!"

"I think you can say *holy fucking shit* right now, Chase," Bran laughs. "The kids aren't out here yet but they're coming."

Turning my head, I see it isn't only the team taking the ice. It's the coaches and staff, the GM and owners.

The second I see Cam, I'm shoving my way from beneath the pile. There's no way I want her walking on the slippery surface of the rink in her condition.

At five months she's barely showing and we're past the danger zone of the first trimester but I'm not risking her or our baby.

Two pushes and a glide and Cam is in my arms.

"You did it!" She smacks her mouth on mine. "You won!"

"*We* won long before tonight."

"Dad!" Whit crashes into me from behind. "Oh my god! Dad!"

Laughing, I lower Cam to her feet, keeping one arm around her to be sure she's steady before wrapping my other arm around my daughter. "Whitbee."

"You have to name my brother Chase now."

"What?"

"Why?" Cam leans around me to see Whit.

"Because we want him to have a strong winner's name and Chase isn't just a Rogue now. He's a hero."

She isn't wrong. We might have earned our place in the finals but winning was never a guarantee and we all knew it. Chase isn't just a Rogues hero, he's going to be the inspiration of every underdog in the world after tonight.

Looking down at Cam, I say, "I'm not opposed to it."

"Chase Nelson Higgison." She ponders that for a moment. "Has a nice ring to it."

"We'll add it to the list."

A list that grows longer every day. A list I'm hoping to use more than once in the future. For now, I'm thrilled to be making a list at all.

For years, Whit has been my greatest joy and the thought of more never seemed possible. Until Cam worked her way under my skin and showed me there was more to life than I had, than I was settling for.

With her love and understanding, Whit and I have the family I secretly wished for. And as my eyes cruise over the players and staff around me I'm thankful for the Rogues and all they've given me.

Without them I wouldn't have the men I now call brothers, or the woman in my arms and the life she's growing inside her.

Beckett and Whitney Higgison were born out of an inexcusable situation. One that could have had devastating results, except like the Rogues, I never gave up, never let the past drag us down.

And from the ashes of a scandalous beginning, we've risen above and beyond all I'd ever hoped for.

Missed the first book in the Hot as Puck series? Check out Walker and Oakley's insta-love, insta-parents story Hot Stuff today!

For what's coming next, latest releases, sales and more, join

Rhian's Royal Readers
http://www.rhiancahill.com/contact/newsletter/

If you enjoyed this book, please consider leaving a review. It only takes a few minutes and you'll be helping other readers find stories they'll enjoy, as well as supporting authors you love.

Acknowledgments

Families come in all shapes and sizes, blood or found, we thrive when we surround ourselves with love.

Schellie, you are a sister of my heart.

Fedora, we'll get that physical hug one day, for now, we'll stick to the cyber ones.

Reader, without you I'm not an author. Thank you for reading! I will never be able to express sufficiently how much it means to me that you would use your precious time reading my books.

xoxo

Rhian

About Rhian Cahill

Rhian Cahill is the alter ego of a former stay-at-home mother of four. With motherly duties rapidly dwindling, Rhian is able to make use of the fertile imagination she used to keep herself sane for all those years of slavery. Years spent living overseas and visiting tropical climates have helped inspire some steamy stories.

Multi-published in erotic romance, paranormal romance, and contemporary romance, Rhian, with the help of Mr. Muse, spends her days and nights writing.

When not glued to the keyboard you'll find her, book or knitting in hand, avoiding any and all housework as much as possible.

For more on Rhian –

Website – http://www.rhiancahill.com/
Newsletter signup – http://www.rhiancahill.com/contact/newsletter/
FaceBook – https://www.facebook.com/RhianCahillAuthor
Instagram – http://instagram.com/rhiancahill/
BookBub – https://www.bookbub.com/authors/rhian-cahill
Goodreads – https://www.goodreads.com/rhian_cahill

Other titles by Rhian Cahill

CONTEMPORARY ROMANCE

Hot as Puck

Hot Stuff

Hot Shot

Hot Damn

Hot Puck

Hot Hook

Hot Date

Love Beach

Summer With a Fake Date

Merry With a Scrooge

Spring Break With a Baby Daddy

Evergreen Lake

Jingle Balls

Winter Lake Series

Love Me Like You Do

Love The Way You Are

When You Love Someone

Let Me Love You

Wild Rush Of Love

Party Games Series

Truth Or Dare

Spin The Bottle

Pass The Parcel (novella)

Are You Game? Series

7 Minutes In Heaven

Catch'n'Kiss

Red Light, Green Light

Hearts Are Wild Series

No More Talking (novella)

Dare You To (novella)

Mad Love

Boys Of Summer

Bondi Beach Boys

Sand, Surf And Sunnie

Only You Series

All Of You

Holiday Romances

Christmas Wishes

New Year's Kisses

Valentine's Dates

Secret Santa

Frosty's Snowmen Series

A Touch Of Frost

A Kiss From Kringle

A Taste For Kandy

Hot and Bothered

Doing Logan

Shut Up And Kiss Me

PARANORMAL ROMANCE

Coyote Hunger Series

Coyote Home

Coyote Wild

Coyote Whispers

Coyote Law (novella)

Coyote Lies

For a full list of available books visit

http://www.rhiancahill.com/books/

For what's coming next, latest releases, sales and more, join

Rhian's Royal Readers

http://www.rhiancahill.com/contact/newsletter/